"No," he said, "you don't look like down. "You look"—his mouth danced across her bruised chin—"absolutely beautiful and more than I can resist right now." The words were as soft as his mouth on her swollen lips.

This was madness. They were on the run in a country that wasn't known for its record on human rights, the secret police were within screaming distance, and all she could think about was his mouth on hers, tasting, soothing, inciting. . . .

A sound ripped through her absorption—a voice calling across the fields in a guttural, incomprehensible language. Randall's hand replaced his mouth across hers; his long fingers stifled any sound as his body pressed her against the wall, holding her still.

*The Maggie Bennett Novels by Anne Stuart*

## ESCAPE OUT OF DARKNESS

*Coming soon from Dell*

## AT THE EDGE OF THE SUN

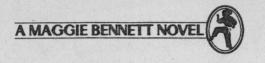

A MAGGIE BENNETT NOVEL

# DARKNESS BEFORE the DAWN

*Anne Stuart*

**A DELL BOOK**

Published by
Dell Publishing Co., Inc.
1 Dag Hammarskjold Plaza
New York, New York 10017

Dell ® TM 681510, Dell Publishing Co., Inc.

ISBN: 0-440-15876-1

Printed in the United States of America

March 1987

10 9 8 7 6 5 4 3 2 1

DD

# prologue

Maggie Bennett lay alone in the king-size bed. She'd been alone for two endless years, ever since Mack Pulaski had been gunned down on a street in Boothbay Harbor, Maine. And she planned to remain alone for the rest of her life.

At the time, she'd been upstairs in the converted shipbuilder's mansion they'd bought, taking a shower and daydreaming of babies, when she heard the gunfire. Even through the pounding water and the thick walls of the nineteenth-century house, she had heard it—and had heard the screams. And she had known what had happened.

She'd raced out of the house, desperate to reach him in time. But the people who had been looking for them for the last year and a half had been thorough. He lay there on the sidewalk in a pool of blood, his eyes wide and staring and curiously peaceful. The April sunshine was beating down, the sky was blue, and the smell of the sea had mixed with the smell of blood, overlaid with the scent of fresh lilacs. Maggie sank down beside him, putting a hand to his still-warm skin, and closed his eyes—those warm, laughing eyes that would laugh no more. And she knelt there in the pool of blood until someone pulled her away.

She'd drawn her strength around her like a protective blanket. Her mother and sisters had flocked to her side, but it was Maggie who had comforted them in their tears and Maggie who had taken over the arrangements and assured her family that it would, eventually, be all right.

And curiously enough, she now thought, turning again in their bed that she hadn't been able to part with, it was all right. For the first month, when she'd returned to New York, she'd slept on the couch rather than face the bed she'd shared for too short a time with Mack. But before long, she'd exerted her common sense, and now she was glad she'd kept the bed. She could remember Mack with warmth and joy and love, but she had the sorrow away where it belonged. *Better to have loved and lost,* she often told herself, taking comfort in the old cliché.

It was three in the morning. She could hear the never-ending New York City traffic outside her apartment, a constant companion to her nights. Most of the time she slept soundly, untroubled by dreams. But every now and then, when her strength was at low, she'd awaken in the darkness and remember, and fresh pain would sear through her. Then she'd have to remind herself once again, *Better to have loved and lost . . .*

Tomorrow she'd be in Chicago, taking her first vacation in two years. Her sister Kate needed her, and Maggie was never one to ignore someone's needs. It must have been the thought of Chicago that had started it again, she thought, burrowing down beneath the cool cotton sheets. Mack had grown up on Chicago's mean streets. Maggie had managed to avoid it since his death, but Kate needed her, and she could avoid it no longer. *Blood is thicker than water,* she thought, adding another cliché to the pile. How tediously trite and maudlin she was getting in her old age.

She rolled over on the bed and stared up into the darkness that surrounded her like a shroud. There was one more cliché, and it was by far her favorite. *Better to light one candle than to curse the darkness.* And she leaned over and turned on the bedside light.

# one

"There's a dead man in my bathtub!"

Maggie just stood there and looked at her younger sister, Kate, standing in the doorway of her Chicago apartment. Kate had always been the practical one, the calm, steady, efficient one. She was the only daughter who hadn't inherited the infamous aquamarine eyes. Instead, hers were plain brown—unblinking, nice, but definitely brown. Her hair was brown, too; her face was attractive but nondescript, and she dressed more with propriety than with imagination. Fair Isle sweaters and discreet pearls were her style more than the urban guerilla chic that Maggie favored.

But at that moment, standing barefoot in the doorway of her apartment, her brown hair a tangled mass around her pale face, her usually calm brown eyes were completely panicked.

"What did you say?" Maggie asked, still staring at her sister in bemusement.

"I said there's a dead man in my bathtub! Don't just stand there, Maggie!" she shrieked, her usually even tones thrown to the four winds. "Come in and help me!" She grabbed Maggie's arm and dragged her into the apartment with strength that was surprising, given that she was shorter and more fragile than her sister.

"Calm down, Kate," Maggie said, automatically efficient. "Sit down and explain to me what the hell is going on. Where's the baby?"

"I took her downstairs to Mrs. Gilliam. She baby-sits for her—Maggie, I don't want to talk about my domestic arrangements!" Her voice was rising again. Maggie pushed her down onto one of the overstuffed sofas in the stylish living room.

"And I don't want to hear about your domestic arrangements," she agreed. "I want you to tell me about the man in your bathtub. But first I think you need a drink."

"Maggie—"

But Maggie had already left her, heading down the narrow corridor to the huge old kitchen with its mammoth ice-making refrigerator. She'd always liked the apartment Kate had shared with her husband. It was huge and prewar, with wonderfully elegant spaces that had taken to modernization with enthusiasm. No expense had been spared, and the place was a showpiece. At least Brian had left her with that much.

She poured each of them a generous glass of whiskey, added a token cube of ice, and headed back to the living room. She detoured to check the bathroom.

Well, Kate was right. There most definitely was a dead man in her bathtub. He'd been shot once, execution style, in the head, and it had made very little mess. Still, it had been a violent death, and Maggie had to grab for calmness that she wasn't quite sure she had. She took a gulp of whiskey as she stared down at the corpse. He'd been a handsome man, and the soiled suit was expensive. She had never seen him before in her life. She wondered if Kate could make the same claim.

"You're right," she said, returning to Kate in the living room and handing her her glass of whiskey. "There *is* a dead man in your bathtub."

Kate drained the whiskey in one gulp, choking slightly. The color came back into her ashen face. Maggie noticed that her small hands were trembling. "What did you think, I was making it up?" she snapped back. "What am I going to do?"

"Do you know him?"

"Of course I know him! Do you think I'd have a dead stranger in my tub?" she demanded in outrage. "His name is Francis Ackroyd. We work together at the studio—or we used to. I guess we won't be now. Is there any more whiskey?"

"I'll get the bottle. Just sit there, Kate. I'll be right back."

But Kate wasn't there when Maggie returned. Maggie looked toward the apartment door, but it was still tightly shut. And then she headed back to the bathroom.

Kate was leaning against the door jamb, her face pale again. "I can't understand why anyone would do this," she said in a small voice that was little more than a whisper.

"Come away, Kate," Maggie said, putting a gentle but inexorable hand on her arm. "We can talk in the living room."

"I don't understand," she said again. And then she made a terrible face. "What is that awful smell?"

Maggie didn't want to tell her, but Kate wasn't showing any signs of moving, and the sight in front of them wasn't the most attractive. "When someone dies violently, their bladder and bowels empty," she said in her most pragmatic tone.

"Oh, God," Kate said in a strangled voice. And clapping a hand over her mouth, she stumbled away in the direction of her bedroom. From the gagging sounds she heard, Maggie guessed that Kate was heading for the other bathroom. Reaching out, she shut the door and the body of Francis Ackroyd out of sight and followed her sister.

"I need another drink," Kate announced when she'd finally managed to stagger from the bathroom on unsteady feet.

"I don't know if that's a good idea," Maggie said. "Some weak tea, perhaps—"

"I need another drink. If we're going to take care of the body, I need more than weak tea to put strength in me," Kate said with a trace of her usual self-possession.

"Take care of the body?" Maggie echoed faintly. "What do you mean?"

"Have you forgotten? I'm in the middle of the nastiest custody fight this side of Gloria Vanderbilt. Brian will crucify me if this comes out. We've got to hide the body."

"Kate!"

"I mean it, Maggie. Only for a couple of days at the most. We go back to court on Friday, and the judge has promised a ruling by then. It'll be too late to do anything about it—"

"Kate, I'm a lawyer. I'm not going to go around obstructing the law by hiding murder victims—"

"Yes, you are," Kate said. Her brown eyes filled up with tears. "This is my baby we're talking about. I can't lose her."

"But why should you?"

"Francis Ackroyd and I had a huge fight this afternoon," Kate said in a flat voice, "in the commissary at the studio, with at least twenty-five witnesses. I told him I wanted to kill him. I told him that very, very loudly."

"Oh, no."

"Oh, yes. It's only a couple of days, Maggie. We can dump him somewhere on the south side and cross our fingers—"

"They'd trace him straight back to you, Kate, especially if you had such a public fight. We're just going to have to make sure no one finds him and starts asking embarrassing questions until the judge has ruled."

Kate looked at her older sister with renewed respect. "What will we do with him?"

Maggie rose from the king-size bed that Kate had shared with Brian before he'd run off and married a twenty-year-old socialite who had forty million dollars more than Kate Zimmerman had. "Go and empty your refrigerator."

"Oh, no, Maggie!" she moaned.

"Oh, yes. Anywhere else, and he'll smell. And decompose, too, for that matter. At least in your refrigerator he'll keep for a while."

Kate turned around and headed back for the toilet. She slammed the door shut behind her.

Maggie shook her head. Disposing of Francis Ackroyd was the most immediate problem. But the moment they had him safely stashed, she was going to sit Kate down and get some straight answers out of her. Like what had they fought over? And when had the body appeared in her tub?

Not for a moment did she entertain the possibility that Kate had done it. Kate was strong, sturdy, fearless, and incorruptible—and completely squeamish. She could no more stick a gun at someone's temple than she could hurt her baby, and

Maggie knew that very well. Someone had framed her, but there was no way she could deal with it until Kate had told her absolutely everything.

It must have had something to do with Kate's job at Stoneham Studios. She'd worked for that small, independent movie studio for the last three years, even when Brian had insisted it wasn't quite the thing for someone of her social background. But Kate had loved it and had clung to her career through thick and thin. Maggie now had to wonder whether it was going to prove her undoing after all.

Moving Francis wasn't a pleasant job. Kate had dumped everything from the refrigerator into the garbage and had put the wire shelves in the utility room. Then she tried to beat a strategic retreat, but Maggie needed her to help to drag the late Francis, wrapped in the shower curtain, to the refrigerator. Fortunately, he'd been a small man, and he fit well enough. But the door wouldn't stay closed, so she propped one of the kitchen chairs against it. Then she sank down into the chair.

It was moments like this, she thought, when one needed a cigarette—even when one didn't smoke. Life's little moments that were fraught with discomfort and despair. She'd considered taking up cigarettes after Mack's death just for something to do, but at the last minute had decided against it. For one thing, every time she inhaled, she choked. For another, it interfered with her suddenly fanatical devotion to making her body as lean and fit as she possibly could. So no cigarettes. But right at that moment, she would have killed for one.

Kate paced back and forth, eyeing the refrigerator with great distrust. "What are you doing, sitting there?" she demanded.

"Keeping the door closed," Maggie said wearily. "I don't think this is going to work."

"Why not? We can just go out to eat."

"Kate, sooner or later—"

The sound of the doorbell shut Maggie's mouth in mid-sentence. It was an elegant, melodious, old-fashioned doorbell, but it cut across their nerves like a buzz saw.

"Who could that be at this hour?" Maggie demanded finally. She shoved the chair under the refrigerator door handle to make sure it wouldn't pop open and spill out its macabre contents.

"It's only eight thirty, Maggie," Kate said, her voice a thin thread of sound. "It only feels like midnight."

"You'd better answer it." The gentle chimes echoed in the kitchen once more.

"Me?" Kate shrieked. "I can't, Maggie!"

"It's your apartment. The doorman knows we're here. We can't just hide away and not answer. Besides, it might be the baby-sitter."

"Oh, God," Kate moaned. She stumbled from the kitchen at a dead run. Maggie raced along behind her.

"Calm down, Kate. I just said it *might* be the baby-sitter. It's probably someone selling Girl Scout cookies," Maggie said. She caught Kate's shoulder just as they reached the door. She turned Kate around and shook her with just enough force to make her sister's eyes open wide. "I said calm down. If we're going to carry this off, you're going to have to get hold of yourself." She gave her another shake for good measure. "Okay?"

Kate took a deep, shuddering breath. The doorbell rang again. Maggie could feel the tension run through her like a live current, but Kate's usual strength of will had taken over. "Okay," she said, and turned to look through the peephole. And then she sank down onto the carpet in the hall. "Help me, Maggie," she said with a note of desperation in her voice. "It's Brian."

The gentle doorbell sound had deteriorated into a loud knocking. It was followed by the charming voice that had fooled more than one susceptible woman, but that had never fooled Maggie. "I know you're in there, Kate. Come on, don't be a child. Let me in."

Maggie grabbed Kate's wrist and hauled her upright. "If

you make it through this," she hissed, "you'll make it through anything. Don't let Brian win, Kate."

"Kate, I know you're in there," Brian continued. His voice was definitely becoming edgy. "If you don't let me in, I'll have the doorman do it. Old Fred's always had a soft spot for me, and you know he'd do it in a flash."

Slowly, Kate pushed her tangled hair back from her pale, sweating face. Her eyes were still wide and shocked, and her hands were trembling slightly. "Hold your horses, Brian," she called out, and her voice sounded calm and prosaic. "You pick the damnedest times for social calls." She took her time fumbling with the locks, and when she finally opened the door, there was a spot of color in either cheek, and to Maggie's amazement, Kate simply looked tired and angry—not as if she'd spent the last hour throwing up and moving a corpse into her refrigerator.

"It's about time!" Brian strode into the apartment, but he stopped short when he caught sight of Maggie. He was a good-looking man, and he knew it; he was a charming man, and he used it. It had always driven him crazy that Maggie hadn't fallen prey to his charm. He immediately smiled his best smile at Maggie, bringing all his perfect teeth into play. "Maggie, how are you? You look terrific."

She stood still for the wet-mouthed embrace she knew was coming. Brian had an almost pathological disregard for the trouble he caused. Not for one moment did he consider that the mudslinging custody battle he'd initiated dimmed his welcome from his ex-sister-in-law. Rudeness on her part didn't make it sink in; ignoring him didn't help, either. So Maggie stood still and let him reach up and slobber on her chin. She moved away as soon as his grip had slackened.

"What do you want, Brian?" Kate demanded from her post by the doorway. "We're going back to court on Friday. Don't you think this is an odd time for a social call?"

"It isn't a social call. I came to see my daughter," he said with quiet dignity that he'd perfected long before.

"Tough. You can't see her till this is settled. You know that perfectly well. I don't want her in the middle of this mess."

"You always were a little pedant, Kate," he said. "I miss Chrissie. Can't you loosen up just long enough for me to say hi?"

"Chrissie's not here," Maggie said, noting the look of panic that briefly swept through Kate's clear brown eyes. "We took her to the baby-sitter's so we could have a chance to talk."

"Why can't you talk with the baby around?" Brian asked with a suspicious tone in his voice.

Maggie stared at him, a chilly, savage stare that had always intimidated Brian and did so now. "Because I needed to talk about . . . Mack—" She deliberately let her voice break. "And we didn't think Chrissie needed to see her aunt Maggie so upset. You know she cries when other people cry."

Brian looked at her skeptically. "Come off it, Maggie. Superwomen don't cry."

Francis Ackroyd almost got company in the refrigerator. Maggie felt her hands clench into fists, but she stood very still and let the rage wash over her and through her. "Good-bye, Brian," she said calmly.

"Aren't you going to offer me a drink?" he demanded.

"No," Kate snapped.

"I'm thirsty, Kate. Don't be such a bloody bitch."

"No."

He glared at the two of them. "I'll get it myself. I used to live here, remember?" And he started for the kitchen.

# two

Maggie considered a flying tackle, then rejected the notion. Brian didn't need any encouragement—he was already slightly suspicious. But there was no way she could keep him out of the kitchen, short of brute force.

Kate cast her a panicked, beseeching look. "Do something!" she hissed. "Brian likes lots of ice!"

"Damn." Maggie raced after her ex-brother-in-law. Kate was close on her heels.

Brian was at the sink—the sink that still bore traces of the milk and juice hastily dumped from the emptied refrigerator. He was drawing a glass of water. Maggie breathed a sigh of relief—one that strangled in midbreath as he turned and headed directly for the refrigerator.

Kate made a muffled sound of anguish as Brian shoved the glass into the outside compartment that set the ice machine in motion. Three cubes plopped into his glass—each one was a death knell. Then he gestured toward the chair holding the refrigerator door closed. "What's wrong with the door?"

"The gasket is broken," Maggie said swiftly. Kate stood in mute panic. "The door swings open and everything gets frosted. Don't worry about it, Brian—the repairman's coming tomorrow."

"I would have thought that a wonder like you could fix anything," he drawled. Maggie stared at him stonily. *Maybe he'd fit in the freezer.*

"I don't claim to be perfect, Brian," she said. "But I do happen to possess an ordinary amount of sensitivity, unlike you. You aren't wanted here. You've started a vicious custody suit against my sister, one that will do nothing but hurt your child, and you don't give a damn. You show up here expecting to be welcomed with open arms, and then you act insulted when you're told to get out. I'll tell you again, Brian. Out of here!"

"You always were a cold bitch," he said.

*Of course, I might have to cut him up in small pieces to get him into the freezer,* she thought, and then she mentally slapped herself. Such wistful fantasies were a waste of time. "Get out!"

"I'm not leaving until my ex-wife tells me to. Even if you can't fix something as simple as a refrigerator door, I'm not so poor a specimen. You know I've always been good at fixing things, Kate." And he reached for the chair.

For a moment Maggie thought Kate might faint. Her brown eyes blinked and her face blanched, but then she suddenly stiffened. "Get your goddamn hands off my chair!" she roared. "Get out of my kitchen, get out of my apartment, and get out of my life! You walked out on me when Chrissie was two weeks old and remarried by the time she was three months. You've severed any rights you had to our life. Get out, and do it fast, or in another moment I'll start screaming!"

Maggie knew the origin of the ragged edge of hysteria in Kate's voice. Brian was mystified but totally convinced. He slammed the glass of water down onto the kitchen table and stormed from the room. His elegant back radiated rage and disapproval. They heard the door slam all the way back into the kitchen.

Maggie met Kate's eyes.

"I *would* have screamed," Kate confessed in a whisper. "And I don't know if I would have stopped."

"I was busy fantasizing about putting the bastard in the freezer," Maggie confessed.

Kate stared at her in shock. And then a reluctant, nervous giggle escaped her. "He would have deserved it more than poor Francis."

"Poor Francis? I thought you threatened to kill him a few hours ago."

"A figure of speech." Kate dismissed it. "Caleb had gotten me riled up over something, and Francis took the brunt of it. Francis and I have always gotten along beautifully. But I wouldn't have minded if it were Caleb in my bathtub. He's been driving me crazy." She took a deep, calming breath. "However, I suppose we're lucky it *was* Francis. Caleb's about a foot taller and fifty pounds heavier. I don't think he'd fit in the refrigerator."

"Thank heaven for small favors," Maggie said faintly. "So who's Caleb and why is he driving you crazy?"

"Caleb McAllister is in charge of finances at the studio," she said with a certain evasiveness. "I'm production, and Francis was creativity. Caleb had been hassling me about some discrepancies in one of Francis's budgets. So I confronted Francis, and he was damnably vague. He was covering something up, I know he was. But when I tried to find out what it was, he just gave me that snooty little look of his." She shook her head ruefully. "I can't even remember which movie caused all the fuss. Probably one of his pseudo–Star Wars epics."

"I think you'd better try to remember," Maggie said. "We're going to have to figure out who killed Francis and who brought him here, and we're going to have to do it soon."

Kate stared at her. "Did you mean to put it in that order? You said 'killed Francis' and then 'brought him here.' Wasn't he killed in my bathtub?"

"I don't think so. I think he was killed someplace else and moved here. He didn't bleed much, but there wasn't a trace of blood in the tub. And his limbs were—"

"Maggie," Kate said in a dangerous voice, "I don't have anything left to throw up. I'll take your word for it."

"And I don't think we have any alternative," Maggie continued.

"Alternative to what?"

"We're going to have to move him back."

"Oh, God," Kate moaned.

"Well, we can't leave him in the fridge," Maggie said with great practicality. "That door really is broken, and sooner or later Francis is going to make an unwelcome reappearance. At best, keeping him in the refrigerator would have only given us a day or two. I've turned the temperature up as cold as it will go—"

"Maggie!"

"But sooner or later we're going to have to move him. What with the door breaking, I opt for sooner."

Kate glared at the refrigerator, as if it were somehow responsible for her current dilemma. "Where to?"

"Back to his apartment. I wouldn't be surprised if that's where he was killed."

"But then why bring him here?"

"You tell me, Katy," Maggie said. "What time did you get home?"

"Not till after seven. And I didn't go into that bathroom until just before you got here—I use the one off my bedroom. I don't know when Francis left work. I didn't see him after our big fight in the lunchroom."

"But he must have been killed sometime before, say, six thirty. Do you know where he lives?"

"Quite close, actually. In the old Carlysle Building, not more than five blocks away."

"Then he was probably killed sometime between five and six thirty."

"How do you know—no, don't answer that," Kate begged. "Do I even want to know how we're going to carry the body five blocks to his apartment building without someone noticing?"

"Got a trunk?"

This was not what she'd envisioned doing twenty-four hours ago, Maggie thought as she hauled the steamer trunk into the service elevator at the Carlysle Building. Her heart was pounding, both from exertion and from nerves, and her abraded palms were sweaty. She was supposed to be on vacation, playing with little Chrissie, providing moral support for Kate as she finished up her messy custody hearing. Brian had brought the suit for nuisance value alone—he'd never had a chance of winning, until now.

She shoved the steamer trunk against the wall with a grunt and punched the elevator buttons, trying to catch her breath. Carting a very heavy dead body all over Chicago in a steamer trunk left something to be desired. She was strong and sturdy, but one hundred and fifty-plus pounds challenged even her energy level. Her legs were aching, her back throbbed, and sweat was pouring into her eyes. Luckily, her denim jumpsuit looked more utilitarian than designer with its zippers zipped and the sleeves rolled down. Tucking her thick blond hair under an old baseball cap helped, and she'd even gone so far as to pilfer ashes from Kate's fireplace to smudge her light complexion. Up close, she wouldn't have passed muster—she'd look like a kid dressed up as a tramp on Halloween. But if God were merciful, no one would see her up close.

The Carlysle's security was wonderfully lax. She'd caught the back door as someone was leaving and had made it to the elevator without anyone accosting her. In moments she was at the service entrance to Francis Ackroyd's apartment on the seventh floor of the building. She leaned against the wall to calm her nerves and catch her breath, and she hoped to God that no one would see her as she picked the lock.

Lockpicking had never been one of her major talents, she thought ten minutes later as she still struggled with Ackroyd's back door. It was a good thing there were only two apartments to a floor, and that the other inhabitants didn't feel like taking out their garbage at this hour. She'd gone through two credit cards, a barrette, and a toothpick, but not until she kicked the door in a sudden temper did it open. It had been unlocked all the time.

The apartment was dark, pitch black—only the streetlights illuminated it. If she had any sense at all, she thought, dragging the steamer trunk into the kitchen, she'd leave the lights off, dump Francis onto the floor, and run like hell.

But she had no sense. If there were blood anywhere in the apartment, that's where she should dump the corpse. But there was no way she could find bloodstains in the dark. She was damned well not going to be alone in an apartment with a dead body and no lights.

At least, she hoped she was alone. That unlocked door meant one of two things. One—the less preferable—was that someone was in the apartment at that very moment, hiding from her, ready to jump out with the same gun that had finished off poor Francis. The second and far more pleasant possibility was that Francis had been killed in the apartment and taken out the back way, and the killer had left the door unlocked.

To hell with it, she thought. He'd find her in the dark just as well as in the light, and she'd just as soon see the killer. She crossed the room and flicked on the light.

It was a glaring intrusion, bright and jarring, and she almost flicked it off again—until she saw the small, barely congealed pool of blood on the quarry-tiled floor of Francis's upscale kitchen.

The next few minutes were ones she didn't savor. She put her brain on automatic pilot, remembered to breathe through her mouth, and left Francis Ackroyd on the floor of his kitchen, his head near the pool of blood.

She'd pulled on gloves, silly white cotton gloves that Kate had unearthed from a bottom drawer. She flicked off the light, plunging the apartment into darkness once more, and tiptoed past the body. "Sorry, Francis," she whispered, and hauled the empty trunk after her, being careful to latch the service door behind her. A moment later, she was in the elevator and gone, out onto the street, where she abandoned the trunk in a pile of old furniture and refuse that was waiting for the dawn trash pickup. It was a chance, but one worth taking. She'd been lucky so far. But she couldn't drag a steamer trunk around Chicago without attracting attention, and by the time they found Francis's body the trunk would be long gone. She moved back toward her car with a marginally lighter heart.

The kitchen at Francis Ackroyd's apartment stayed dark for no more than forty-five seconds after Maggie had shut the door behind her. The light flickered back on, and a tall, dark figure stood in the doorway, staring down at the late Francis, staring back at the closed door. He moved forward into the light, and his dark, fathomless eyes looked down at the corpse at his feet.

"Well, well, Maggie," Randall Carter said in a low, meditative voice that held no surprise at all. "What have you been up to?"

Maggie's steps quickened as she headed down the elegant hallway outside Kate's fourth-floor apartment. Chrissie would have been retrieved and settled for the night by now, and the apartment would be quiet. Maggie could kick off her shoes, pour herself another, much more generous drink and collapse on the couch for at least half an hour before she had to figure out their next step. The idea of the couch and the drink was so enticing that she was almost dizzy with longing. She fumbled with the key and then practically stumbled in the front door.

"Mission accomplished," she sang out, heading into the well-lit living room. She stopped short. Kate wasn't alone.

She wasn't happy, either. She looked like a small, fierce terrier confronting a St. Bernard. Actually, an Irish wolfhound would be a better description. Kate's companion was definitely shaggy; his Celtic ancestry was clearly proclaimed in the sandy red hair, in the huge body, and in the incongruous trace of freckling across his broad, earnest face. He was dressed in a dark business suit. His tie was long since gone, his hair was rumpled, and his blue eyes were still frustrated as he turned to look at Maggie. The frustration faded and was replaced with surprise tinged with amusement.

Maggie was used to seeing surprise on men's faces. She was

a healthy, six-foot-tall woman with curves, muscles, and long, rippling blond hair. The mere sight of her had a tendency to daze mortal men. But amusement was something new—until she remembered the baseball cap on her head and the soot covering her face.

"Who's the street urchin, Kate?" he inquired. Maggie liked his voice. It was warm and low-pitched, with a flat Midwestern accent that somehow added to its charm.

"My sister," Kate said flatly. "Maggie Bennett, this is Caleb McAllister." She placed a slight emphasis on his name, and Maggie took a second glance. During her short drive back to the apartment, she'd decided that Kate's nemesis Caleb was her most likely suspect in Francis's untimely demise. But casting another glance over Caleb's rangy figure, she quickly revised her original suspicion. She wouldn't rule him out, but at the moment he seemed very *un*likely—even if he looked now as if he wanted to wring her little sister's neck.

"Did I interrupt something?" Maggie inquired coolly, kicking off her shoes and sinking onto one of the white couches. Her hand left a nice sooty imprint. She brushed at it with little success. At least it wasn't blood.

"Caleb insists on interrupting my home life to discuss business," Kate said in an icy tone, "to find out what our colleague Francis had to say this afternoon."

"Had to say about what?" Maggie asked, wiggling her bare toes.

"Studio business," Caleb said, staring at her toes with unwilling fascination.

"About budgets," Kate said at the same time, watching Caleb watching Maggie's feet and not looking pleased. "Francis was way over budget on *The Revenge of the Potato People,* and his figures didn't add up. Caleb decided to see me about them instead of going directly to Francis."

"You're in charge of production, Kate. It's your job," Caleb replied with maddening patience.

"You're in charge of finances—it's just as much your job to find out where the money went," Kate snapped.

"I don't want to argue about it. I want to know what Francis had to say."

"Why don't you ask him yourself?" Maggie inquired smoothly, curling her bare feet under her and rolling her sleeves back up.

Caleb cast her an irritated glance. "Don't you think I haven't tried? He hasn't been home all evening. I've called—I even stopped by—but there was no one home."

"Why didn't you ask him this afternoon before he left work?" Maggie persisted gently.

"Because he disappeared right after he and Kate had their battle in the lunchroom, and he didn't bother to leave word with anyone about where he was going," he said, telling Maggie exactly what she wanted to know. He turned back to her sister. "I need answers on this, Kate. The end of the fiscal year is only a month and a half away, and I—"

"You know what you can do with your fiscal year, Caleb," Kate said sweetly.

Time to take a hand, Maggie thought, stretching her feet out in front of her and rising with all the languid grace she could muster—which wasn't much, given her recent activities. She smiled up at Caleb McAllister, who had to be six foot four or five at least, and was pleased to see that she could still summon forth an appropriate male response. It had been years since she had tried, but right now she needed to get Caleb out of there and Kate settled down with a good book and a Valium.

"Why don't you ask him tomorrow morning, Caleb?" she inquired, dropping her voice a note or two. "It's after eleven already. By tomorrow, I'm sure Francis will turn up with all the answers. He's probably just spending the night at a girl friend's—"

Kate shook her head. "Boyfriend's," she supplied.

Maggie shrugged. "Anyway, I'm sure everything will be cleared up in the morning. As you said, you have a month and half to get the answers. Surely a few more hours won't make any difference?"

Caleb looked torn. Maggie's low, soothing voice was having a predictable effect, and he was warming to it while still trying to keep his attention on her embattled sister. "You call Mrs. Stoneham," he ordered Kate.

"Did she send you out here?" Kate demanded. "I don't believe you."

"She was worried about you, Kate. When she called me tonight, she asked me to check on both you and Francis. She said she'd never seen you as angry and upset as you were in the lunchroom."

"Then clearly she's never seen me around you," Kate said angrily, and once more Maggie intervened.

"Mrs. Stoneham can wait till tomorrow, too," she said, taking Caleb's strong arm in her hand and pulling him gently toward the door. "I don't see what all this fuss is all about. Life must be extremely peaceful at Stoneham Studios if a little lunchroom argument can cause so much worry."

A reluctant smile creased Caleb's expression, and the change was a revelation. Maggie cast a surreptitious look back at her sister to see if she had any reaction to that glorious smile, but Kate was looking, if possible, even angrier.

"Peaceful, it isn't," he said. "All right, it can wait till tomorrow. Be in my office at nine, Kate, and bring Francis with you."

Maggie coughed at the sudden vision, but Kate rose to the occasion magnificently. "Caleb, I'm not your employee, I'm your co-worker. If you want to meet with me tomorrow, you can check with my secretary for an appointment, and you can damned well find Francis and bring him along yourself!"

Caleb sighed ostentatiously. "You could learn some manners from your sister here. I'll be in your office waiting for you at nine o'clock tomorrow morning. Be there."

The apartment was very quiet once the door had closed behind him. Maggie turned an inquiring gaze back to her sister and was amused to see temper still lurking around her eyes. At least it chased away the haunted, frightened look that Francis had engendered.

"I think he's charming, Kate," Maggie said mischievously.

"You can have him," she snapped back. "He'll be the death of me yet."

"I don't think so."

"I beg your pardon?"

"I had thought he might be the most likely suspect, but now I've changed my mind. He might kill someone in a white-hot temper, but he wouldn't go to all the trouble of hiding the body and then framing someone else."

"Caleb?" Kate echoed. "Caleb wouldn't hurt a flea."

"Then what's your problem?"

"He wants me," Kate said in a depressed tone of voice.

"So I noticed. I still don't understand the problem."

"I don't want him," Kate said. "I've had enough of men to last me for quite a while, thank you. Brian soured me for a good long time. I'm not about to go from a marriage to motherhood to a divorce to a custody battle to marriage again in the space of one year. Forget it."

Maggie smiled. "I don't know if Caleb will. He looks like someone who's used to getting his own way."

"Not this time," Kate said firmly.

"Even if it's what you want, too?"

Kate cast her a frustrated glance. "You don't have to be so know-it-all. Why don't you wash your face and find us what's left of that bottle of whiskey while I check on Chrissie? It's going to take a lot of Jack Daniel's to get me to sleep tonight."

"Me, too. Okay, little sister. We'll get drunk together, and you can pour out your girlish heart," Maggie offered.

"Stuff it," Kate replied sweetly. "Bring the Scotch, too. It's going to be a long night."

"It has been already."

"Amen to that," Kate said. "And no ice."

# three

It took her a moment to remember where she was. The guest room in Kate's apartment was large, and Maggie had kept the bedside light burning all night. It hadn't kept the nightmares at bay, though—throughout her disturbed sleep, Francis Ackroyd had waltzed, pale and macabre, doing a graceful dance of death that left her clawing at the pillow and sweating in her sleep. And then, strangest of all, Randall had invaded her dream.

It had been years since she'd even thought of him, longer still since she'd dreamed of him. Randall Carter was one of the weak, unpleasant parts of her life, symbolic of stupid mistakes that she'd always regret. She'd learned long since that the only thing you could do with hideous, embarrassing mistakes was to accept them and then dismiss them. She'd done that with Randall and had been happily free of him since she'd met Mack. Why he'd suddenly returned to haunt her dreams was beyond her comprehension.

Still, she had to admit he was a better nocturnal companion than Francis Ackroyd's restless ghost. She'd rather dream of Randall than remember the pale corpse she'd spent too much time hauling around town. She could almost be grateful for the distraction. The thought made her laugh ruefully as she pulled herself out of bed. Never in a million years had she thought she'd be grateful to Randall Carter. It just went to show that you couldn't be certain of anything in this life.

There was no sign of Kate when Maggie staggered sleepily into the deserted kitchen. It was well past nine—she must have dropped Chrissie off at the baby-sitter's and headed to the studio to face Caleb McAllister. Maggie only hoped she'd be able to keep her cool. Caleb was so enamored of Kate that it would be a simple enough matter to distract him, but that seemed like the last thing her sister was willing to do.

The coffee was made, and Maggie wandered around the kitchen, sipping at the unaccustomed bitterness of the milk-less brew. Not once did she make the mistake of opening the refrigerator door. Kate had left a note—an early call to the building superintendent had resulted in prompt repairs while Maggie had slept the sleep of the just. The appliance stood there, a mute white monolith, a silent reproach; it made her want to return to the quiet guest bedroom. But Maggie was made of sterner stuff than that. She made toast in the kitchen, sipped her coffee, and ignored the temptation to glance over her shoulder. But then she grabbed the grapefruit marmalade that she and Kate shared a passion for and headed into the living room. She didn't notice until she had settled herself on the overstuffed white sofa that she had been holding her breath.

Thank heaven they had rescued the marmalade when they'd emptied the refrigerator! The tart flavor soothed her with its familiarity. She could remember Mack teasing her about her fanatical devotion to it. For that matter, she even remembered that Randall had once presented her with a couple of jars of it when they had been trapped together in a dingy little apartment outside of Gemansk. God, why was she thinking of Randall again?

She drained her coffee and for a moment thought longingly of a refill. But the coffeepot was on the counter next to the refrigerator, and not even for another much-needed jolt of caffeine did Maggie feel like returning to the kitchen. The coffee could wait. In the meantime there were things to be done.

She moved over to Kate's delicate Louis Quatorze desk and picked up the telephone. She punched in numbers that she knew by heart and wished she didn't have to use. But this time she didn't see any alternative.

"Central Intelligence Agency," the anonymous voice announced smoothly.

Maggie considered hanging up. But there was no choice—not this time. "Bud Willis, please."

It was a mercifully short conversation. "Hi there, sweetcakes," his hatefully familiar voice drawled over the line from Langley. "How's the black widow doing?"

"Just fine." She'd inured herself to his jibes years ago. "I need something from you."

"Listen, any part of me is yours for the asking. I've got more than enough to go around."

"I'm sure you do. What I need is information. I need to know if you have any information on a Francis Ackroyd, or a Stoneham Studios in Chicago."

"Now why would you want to know that, honeylips? You interested in becoming a movie star like your mama? You don't have her knockers."

"Willis, Third World Causes has an agreement with the government, and you're part of it. You're supposed to help me —no questions asked—when I need it. I need it, and you can stuff your damned questions."

"Whatever happened to that sweet, ladylike demeanor?" he drawled back. "Not getting enough lately, that's your problem. You just take a little trip to my apartment, and I'll fix you up so you'll be walking bowlegged for a month."

"Charming. I'll leave you my phone number, and I'll expect to hear from you in the next twenty-four hours."

"Or what?" Willis taunted.

Maggie nobly controlled the very graphic revenge that immediately formed in her mind. "Or you'll be sorry, Willis," she said gently.

"Oooh, I'm frightened. Don't worry, Mrs. Pulaski," he said, mocking the married name she'd always been too stubborn to take. "I'll find out what you need to know. I may even have the information hand-delivered."

"Willis, I don't want to see your ugly face—"

"Not me, sweetlips. I've got too many things going on. I'll be in touch."

The man was pond scum, Maggie thought, stretching out on the sofa and looking at the Chicago skyline. But useful pond scum. She never did understand why he had decided to go back and ally himself with the CIA again, nor did she care. What mattered most was that she could, for some reason, trust what he told her. If Francis Ackroyd were involved in anything, Bud Willis could find out what it was. And Maggie's oddly reliable instincts told her there was something going on.

"How are you surviving?" Kate's voice was on the telephone, hours later, and if the edges were a little ragged, only Maggie knew her well enough to recognize it.

"Fine, but I'm not on the front line. How are you doing?"

Kate sighed. "Okay, I guess. Things are absolutely crazy around here—so crazy that no one notices if I'm a little distracted. They probably just figure it's the court case."

"What do they think happened to Francis?"

"No one knows. Someone's been calling his apartment hourly, but of course there's no answer. To top it off, Alicia Stoneham has shown up with a new investor, and we all have to make nice to him. The studio's in deep financial trouble, and no one can afford to be rude, but he picked a hell of a time to make a visit."

"Well, that's not your concern. How soon can you get home?"

"I don't know."

"Take your time. Everything's under control. I've called a contact I have in Washington, and he's promised to look into it and let me know."

"Look into what? What's Washington got to do with a murder?" Kate demanded.

"Shhh, darling. No one knows anyone's been murdered. At least, not yet. And it's just a hunch I have. If there's anything to know, Bud Willis can find it out. I've also called our dear mother." Maggie's voice had the fondly mocking tone it always took on when she referred to Sybil Bennett.

"What for?"

"I thought she might come in handy looking after Chrissie. You know Sybil—she loves to pose with pretty infants, and Chrissie is a very pretty infant. I thought that if things got rough, the baby might stay with her. She's getting a suite at the Mandrake and bringing her usual retinue, including Queenie. Chrissie couldn't be in better hands."

"I suppose it's a good idea," Kate said morosely. "God, I feel as if I'm caught in a nightmare. Listen, I'll be home as soon—oh, no!"

"What?"

"Mrs. Stoneham just appeared in the hall outside my office. She's clinging to Caleb's arm and weeping. And there's a policeman with them."

"Looks like they found Francis," Maggie said.

"Looks like they did. 'Bye." The phone went dead. Maggie sat and looked at it. It did feel as if they were caught in a nightmare. But Maggie had dealt with nightmares before, and she'd deal with this one, too. In the meantime all she could do was sit tight and wait for Bud Willis to get back to her.

It had taken all her nerve, but she'd gone out and restocked the refrigerator. Kate had already done the dirty work the night before—she'd cleaned both it and the bathroom while Maggie had been hauling the steamer trunk to and fro. The newly repaired handle worked perfectly. Thank God there was no trace of the late Francis in the refrigerator—only some grapefruit marmalade that clung to the pristine white walls had escaped Kate's eagle eye. Maggie had scrubbed it off, then refilled the fridge with every treat she could think of, from Hostess Twinkies to fresh-baked croissants, from French yogurt to chocolate milk. And then she had spent the afternoon sitting by the telephone and eating all the food she'd bought.

She still stayed away from the now-spotless guest bathroom; she'd even locked the door. Not that the room looked suspicious, although the brand-new shower curtain didn't quite match the decor. Maggie simply couldn't bring herself to examine the tub more closely, either, trusting in her sister's efficiency.

She was in Kate's bathroom, applying enough rouge to make her look cheerful, when she heard her sister return home. She raced into the hallway, about to demand what happened, when Kate's loud voice forestalled her.

"Maggie, I've brought someone home with me," she announced. "Come out and meet Stoneham Studios' new investor while I make us some drinks."

*Damn,* Maggie thought, slowing her headlong pace. Just their luck to be saddled with some star-struck magnate when they needed to make plans. "I'll be right there," she called, darting into her own room to slip on a pair of sandals and grimace at her reflection. The blond hair was a flyaway mane around her narrow face, and her aquamarine eyes were defiant and slightly scared. Well, all she had to do was charm the investor, and that was something she could do with only half her brain. Then they'd get rid of him as soon as possible.

The living room was in shadows—the sun was sinking behind the city skyline—and at first Maggie didn't see their visitor. But then, over by the window looking down on the city, she saw a tall man clad in an impeccable gray suit that fit his body better than any suit had a right to. His dark hair was cut to shape his beautiful head. In fact, everything about the man who was turned away from her was perfection. But a sudden flash of horror and denial swept through her as she recognized that perfection. And she would have rather seen Francis Ackroyd propped up in the living room.

She hadn't made a sound. Her sandaled feet were silent on the thick carpeting, and even if her heart had slammed to a stop and then began to race, there was no way he could have heard. But he turned, very slowly, and she knew he had been expecting to see her.

"Hello, Maggie," said Randall Carter. And for the first

time in six years, she looked into the still, dark eyes of the man she hated most in the world.

"What the hell are you doing here?" Somewhere she found her voice. It came out scratchy and raw, but it was there all the same. She didn't move any closer but just stood staring. A distant part of her marveled at the fresh waves of hatred that washed over her. She wasn't a hating woman, and yet here she was, immersed in hate, awash in it, hating Randall Carter as if it were only a week ago that he'd broken her heart and smashed her ideals without the slightest feeling of remorse. There was no remorse in him now—just a waiting, watchful expression on his narrow, clever face.

"I thought your sister told you," he said. His low, even voice brought other memories of rage and pain. "I'm thinking of investing in Stoneham Studios. I decided to come here and check them out."

"When did you decide? Sometime after ten this morning, I suppose?" she demanded. Willis must have sicced him on her —he *must* have.

Randall shook his head. "I've been in Chicago for three days now, Maggie."

Kate bustled in, a tray of drinks in her slightly trembling hands. "I see you two have met," she said brightly. "I'm so glad—I hate to make formal introductions."

"We've met," Randall said quietly, his eyes still unfathomable as they watched Maggie. "Did your sister tell you about the excitement at the studio today?"

"Excitement?" Maggie echoed innocently.

"One of my co-workers was found murdered," Kate said, and if her voice shook slightly, that was an understandable reaction. "His name was Francis Ackroyd. I don't think you ever met him, Maggie. Someone shot him."

"How perfectly ghastly," Maggie said, taking the proferred drink and forcing herself to sip it lightly. She was experienced at dissembling; she was much better at it now than she'd been when she'd first known Randall. But somehow those dark

32

eyes of his made her feel suddenly gauche and uneasy. "Do they know who did it?"

Kate shook her head. "They've ruled out robbery—nothing was taken from his apartment."

"Is that where he was killed? In his apartment?"

"That's where he was found, Maggie," Randall said, and she told herself that she was only imagining the wealth of meaning in his slow, deep voice. She moved away and turned her back on those eyes that she hated.

There was a long, uncomfortable silence. Kate broke it with sudden chatter. "Everyone was completely freaked out, Maggie! The police were all over the place, asking questions, and Alicia Stoneham was prostrate—"

"The poor woman," Maggie tried to interrupt her sister's nervous spate of words. "She's been through so much the last few years, what with losing her husband and trying to keep the studio together. She doesn't deserve this sort of thing."

"No one does," Randall said. "I would think it would be harder on the victim."

"I don't know. At least it's all over for the victim. He doesn't have to deal with the horrible aftermath of violent crime. He's well out of it."

"I think I'd prefer to deal with the horrible aftermath," Randall said.

"You *would,*" Maggie shot back. Kate stared at her in sudden surprise, no doubt shocked by her rudeness to the supposed stranger. Maggie considered explaining to Kate that she'd known Randall in her scarlet past; she considered it, and then dropped the idea. Kate didn't need anything new to worry about, not when she looked as if she were on the edge of collapse already. It could wait until Maggie found out why Randall really was there. His story about investing in Stoneham Studios was so farfetched, it was a joke. Randall never did anything that didn't make piles of money, and it would be a long time before Stoneham turned a profit once more.

"Do you suppose we could change the subject?" Kate inquired faintly. "I've had about as much as I can take this afternoon."

"Of course, darling," Maggie soothed instantly. "Why don't you sit and relax? By the way, where's the baby?"

"Still at the baby-sitter's. Mrs. Gilliam is bringing her up at six. That reminds me, I'd better call . . ." Kate disappeared before Maggie could stop her, and she was left alone in the lofty confines of the old apartment, alone with her nemesis, who made even Bud Willis seem less reprehensible.

Hell, she was an adult. There was no reason on this earth why Randall Carter should still have the ability to elicit such emotions from her. She'd be civil, cool, and remote. There was no way in hell he'd ever have to know that a small, secret part of her soul was still lacerated from her last encounter with him.

She gave him her brittle, polite smile. "So tell me, Randall," she said, "are you still messing in other people's politics for kicks?"

He just looked at her. His was an arresting face, not particularly handsome, but striking. His nose was long, elegant, and aquiline; his mouth was equally aristocratic and thin-lipped. His cheekbones were high, almost Slavic-looking; that trait that had served them well six years before, when their lives had depended on passing as Eastern Europeans. His eyes were a dark, stormy color somewhere between blue and gray. They never laughed, and they never warmed with life and tenderness. They stayed cold and stormy and slightly mocking even at the very best of times, and yet they pulled her. As they'd pulled her six years ago, when he had been married and she had been fighting her hopeless attraction to him—an attraction that he'd done everything to encourage.

"Other people's politics aren't as much fun as they used to be," he said slowly. "I've spent the last few years making money that I don't need."

"Poor Randall," she mocked gently, inordinately pleased that she could do so.

"And what about you, Maggie? You've been through a lot

since we were together. A divorce, an affair, another marriage. How are you surviving widowhood?"

"Surviving," she said. "I'm surviving. I don't believe you just happened to show up, Randall." She changed the subject quickly. "Why are you here? Who sent you? What the hell is going on at Stoneham Studios?"

He moved then, and she'd forgotten his peculiar grace and speed. She stood her ground as he advanced upon her, determined not to give way, but as he closed in on her, she felt trapped, smothered, diminished. He was only just over six feet tall, and yet he dwarfed her. She could sense the tension radiating through his body, beneath that perfect gray suit of his, and his tension reached out and caught hold of her own nerves, twisting them into knots.

"So many questions, Maggie," he said softly, his voice a silken threat. "I'll answer them if you'll answer one of mine."

"Shoot," she said defiantly, and then winced at the horrible appropriateness of her word.

His oddly sexy mouth twisted into a reluctant smile. "I couldn't help but overhear the police discussing the case. It appears that Francis's body was in a very strange condition. He had multiple bumps and bruises that had clearly been inflicted after death. And the tips of his fingers, his ears, and his nose were frostbitten."

Maggie kept her face stony. "So?"

"So I wonder what could have caused it. You remember how curious I can be. But there was something even more interesting, Maggie." He moved even closer, so close she could smell the faint tang of whiskey on his breath, so close she could see faint lines of gold fanning out in his gray-blue eyes. "I'll tell you what I'm doing here," he said, "when you tell me why Francis Ackroyd had grapefruit marmalade on his shoulder."

# four

"You know, I like him," Kate said three hours later. She was curled up on one of the living-room sofas with an afghan draped around her small body and her head resting on a pile of pillows.

Maggie stared at her for a long moment. She was stretched out in a chair, barefoot. Her second glass of whiskey and water was making no dent on memories she desperately wanted to drown. "Who?" she said finally.

"Randall Carter."

"You're out of your mind," she said flatly. "He's a cold-blooded, arrogant bastard, with ice water in his veins. He'd sell his own mother if the price was right."

Kate roused herself enough to peer at her older sister. "You figured all that out in the space of an hour? You're a quick judge of character."

Maggie decided to go on the attack. "I figured out I like Caleb McAllister in less time than that."

Kate's mouth thinned into an angry line. "You're welcome to him."

"And you're welcome to Randall Carter."

"There's no comparison," Kate shot back.

"Isn't there?"

There was a long silence as the two sisters stared at each other. "I don't think we need to be obscure," Kate said finally. "Our situation is difficult enough without talking at cross-purposes. Does Randall Carter mean something to you? Do you know him from before?"

"Randall Carter means absolutely nothing to me. Less than

nothing," Maggie said in a flat voice. "And yes, I know him from before."

"Aha!"

"Aha, what?" she snapped. "I can't stand the man. He's a sleazoid, he's a worthless piece of garbage, he's—"

Kate giggled. "I can't imagine someone as elegant as Randall Carter being called garbage."

A reluctant smile played around the corners of Maggie's generous mouth. "You're right. The man reserves all his emotion for his wardrobe."

"How would you know that?" Kate asked. "Were you in a position to ask for his emotions?"

"I'll tell you what, Kate," she said in a friendly voice. "I won't pester you about your convoluted feelings for Caleb, and you won't interfere in my past relationship with Randall. Believe me, it's very past, very old, and very dead. The only thing I feel for him is contempt."

"It's a deal—if you answer one question."

*Here we go again,* she thought with a shudder. At least it couldn't be as horrifying as Randall's unanswerable question. "All right."

"Was it six years ago that you knew him?"

Maggie looked at her sleepy younger sister with surprise. "Why do you ask that?"

"Because the whole family knows that Maggie the Indestructible self-destructed six years ago. And no one ever knew what or who caused it. Was it Randall?"

That was almost as horrifying as Randall's question, she thought grimly. She considered denying it. She considered getting up and walking out of the room. But Kate was right— they were in too much trouble as it was. Kate didn't need to know just how much Randall suspected. Maggie herself didn't even know—Kate had walked into the room immediately after that bombshell of the grapefruit marmalade, and he'd been polite, charming, and distant and had left a courteous half-hour afterward without another word about Francis's demise. But his silence wouldn't last forever.

Maggie looked over at Kate's sleepy face. "It was Randall," she said. "Go to sleep."

Kate's muffled sound of protest deteriorated into a quiet little snore. Maggie sat watching her sister and took another sip of whiskey. It had been Randall, indeed, she thought, and gave her weary mind over to the memories that the alcohol couldn't keep at bay.

She'd been so damned young six years ago, younger than her twenty-eight years at the time, and she still had an extraordinary faith in human beings that was downright stupid, when she looked back on it. She'd gone through a disrupted childhood that had included a mother who was feckless and charming and never there when you needed her, a father who was cold and distant, three stepfathers, and innumerable honorable "uncles." She'd been forcibly introduced to sex by one of her drunken stepfathers, and if the psychologists that her outraged and suddenly maternal mother had provided had managed to convince her that it wasn't her fault, she had had yet to prove to herself that she could do more than just manage a physical relationship.

But still and all, she had somehow expected the best from people, despite their lapses. Maybe Granny Bennett had taught her that before she died; maybe Queenie had managed to instill it in her. She'd learned to look past her mother's selfish irresponsibility to the very real love beneath it, and she'd learned to accept her father's distance. She'd learned to be strong and loving to her younger sisters, generous with her mother, and accepting of human frailty—until she made the mistake of falling in love with a man who didn't deserve her.

Why she'd ever been fool enough to work for the CIA was another matter. She'd been restless and bored and had needed a better outlet than law school for her razor-sharp intelligence and her longing for excitement. All her life she'd been torn between her need for security and her need for adventure. She needed the security to balance her disrupted childhood, and most of the time that part of her was ascendant. But her mother's gypsy blood made her break out every now and then, longing for something more exciting, and that impractical longing had made her drop out just before her law boards and give in to Mike Jackson's importunities and work for the Company.

Who would have thought they would both end up in a peaceful, nonprofit organization like Third World Causes, Ltd.? she thought with a lazy grimace. She'd gotten out of the CIA sooner than Mike. It had taken less than a year to become thoroughly disenchanted with the way the Company worked. She could thank Randall Carter for that, she supposed. He did have his uses.

She had still been in training six long years ago when she had met him, was still doing the myriad paper work and secretarial work that somehow was supposed to be suited to female trainees but not male ones. She'd been sent up to Jackson's office, her arms full of secret files involving Yugoslavian terrorists, and even though she knew that the deep, rich voice that was telling her to enter wasn't Jackson's, she had still been unprepared for her first sight of Randall Elverston Carter. She'd almost dropped the files on the carpet.

It had an eerie similarity to today, she thought, burrowing down into her chair. He'd been alone in the office, staring out the window, and he'd turned when she'd entered. His dark eyes had narrowed as they swept over her suddenly gawky figure. He'd had the uncanny ability to make her feel too tall, too gangly, too clumsy. And yet later he hadn't made her feel that way at all.

"There you are, Maggie." Mike had come up behind her. "This is Randall Carter. He's a friend of the Agency's; he helps out every now and then in an unofficial capacity. Randall, this is Maggie Bennett."

Randall had nodded, his elegant head inclining regally. All the while those dangerous eyes had watched her.

Jackson had continued on. "We're sending you out on your first mission, Maggie. It's simple enough—you're to provide cover for an operative traveling through Eastern Europe.

You'll pose as his wife. The whole thing shouldn't take more than a week—ten days at the most. Just a chance to get your feet wet."

Maggie had turned to look at Randall, aquamarine eyes into stormy gray, and there was an unspoken question on her face.

He shook his head. "Not me, I'm afraid," he'd said in that rich, deep voice that was unexpectedly delicious. "Mike's agent is a man named Jim Mullen. He's going to be acting as a sales rep for one of my companies. It should prove a good enough cover."

"One of your companies?" Maggie couldn't help but echo.

"Randall's our quintessential capitalist pig, Maggie," Mike had announced genially, dropping into his desk chair. "Born with a pedigree and a silver spoon in his mouth, and no matter what he does, he just keeps making money, don't you?"

Randall inclined his head once more. "It gets boring."

"I imagine it does," Maggie said faintly. His eyes still hadn't left her. Even after she turned and tried to concentrate on Jackson, she could feel them, feel their pull—a pull she recognized, even with her limited experience, as purely sexual.

"So poor Randall gets his kicks helping out," Jackson had said, and his gaze flew back and forth between the two of them, not missing a thing, neither Maggie's averted face and stiff back nor the intense, unreadable expression on Randall Carter's aristocratic face. Jackson knew how to read faces, and he didn't like what he saw. He didn't like complications. "But you two won't be working together," he added abruptly. Randall finally looked away from Maggie and turned a quizzical expression toward the older man at the sudden change in plans. "Maggie, I can brief you just as efficiently as Randall can, and we don't want to bore him with details." He smiled his friendly smile that hid his barracuda nature. "Randall's easily bored," he added to Maggie. "As long as we keep him reasonably entertained, he'll help us. So we try to spare him all the nitty-gritty of everyday life."

"I don't think I'd find Maggie boring." His voice was low

and mesmerizing, and Maggie lifted her head and looked straight into his eyes.

It was a heady experience. A sexual current was flowing between them, a hypnotizing threat that Maggie wanted nothing more than to succumb to. She'd avoided romantic involvements when they'd proved to be more trouble than they were worth. The man staring at her now was nothing but trouble, sheer, terrifying trouble, and normally she would have run. But not this time. She turned and faced him, an unconscious offering that said she was ready for the first time in years to take a chance.

"How's the wife, Randall?" Mike said.

Randall had already learned to be impassive. He didn't even blink. Maggie flinched and withdrew, physically, mentally, emotionally, pulling in on herself. "She's fine, Mike. You already asked after her."

"Did I?" Mike murmured. "I must be getting forgetful. Maggie, we'll go over everything you need to know tomorrow. You won't be heading out until next week—we've got plenty of time to get you settled."

Randall wasn't one to give up easily. "I think I'd do a better job," he said. "And I'm at loose ends right now."

But Maggie had skittered away, nervous and remote. Jackson gave her an approving smile. "We wouldn't think of bothering you, Randall. Maggie and I will handle this just fine."

But Randall had pursued her and had done everything he could to feed her attraction. He'd wanted her, wanted her like he wanted one of those damned works of art he collected, and he'd gone after her. And in the end he'd gotten her.

The quiet snore from the sleeping figure opposite her startled Maggie out of her memories. This wasn't how she'd envisioned spending her first vacation in years, she thought with self-deprecating amusement, which was only a defense against the pain. Hauling bodies around and then wallowing in unwanted memories of Randall Carter. It would be enough to depress even the cheeriest person.

She reached for the bottle of Cutty Sark on the floor next to her chair, refilled her glass, and took a deep drink. She wasn't used to drinking, and she would probably have a hell of a hangover tomorrow—when she'd have to handle the usually overwhelming arrival of her mother. But she'd be even more exhausted if she had no sleep at all, and the sudden reappearance of Randall in her life needed more than willpower to banish. Why the hell did he have to show up now, asking questions about grapefruit marmalade?

And why had he had to show up in Eastern Europe six years ago, just as everything was falling apart?

She'd managed to avoid him during the week before she left. Oh, he'd shown up in the office every now and then when she'd least expected it, and the feel of those dangerous eyes would pull her attention away from the maps and data she was trying to study, and she'd look up to see him, tall and perfectly clothed and somehow more threatening than any half-dressed savage. But Mike had run interference, more out of self-interest than the goodness of his heart, and Maggie had managed to keep her distance. She hadn't been able to keep her imagination and fantasies under control, but no one knew. Except perhaps Randall Carter himself, who seemed to have the uncanny ability to read her mind.

She'd found out about his wife. It had been easy enough to do—Marilyn Carter was a beautiful, socially prominent brunette who appeared often enough in the social pages of the *Post* for Maggie to memorize her patrician features. She'd even cut her picture out and stuck it to her refrigerator door during that endless, hellish week, to remind herself. She should have cut Randall's half of the picture off and thrown it away.

She'd taken off for Eastern Europe with a sigh of relief. Margaret Mullen, off to meet her husband Jim, a representative for Carter Industries who was currently scouting the market for exported automobiles. It would be an easy job, Mike had promised, more a vacation than anything else. Mullen would have done the hard part by the time she got there, and the detailed plans for several Eastern European missile bases would already be making their way back to Washington via another messenger. All she had to do was provide cover for Jim Mullen while they spent an innocent two days touring and then flew back to Washington.

Of course, it hadn't worked out that way. No one had been at the small, seedy airport outside of Gemansk. It had taken her three days to find Jim. He had been holed up in a caretaker's shed in a cemetery that was gruesomely appropriate. His shoulder where the bullet was lodged had already begun to swell and redden.

During those three days, she'd sent word back to Mike. She wasn't supposed to rely on her own abilities—her orders had been exact. If there was a problem, she was to call them with the prearranged code and wait for further instructions. By the time she found Mullen, those instructions had come through: *Wait for rescue.* Someone would be coming.

First aid had been limited during the thirty-six hours she hid out in the shed with the wounded agent. Mullen had been in and out of a mild coma. He had ordered her to leave him when he regained consciousness and had lain sweating and shivering when he was out. Maggie did her best to warm him, did her best to clean the wound that had spread raw, angry red streaks down his torso, and tried to ignore the smell of rotting flesh as she waited in the darkness with tears streaming down her face. She had waited for rescue, hating her own impotence.

"Hey, Maggie." It had been just before dawn, and Mullen was conscious again, if just barely so.

"Yes, Mullen," she had said, pulling herself together and moving back to his bedside. She'd known him only casually in Washington, but in the last thirty-six hours he'd become intensely important to her. Somehow, some way, she had to get him home safely. Her peace of mind, her faith in herself depended on it.

"You gotta get out of here."

"We've spent the last day and half arguing about this. I'm staying."

"Look," he said—and she could see the effort the words cost him—"even Vasili had the sense to get away after he brought you here. He can't help the Resistance if he's dead, and neither can you. You're just going to go down the tubes with me—and for what? It's too late for me; you know it and I know it. The only thing you can do for me is to get away from here safely."

Maggie mopped his pale, sweating brow—a useless gesture that soothed her more than it did him. "I've told you before. My orders are to wait here for rescue. Mike Jackson would have my skin if I disobeyed, and you know it."

He'd even managed a weak laugh. "He's going to have mine, for screwing up so badly. Damn it, Maggie, you've got to leave."

"I'm not going anywhere."

"Yes, you are." She hadn't heard him enter. Some secret agent she was—someone could sneak up on her without her noticing. He stood in the doorway of the shed with the dawn sky lightening behind him; it cast his tall body in shadow. She didn't need the light to tell her who it was. She'd known, with a sense of fatality, who it would be.

He moved across the dirty little room and squatted down beside Mullen's supine body. "How are you doing, Jim?"

"Randall." There was relief in his voice, relief and resignation. "It's a code thirty-seven, I'm afraid."

"You sure?"

"What's a code thirty-seven?" Maggie had demanded, and Randall looked up at her from his position beside Mullen.

"That's only for senior agents," Mullen said with a grim smile. "You'll get her out, Randall?"

"I'll get her out. Have you got everything you need?"

"I'm set. Take care of her, will you? She's a good woman."

Randall had managed a cynical smile. "Now what the hell would I do with a good woman, Jim?"

And Mullen had laughed. "You'll think of something. Thanks, Maggie."

She'd stood there, uncertain, exhausted. "Aren't you coming with us?" She'd been too tired to see the look that had passed between the two men.

"He's coming later," Randall said, patting Mullen's clenched hand and rising to loom over her in the predawn light. "We've made special arrangements."

"Maybe I should wait—" She didn't even bother to finish the sentence. His hand had clamped down over her wrist, and his face had been remote, implacable.

"Maybe you should come," he interrupted. "Good-bye, Jim."

"Good-bye, Randall." His voice was stronger than it had been in the thirty-six hours she'd been attending him. "Take care, Maggie."

"You, too." She'd had no choice but to follow Randall, what with that manaclelike grip on her wrist. She'd climbed into his Mercedes and sunk into the leather seat with mingled relief and doubt.

Randall had said nothing as he started the car and drove out of the graveyard. She allowed herself a furtive glance at him as they drove down the road, then leaned back against the seat. It was out of her hands. There was nothing she could do to fight it, not at that moment. And closing her eyes, she'd fallen asleep, never guessing what they'd left behind in that tiny shack.

*But I know now,* Maggie thought, stretching her cramped legs out in front of her and pouring herself another glass of Scotch. She knew, and would always remember, exactly what she'd left behind in that cemetery. And she'd remember that Randall had had full knowledge, damn his soul to hell. Holding up her glass, she drank a silent toast to the memory of Jim Mullen.

# five

There were few things Randall Carter detested more than hotel rooms. No matter how spotless, no matter how luxurious, they all had a mass-produced feel that left his skin crawling and his spirits edgy.

Not that that was unusual nowadays, he thought, stretching out on the king-size bed that was much too big for one person, even for someone as tall as he was. There were times when it seemed as if he'd spent his entire adult life waiting for something, working for something, only to have it become worthless once he had it in his hands. Except for Maggie Bennett. He hadn't had a chance to lose interest in her. He'd been careless, damnably careless, and she'd slipped away like a wisp of fog, and during the last six years there'd been no way he could get back to her, to find out why she had this incomprehensible effect on him. Until now.

He could remember the first time he had seen her, standing in Mike Jackson's office, long and leggy and curiously untouched, like a young colt, with those magnificent aquamarine eyes staring up at him. If he believed in love at all, much less in love at first sight, he would have known what it was that had knocked him sideways. But he didn't believe in those things; he called it sex, and he was determined to get her.

His wife's existence was a minor inconvenience that he intended to ignore, as he'd ignored it before. But he'd seen Maggie's withdrawal when Jackson mentioned her, and he had known it wasn't going to be easy.

And it wasn't—which only made him more determined. He was very careful not to hound her. He'd simply appear when she least expected it, making no demands. He'd just watch her, knowing she felt the same pull he felt. Knowing that sooner or later she'd get tired of fighting it, and he'd have her.

He thought he'd have more time. He'd made his plans carefully, baiting his trap, waiting for her to return to Georgetown after her first easy mission. But that easy mission had gone suddenly, horribly awry, and he'd taken off in the dead of night to try to salvage some part of it. And the part he wanted most to salvage had been Maggie Bennett.

He loosened his tie, kicked off the handmade Italian shoes, and sipped the brandy that was older than he was. The hotel room was the best money could buy, but it was barren, anonymous, and empty. *Lonely* was a word he never used, refused to use, but it was dangerously apt. He took another slow sip of the brandy, leaned back against the feather pillows, and gave himself up to the indulgence of remembering Maggie.

"I don't feel right about leaving Jim," she'd said when she'd woken up two hours later. It had been almost six in the morning, and she had looked like a sleepy kitten, rumpled, hungry, and utterly delectable. Randall had always liked sleek, well-groomed women, every hair in place, makeup perfect. Maggie's wheat-colored blond hair was a tousled mane around her pale face, and when she yawned, stretching with uninhibited abandon, he'd almost driven off the side of the road.

"You didn't have any choice in the matter," he said repressively.

She looked up at him. "No, I suppose I didn't. How long before they pick him up? I hate to think of him alone there when he's in such pain."

"They?"

She was bright enough, he had to grant her that. She simply didn't have much experience with how brutal intelligence work could be. "They," she repeated. "Your backup people. The ones sent over to rescue us. The ones who are going to get

47

Jim out and get him back to the States and to medical treatment."

"I'm the only one who was sent over."

She'd stared at him, her face growing paler. "His contacts had disappeared. They couldn't help him."

"No."

"Then you were willing to let him be picked up by the local police? He's been in and out of a coma—how do you know he won't say something incriminating?" she demanded. "And how long will he have to wait there for help?"

He'd considered lying to her. But it wouldn't work—he could see there in the back of those wonderful eyes that she knew. She just didn't want to believe it.

"He won't need any more help," he said, and his voice sounded cold, distant. He'd known Jim Mullen for five years, had worked with him, had his life saved by him. He was damned if he was going to let the woman next to him know what he'd gone through in the last few hours. Knowledge was power, and he couldn't afford to give her that power. His long, slender hands clenched the steering wheel of the Mercedes, then relaxed. "Jim's dead," he said.

"What the hell are you talking about?"

"Don't be naïve, Maggie. You saw what kind of condition the man was in. Even with the best of American medical technology, he wouldn't make it. He'd been holed up in that shack for days before you got there. If we had tried to take him with us, we would have walked straight into the arms of the secret police."

"At least then he would have gotten some help."

Randall laughed, a singularly unpleasant sound. "He would have been tortured to death, Maggie. It's better this way, and Mullen knew it. It sounds melodramatic, but cyanide capsules are standard issue on any undercover mission, no matter how innocuous they seem."

"Code thirty-seven," she said in an odd little voice.

"Exactly."

"And you let him do it," she said, her voice rich with loathing. "You did absolutely nothing to try to help him, to get him out of there. You just left him to die."

He looked across at her, his face enigmatic. "I brought another capsule in case he'd lost his."

She hit him then. She'd gone for him, dry-eyed and furious, pounding on him, scratching, punching, but in her exhausted state it had taken little effort for him to subdue her, even with having to control the vehicle at the same time. He drove into a ditch, slammed it into park, and caught her arms. He twisted them just enough to bring sanity back.

Finally she had subsided, sinking back against the seat limply, her eyes still wide with dazed hatred. "You're a murderer," she said in a low voice.

Slowly he released her arms. "Yes," he agreed. "Though not in this case."

It had shocked her out of the last remnants of fury. She was looking at him, he thought, as if he were Dracula about to bite her neck. The idea had a certain charm. He found that the deathly depression that had settled around him when they'd left Mullen was beginning to lift. "Life is like that, you know," he'd continued. "It's not clean and pretty and fair. Good people die, bad people prosper, and you do filthy, rotten things to survive. And if you can't accept that, can't do the same, then you've picked the wrong career."

She didn't hesitate. "I picked the wrong career," she said. "Where are we going?"

"A little industrial town near the western border."

"Does it have an airport?"

"It does. We, however, are not going to make use of it. At least, not right now."

"What do you mean?"

"Jim's body will be found within the next few hours, and then the hunt will be on. They'll suspect he wasn't here alone, and they'll be wanting to find out who was with him. We'll have to lie low for a day or two, until they decide he didn't have anyone with him."

"Oh, God."

The quiet sound of those words had sent an answering surge of tension through him. "What?"

"I left my phony passport behind. Jim took it when I got there, and I don't even know where he hid it. Should we go back?" She shuddered at the thought.

"No."

"Maybe they won't find it."

"They'll find it. I suppose it has your picture on it?"

"Most passports do," she snapped.

He nodded. "All right. There's nothing we can do about it for now. We'll figure something out once we get to the safehouse."

"Is there such a thing?"

"Our friend Vasili arranged for an apartment down by the railroad tracks. People leave you alone down there, he said. As long as we lie low, we'll be all right."

"For how long?"

He'd looked at her then, at the stubborn, angry set to her mouth, the pain and sorrow still lingering around her fine eyes. "That'll depend on how long it takes to get you another passport."

"In other words, it's my fault."

"In other words, don't complain if it takes awhile," he said evenly, his voice showing none of his feelings. He'd seen the apartment—Vasili had insisted on showing him before he went to fetch Maggie. It was one room, with a table, two chairs, and a double bed. Randall had every intention of using that bed to good advantage while they were holed up waiting.

He saw the dislike in her eyes, and he knew why it was there. She was keeping it in place to fight off her attraction to him. He knew women too well not to recognize when one wanted him, and he knew Maggie Bennett wanted him as much as he wanted her. A day trapped in that dingy apartment hiding from the police, and middle-class morality was going to fly out the window. It was the only thing that could push Jim Mullen's white, sweating face out his mind.

Randall sat up, staring around his luxurious hotel suite with unseeing eyes. For a moment he'd been back in that tiny little room with the cracked plaster, sagging ceilings, and the smell of cabbage embedded in the walls. And Maggie had been there, staring at him out of those eyes of hers, a mixture of anger and panic and something far more pleasant warring for control. He'd broken that control once, and he could do it again, fighting through her defenses until he had her exactly where he wanted her. And he would do it again, and again, and again, until he finally understood and grew tired of her—and brought the whole tangled affair to his own end.

That must have been the problem, he'd told himself more times than he could remember. He couldn't get her out of his mind because it wasn't over. He'd walked out on her with unfinished business between them. And because they hadn't settled it, he'd been unable to get on with his life. But that would be over, soon. And then maybe he'd get rid of the aquamarine eyes that haunted him.

In the meantime, maybe remembering wasn't such a good idea after all. Nor was lying alone in an empty hotel room thinking about her. He needed to be out among people; he needed distraction. He moved from the bed, headed toward the telephone, then stopped. There was no one he could call, no one he wanted to call. He was trapped, waiting. As he'd been waiting six years. With a silent curse, he turned back to the brandy.

She was getting drunk. It was a pleasant enough feeling, Maggie thought, sipping at the Scotch and smiling at the darkened living room and the sleeping figure of her sister. Hell, she deserved to get drunk—she'd faced the ghost of her past and survived. Randall Carter, in the flesh, was something she'd assiduously avoided for so long, it had become second nature to her. Then he'd shown up, the skeleton at the feast, when she was least expecting it, asking questions about grapefruit marmalade. Fancy he'd remember that, she thought, shifting around in the chair with careful deliberation, not spilling a drop of her umpteenth drink. Why would he remember it after all those years?

The apartment had been small and squalid. Randall had left the Mercedes on a side street, where Vasili would pick it up and return it, no questions asked. They'd made it down the narrow, depressing streets and up the three flights to their room without running into anyone. And there Randall had abandoned her, with nothing but the hot plate, chairs, and the bed, while he went off and met with the underground.

If the thirty-six hours by Jim Mullen's side had seemed endless, these were even more so. She sat in the sturdier of the spindly chairs, staring out the window into the depressing streets of Gemansk, and tried to stay awake.

In the end it had been a useless battle. She crawled into the bed, just for a few moments, and then exhaustion took over, followed by a deep, drugged sleep.

She would have been fine without the dreams, she told herself later. She'd done a great job of fending off Randall, of ignoring the insidious attraction that he'd been trying to feed. But dreams pay no attention to common sense, and she lay on the sagging bed in a cocoon of sleep, prey to the erotic fantasies of her subconscious mind. The dream was so different from any of the unpleasant sexual realities she'd experienced that she awoke, flushed, sweating, completely aroused, to hear the sound of a key in the thin panel door.

It had been dark in the hideout. Fitful light filtered in from the streets, and through the thin walls and ceilings Maggie could hear footsteps, voices, babies crying. Randall stood in the doorway, illuminated by the dim light bulb from the hall, and for the first time since she'd known him, he wasn't wearing one of his impeccable suits. He was dressed like the workers on the street, in rough clothes and work shoes; his black hair looked longer and scruffier around his head, setting off the Slavic cheekbones. He shut the door behind him, plunging them both into semidarkness, and he came across the room to the bed, dumping a bag on the rough little table as he moved. He still had that peculiar grace of his; it would have set him apart from the workers of Gemansk, but she had little doubt that he'd corrected that in public. She lay on the bed, bemused and unmoving, as he approached her.

"I've brought you some clothes," he said, and his low, rich voice danced along her nerve endings. "Vasili will be by after midnight with some food. Until then, there's nothing we can do but wait."

She nodded, then thought that perhaps he couldn't see her, so she tried to speak. Her voice came out a little hoarse. "Yes."

She could see the flash of teeth in the dim light. The big bad wolf, she thought fancifully. What did he find to smile about in their current situation? "We have to keep the lights off. This apartment's supposed to be empty. We don't want any of our neighbors coming to investigate."

There was nothing else she could say. "Yes."

He moved closer, so that his long legs were touching the bed, and she could see that his shirt was open, exposing a strong, tanned chest. It made him desirable, and it made him irresistible. She stared up at him, her face mirroring all of her thoughts.

He knelt down beside her, and his hand reached out to touch her face. It was still his hand, strong, thin-fingered, ringless. That didn't mean he shouldn't be wearing one, she tried to remind herself, but failed. His hand gently stroked the side of her face, and his fingers brushed her lips. And then it was too late—his mouth was on hers, his hands had claimed her, and the darkness of the Gemansk night closed around them.

"Yes," she said. "Yes."

Why the hell couldn't he stop thinking about her? Randall began pacing back and forth over the thick wall-to-wall carpeting of the hotel room, trying to blot the memory of that look from her eyes when he'd come back and found her waiting for him. Panic, anger, and wanting had all been mixed up. He'd known how to use all three. He'd known how to use her.

She'd been strangely docile as he'd stripped the clothes off her, but he'd liked that. He'd liked kissing her, arousing her, playing with her until she was lying in his arms, shivering and gasping and trembling, reaching for him with desperate hands that were clumsy and untutored and infinitely arousing despite, or because of, their innocence. He had half-expected to find her a virgin, was almost disappointed when he finally took her, plunging into her with a deep, almost savage stroke and finding no barrier. But disappointment was the farthest thing from his mind as she tightened around him, clinging to him, strange, moving little sounds of both panic and desire coming from the back of her throat. It hadn't taken him long to bring her to the peak—she was starved for it, desperate for it, and he exulted in his sense of power, bringing her to ecstasy again and again, until she was weeping against him, begging for him, and he'd finally dropped his iron control and given himself to her, plunging deep and losing himself as he seldom dared to do.

If she'd looked shell-shocked, still half-panicked, it was nothing compared to what he felt when he finally pulled away from her. Suddenly he was exposed, naked, and vulnerable. And his panic matched hers.

Slowly he sat up beside her and waited until his voice was steady and his breathing had quieted. "If you're that good already," he drawled, his voice cool and distant, "I can't wait till you've had a little practice." And he'd sat and watched her withdraw, close in on herself without a word. And then he'd watched her as she slept.

Randall tossed back the brandy with less than his usual respect, slammed the snifter down on the fake antique furniture, and headed for the bathroom. Damn Maggie Bennett. By the time this was over, he'd be able to forget her. That was a promise, and he never broke his promises to himself. To others, perhaps, but not to himself.

But he never lied to himself, either, not if he could help it. As he stood under the icy beads of a cold shower, he wondered whether it was going to be a promise he had any chance of keeping.

# six

When Maggie awoke the next morning, she was lying fully clothed in the guest-room bed. The sheets were tangled around her body, and she had no memory at all of how she had got there. Her head was pounding and throbbing, her mouth tasted like dust, and her spirits had plummeted even lower. For a moment she considered burrowing down under the sheets, bursting into tears, and hiding away from everything she didn't want to face. But Kate would have left for work hours ago—there was no one to witness her weakness. And Maggie Bennett was made of stern stuff. She threw back the covers and staggered, moaning, to the shower.

She was standing in the tub and turning around under the stinging spray of the shower when full consciousness returned. And she remembered what shower she was standing in.

She screamed and jumped out of the tub, bringing down the new shower curtain that Kate had bought the day before, and then collapsed on the toilet seat, shaking. "Hell and damnation," she said out loud in a shaky voice, pushing her sopping hair away from her face. She was tough, but nothing on this earth was going to make her get back in that shower.

She leaned over, turned off the spray, and headed down the hallway to her sister's bathroom to finish her shower. Her wet feet left a trail of footprints on the pale gray carpet. The living room curtains were open letting in a flood of pale yellow sunlight, and Randall Carter sat on the couch watching her.

Her Scandinavian blood had left her essentially unconcerned about her nude body, but having Randall see her was another matter. She would have preferred Jack the Ripper. She could feel the flush covering her pale skin as she met his incurious gaze. "Pervert," she said, and kept walking. His soft laugh followed her.

By the time she climbed into Kate's shower, she was well and truly awake. She stalled as long as she could. There was no question but that Randall would be there when she emerged, but she intended to be completely in control before she made her second appearance of the day. Kate kept aspirin in her medicine chest, makeup under the sink, perfumes and skin creams and everything a sybaritic female could want. That Kate usually had only minimal interest in such things didn't pass Maggie unnoticed.

Maggie washed her hair, blew it dry, shaved her legs, flossed and brushed her teeth, rubbed Chanel 22 body cream all over her skin, gave herself a manicure, a pedicure, and a facial mask, discovered a partially done crossword puzzle in the trash and completed it in eyebrow pencil, and finished it all with stretching exercises. It was damned hard to stretch an almost-six-foot-tall body in a six-foot bathroom, but she managed—the thought of Randall in the living room waiting spurred her on. She tried not to think much about Randall Carter, but one thing was indelibly etched in her memory: He hated, he absolutely detested, to be kept waiting. She doubted he'd learned patience in the last six years.

She had no choice but to make use of Kate's silk Chinese bathrobe, which didn't do much to cover her statuesque proportions. Now, if she really had guts, she told herself, she'd walk back down that hall stark naked, just to show him how little he mattered to her. But that much guts she was sadly lacking, and even the skimpy turquoise silk bathrobe was too revealing to be completely comfortable.

He was still sitting where she'd left him, immaculate and at ease, the Italian gray suit fitting him to perfection. He'd helped himself to coffee, in Kate's best Limoges cups, of course, and he lounged, if Randall could ever be said to lounge, on the wide white sofa with his long legs stretched out in front of him.

He looked up when she reappeared in the hallway, and his gray eyes swept over her, impassive as always.

"Still here?" she demanded.

"Still here," he replied. "Did you expect otherwise?"

"No. But one always hopes." The animosity in her own voice startled her. She wasn't that sort of person. But her outward hostility disturbed her far more than it seemed to disturb him. Carefully she pulled her self-possession back around her. "You could get me a cup of that coffee while I dress. I drink it with cream."

His faint smile was hardly reassuring. "I remember," he said. "Do you want anything to eat? Your sister left some croissants."

"Sounds good," she said with equal courtesy. "I'll take one with grapefruit marmalade." Better to attack, she thought, than to wait for him to bring it up.

She didn't waste any time dressing, making do with faded jeans and an oversize cotton shirt. Randall hated jeans, hated casual clothes. She left her feet bare as a final act of defiance.

In the full daylight of her sister's living room, she got her first good look at him in six years. He'd aged, of course. That handsome face of his had new lines, lines that certainly hadn't come from smiling, she thought as she accepted the coffee, being careful not to touch him. No gray in his hair yet, no drooping of skin and muscle. It was his eyes that were old, she realized. Their expression belonged to a man twice his age. He'd already seen too much when she'd known him before—what more had he seen in the last few years?

He waited until she'd seated herself in the overstuffed chair where she'd spent most of last night, then went calmly, gently on the attack. "Why did you scream and rip the shower curtain down?"

She'd taken a sip of the coffee, and the blissfully strong caffeine was flowing through her veins. She didn't even falter;

she lifted her eyes to meet his. "The hot water shut off, and I got a blast of ice water," she said.

"How long did it take you to come up with that answer?"

"I would have had plenty of time while I was in Kate's room," she replied. "But actually, I just thought of it right now. Pretty good for spur of the moment."

"Not good enough. Did you kill Francis Ackroyd in that bathtub?"

She leaned back, considering him for a moment. "Did Bud Willis send you here to extricate us?" she demanded, refusing to answer his question.

"No."

"Let me rephrase that. Did Bud Willis send you to Chicago three days ago?"

"Bud Willis doesn't send me anywhere."

"Dammit, Randall," she said, her spurious calm vanishing, "why are you here? And don't tell me it's coincidence—I won't believe you."

"I wouldn't lie to you, Maggie—"

"Bullshit," she said inelegantly.

"I'm here because of Francis Ackroyd," he continued smoothly, ignoring her outburst. "But not because of his death. He was selling government secrets to the Eastern bloc. We were trying to put a stop to it."

She blinked and digested the information in no more than a moment. "How?" she demanded. "How was he getting the information in the first place? How was he managing to pass it?"

Randall gave a long-suffering sigh. "If we knew that, dear heart, I wouldn't have to be here. No one knows how he was doing it or who was helping him. He couldn't have been doing it alone—that much is certain. The question is, who else was involved? Your sister seems a good possibility."

"What!" she shrieked. "You're out of your mind, Randall! Not that I didn't already know that. Kate is the sweetest, most innocent, most loyal—"

"Kate's in the midst of a nasty custody battle. Such things

are notoriously expensive, and espionage pays quite well. She may not have known what she was getting in to, and then when she found out, she had a blowup with Francis at work, lured him back to her apartment, and murdered him."

Maggie controlled her temper. Randall was very good at infuriating people, just to see them lose control and let something important slip. She wouldn't give him that pleasure. "You don't believe that."

He smiled faintly. "No, I don't believe that. But it's a possibility."

"What makes you think Kate had anything to do with Francis's untimely death?"

"I happened to be in his apartment when you lugged his body back and dumped it onto the kitchen floor. That aroused my suspicions."

"Damn you, Randall. Why didn't you call the police and have me arrested?"

"The less the police are involved, the better. Let's stop fencing, Maggie. I'm here, I'm involved, and there's nothing you can do about it. I want to know what you know, and then I want your word that you'll keep out of it."

"I thought you wondered if I'd killed Francis myself," she shot back.

He shrugged. "Did you?"

"Do you think I could kill a man in cold blood?"

"Undoubtedly. Particularly if it were me."

"Don't flatter yourself, Randall. I couldn't care less about you one way or the other."

"Then why are you clutching that cup and saucer like it's about to fly out of your hands?"

She considered that for a brief moment and was tempted to throw them at his sleek, handsome head. Carefully, she loosened her tight grip on the china, smiling sweetly. "I've got a hangover, Randall. It makes me edgy."

"You didn't used to drink too much."

"Give me strength," she muttered imploringly to the dregs of her coffee. Her eyes met his, calmly. "I don't drink too much as a general rule, Randall. Not that it's any of your damned business if I want to become a lush."

"It is when you're involved in something I'm working on." His voice was rich, smooth, unconcerned. She could almost believe it was pure self-interest that prompted him.

"Why are you working on it? Why didn't they send someone else—why pick their handy elitist volunteer? I presume this is still volunteer work—you haven't joined the CIA yet?"

"It's still volunteer work. You know I never cared for joining groups."

"Still the aristocrat. Why are you here, Randall?"

"We figured I'd be useful because of my connection with Kate's family."

"What connection with Kate's family?" She racked her brain for some distant kinship with Brian's silver-spoon relatives. No wonder she'd never trusted him.

"You."

Maggie set her coffee cup down carefully. "Any connection with me is ancient history. I realize that half the intelligence network of the world knows all the sordid details—"

"Never sordid, Maggie."

"Sordid," she said firmly. "But they should also know that I haven't even seen you in six years."

"It still provides decent cover. I don't necessarily have to be investigating Francis's proclivities. I could be here to take up where we left off in Gemansk."

"It'll be a cold day in hell," she snapped.

He raised an eyebrow, that quiet, elegant gesture that used to defeat her. But not this time. There was no way he could touch her, no way he could demoralize her, she promised herself fiercely.

"I didn't say we were going to, Maggie dear. I just said it could look that way."

"You'd need my cooperation for that."

He smiled that cool, mocking smile that still managed to cause an occasional nightmare. "Oh, I'm counting on that."

"And why would you be so foolish as to do that?"

"Because your sister's at stake. We can protect her—I can protect her, if I want to. Or I can throw her to the wolves. It's not an opportune time for your sister to be charged with murder. Or at the very least with obstructing justice. It does happen to be against the law, you know, to drag murdered bodies around Chicago."

"Is it really?" She kept her voice cool and remote, not for a moment showing her inner panic.

He nodded. "Not to mention freezing them first. Really, Maggie, how unspeakably tacky. Couldn't you have tossed him into the trunk sooner?"

"It was spur of the moment," she said faintly. "What do you want from me, Randall?"

He smiled briefly, that chilly, slightly mocking smile, and for a moment she stared at him in complete confusion. How could she have ever thought herself in love with such a man? He had no warmth, no love, no tenderness at all—qualities that Mack Pulaski had had in abundance. Randall Carter was a cold, calculating man, permanently bereft of any trace of human kindness. The thought of making love to such an automaton was distasteful, and she wondered how she could have done it. And how she could have become so obsessed with him in such a short time. Thank God all that was in the past, more like a bad dream than a memory. There was no way he could touch her, ever again. Not with the memory of Mack's real love like a talisman to guard her against evil.

"Cooperation," he replied. "Simple cooperation, Maggie. I want to know what you know about all this, and I want you to keep out of it from now on. No more lugging bodies around, no more phone calls to Bud Willis, no more snooping and prying. Leave it to me."

"Screw yourself, Randall," she said pleasantly. "The only thing I'd leave to you is the *Titanic.*"

He moved so fast, she didn't have time to react. One moment he was staring out the window, the next he was looming over her, his hands gripping the arms of her chair, his long arms imprisoning her. He didn't touch her, but the threat was very real, tangible, and faintly, perversely erotic. "Don't be tiresome, Maggie," he murmured. "What do you know about Francis Ackroyd?"

She stared up at him, determined not to be intimidated. But he wouldn't move away until he got the answers he wanted, and she needed him to move quite desperately. "Nothing. He and Kate had a fight over some discrepancies in the books at Stoneham Studios. I think it was Caleb McAllister who first discovered the problem."

"I've met him." He stayed where he was, unmoving.

"According to Kate they had a massive blowout, screaming and yelling at each other in the studio commissary with many witnesses," she continued. Her voice was low-pitched and nervous, and there was nothing she could do about it. "Francis disappeared shortly afterward. Kate worked late. When she got home, sometime after six, she found Francis in the guest bathtub with a bullet in his brain."

He nodded. "That explains your distaste for the guest bathroom. When did you appear on the scene?"

"An hour later. I was flying in to stay for a few days to give her moral support during the court hearing."

"And instead you've been serving as impromptu undertaker. Whose idea was it to hide the body?"

"I don't know." She reached up a hand to push her hair out of her face, and it brushed his gray suit jacket. She pulled her hand back quickly, and her breathing was ragged. "Would you mind moving back a little, Randall? I don't like being crowded."

"In a moment." He remained where he was, and she considered kicking him. She would have if she weren't so afraid of touching him. No, that wasn't it. She wasn't afraid of anything. She just didn't want to. "So you shoved him into the refrigerator, and then carted him back to his apartment. How did you know he was murdered there?"

"I didn't. It was an educated guess. Randall—"

"Do you think your sister told you the truth? Do you think she killed him?"

"Of course not! Kate wouldn't hurt a fly."

"Then why do you think someone dumped him here? Do you think she's involved?"

"How do you expect me to answer that, Randall?" Maggie snapped. "She's my sister, for Christ's sake!"

"I want you to answer it honestly, Maggie. I wouldn't expect anything less from you." He still hadn't moved. She found that her hands were shaking in her lap.

"I don't think she has anything to do with Francis's activities or his murder," she said finally. To her amazement, Randall nodded.

"But why was he dumped here? Why wasn't he left where he was murdered?"

"To frame Kate."

"Why?"

"Because she was there," Maggie snapped. "Because she happened to have had a very public fight with him a few hours before he was killed, a fight in which she threatened to kill him. It was a situation tailor-made for a setup. Don't give me that look, Randall. I know it's farfetched, but having a dead man turn up in your bathtub is equally farfetched."

"I think you're probably right."

"Besides, I wouldn't jump to any conclusions. . . . What?"

"I said I think you're right. Your sister checks out completely clean. And I know you well enough to know that you wouldn't cover for her. If she were involved in something illegal or traitorous, you'd drag her in, kicking and screaming, and stand by her all the way. Wouldn't you?"

"Yes."

He moved then; his arms released her from the psychological prison, and slowly her pent-up breathing returned to normal. "So the question is, what are we going to do now?"

She looked up at him, throwing back her mane of wheat-blond hair. "I don't know what you're going to do, Randall, and I don't give a damn. I'm going to find out who tried to frame my sister. If I also find out who's been helping Francis sell information to the communists, I'll be glad to tell you all about it."

"Don't challenge me, Maggie," he said softly. "You won't win."

"This time I might. I'm a lot tougher than I used to be, and I don't take shit from anyone. Especially not from you."

She could see the real effort it took him to control his temper. "It's not going to do anyone any good, working against each other."

"Are you suggesting we work *with* each other?" she countered.

"Heaven forbid. I work alone."

"So do I," she snapped, but the calmer, saner part of her remembered his connections that could prove invaluable. "The last thing in the world I want to do is work with you again."

"I agree," he said promptly.

She stared up at him. "But I might have to make an exception this time," she said slowly.

"Maybe you will. Give me one good reason why I should."

"Because you need me as cover. You have your choice, Randall. Either cut me in, or I'll tell everyone exactly why you're here."

"You'd do it, wouldn't you?"

"I wouldn't hesitate for a moment," Maggie said, lying through her teeth. When it came right down to it, she had no idea whether she'd blow his cover or not. All that mattered was that he think she would.

"So you're not giving me much of a choice," Randall said in that rich, low voice of his, his face distant. "Will you keep your mouth shut and do as you're told?"

"Have I ever?"

He sighed, turned away from her, and stared out the window. His back was tall and straight and slim in the perfect gray suit. "It appears I have no choice in the matter. I guess we're partners again."

Maggie couldn't resist a smug little smile. "I guess we are," she agreed, reaching for more coffee.

Randall watched her reflection in the window and smiled his own smugly triumphant smile.

# seven

"Don't you think a cocktail party is a little macabre?" Maggie muttered under her breath a few hours later, looking around the chattering, well-dressed people on the bare sound-stage at Stoneham Studios.

"It's not a cocktail party, it's a wake," Randall said in a reproving voice. "Haven't you noticed? Everyone's wearing black."

"Even me." She looked down at her clinging silk dress with a disconsolate eye. It was Kate's, and it was too small for Maggie's long-limbed body. The black hem showed far too much leg, the bodice clung almost indecently, and the sleeves pinched her arms. But it was black, and at least somewhat formal, and that was all that mattered.

"There you are." Kate bustled up, breathless, pale, and edgy. "I was afraid you weren't going to make it." Her look at Randall was a combination of awe and surprise; Maggie could well understand both. As for her awe, Randall Carter in black was even more impressive than Randall Carter in dove gray, and he was easily the best-dressed man in the room, which was full of well-dressed men. But that was nothing new.

Her surprise, Maggie knew, was for his date. Ever since Mack's death, she'd kept herself away from men. Not out of any misplaced sense of mourning—she was too well-adjusted for that. It was simply that no man had interested her.

Randall was a hell of a way to start dating again, she thought morosely. But then, she had had no choice in the matter. Kate had called Maggie and Randall separately, inviting them to the party, and she could think of no good reason not to go with him. She'd done her best to remove any illusion that they might actually be socializing by alternating snappishness with silence, until Randall had finally snapped back.

"Your charm, Maggie dear, leaves a lot to be desired."

"I reserve my charm for those who deserve it," she said, knowing her voice sounded sulky but unwilling to do anything about it.

He'd paused at the entrance to Stoneham Studios. It was a huge warehouse on Chicago's West Side, and it was just after six on a sultry summer evening. The heat lay heavy in the air, heavy along her nerves. "I thought we were going to cooperate with each other."

"I'm cooperating," she said. "I'm just not friendly."

He'd raised that damnable eyebrow again. "Really? You could have fooled me." His hand reached out to politely take her elbow, but she yanked herself out of his reach before he could touch her.

This time when he took her arm, she couldn't pull away, not in a crowd of people. Not that she didn't try, but his long, thin fingers bit into the soft flesh above her elbow, and her choice was to make a scene or relax. She promised herself that the scene would come later. Kate was staring at them, her brown eyes wide, and Maggie quickly placed a grim smile on her mouth.

"Maybe you'd better introduce us to our hostess," she said sweetly, moving her high-heeled foot purposefully toward Randall's instep.

"And then we'll mingle," Randall added, side-stepping her attack neatly, his fingers tightening. "Come along, Maggie."

Alicia Stoneham was a great, cheerful, horsey woman with rawhide skin covered with freckles, red hair that was graying in patches, large, tobacco-stained teeth, and a fuschia-colored mouth that often gave way to a braying laugh that had the uncanny ability to make other people laugh, too. She was sitting on the strangest couch Maggie had ever seen, composed of chrome and hot pink plastic, with horns and tendrils and other strange protuberances. Alicia caught Maggie's look

of astonishment and emitted her braying laugh as she surged
to her feet to look her directly in the eye. Which meant she
was over six feet tall, since she was barefoot and Maggie was
wearing heels, Maggie thought as she took the huge, hamlike
hand that Alicia thrust at her.

"It's a prop," Alicia announced in a voice that still maintained a western twang, gesturing toward the sofa, "from one
of Francis's sci-fi epics. Damn, I'll miss that boy." She shook
her head sadly, and the diamond drop earrings, entirely real
and worth a small fortune, shook with her. "You're little
Kate's sister, aren't you? You've got the look of your Ma
about you."

Sybil Bennett was almost a foot shorter and much more
lushly built than Maggie, and she had carefully retouched
raven hair, but Maggie nodded anyway. "So I've been told.
You've met Randall Carter?"

Alicia eyed him approvingly. "You sure work fast, boy,"
she brayed. "Are you going to be as fast coming to a decision
about the Studio?"

Randall smiled his chilly smile. "I never talk business after
hours, Mrs. Stoneham," he said in the wintry voice that had
quelled many a lesser person.

Alicia Stoneham was made of sterner stuff. "Hell, call me
Alicia," she shouted, slapping the elegant Randall on his elegant back. "Mrs. Stoneham's my mother-in-law, may she rest
in peace. Not that she will, of course. That woman was a
troublemaker from way back. I don't doubt she's stirring up
St. Peter something fierce."

"What makes you think she isn't stirring up the devil?"
Maggie asked, feeling immediate fondness for Alicia Stoneham. Anyone who pounded Randall Carter deserved high
marks.

"Hell, that woman was so damned good, she'd make a nun
feel guilty," said Alicia, gesturing with her cigarette and dropping ashes all over Randall's shoes. "Now me, I'm a hell-
raiser from way back. I never let a little morality get in the
way of what needs to be done. It's a lesson you all could

learn." She gestured to the group around her. Maggie could see Caleb in the background; he had a disapproving expression on his long, dour face, and she flashed him a friendly smile.

The fingers tightened again, and she turned to glower at her unwanted escort.

"Who the hell is that?" Randall demanded.

Maggie smiled sweetly at him. Her tallest heels didn't quite bring her up to his height, but she arched her neck and looked him straight in the eye. "Alicia Stoneham."

"I mean the man you were grinning at."

Maggie's smile widened. "Caleb McAllister."

"Good."

"Good?" That wasn't quite the reaction she'd been hoping for. But what *had* she been hoping for? she demanded of herself. "Why 'good'?"

"Because if he's busy here, I can go search his office."

"Guess again, Randall. *We* can go search his office. What are we searching for?"

He stared down his long, elegant nose at her, disapproval radiating through him. "We're looking for anything pertaining to Francis's last project. You know, you'd be a great deal more helpful if you stayed here."

"Why don't you stay here, and I'll go search his office?" Maggie countered brightly. "And if you don't take your goddamned hand off my arm, I'll kick you so hard you won't be going anywhere."

He didn't even blink. "You're welcome to try anytime, Maggie. I haven't slowed down in the last five years."

"Six," she said, and could have shot herself.

He nodded, expressionless. "You're right. It has been six years." He released her. "I thought we weren't going to waste our energy fighting each other."

"I'm not fighting you, Randall. I'm just going to help you search Caleb's office."

He sighed, a put-upon sound that didn't quite match the

deep intensity of his stormy eyes. "What did I do to deserve you?" he murmured.

"You want me to remind you?" Her voice was still and cold.

Randall looked at her, suddenly wary, and she could see there was no need for reminders. He hadn't forgotten a thing. "We only have a few minutes, Maggie. Do you want to spend it on nostalgia or on finding out who framed your sister?"

Her smile was ice cold. "The nostalgia can wait, Randall. Show me Caleb's office."

Their affair had been a mistake from the first. Maggie had known that, just as she'd also known it was inevitable. From the moment Randall had shown up at the cemetery—No, from the moment she'd walked into Mike Jackson's office and seen him—she'd recognized the inevitability of it all.

But that was no excuse. She should have fought, and kept on fighting, and never let him close enough to touch her. It wasn't the physical touching that had done her in, though that was powerful enough. It was the psychic reaching, deep inside her soul, something that cried out to her from some part of Randall that was carefully locked away.

Damn, she'd been a fool to believe such things. The only thing Randall Carter had locked away inside him was a stone-cold, flint-hard heart the size of a walnut. She'd had more than enough proof of that.

She'd learned to forgive herself for her stupid mistakes. She had been alone and frightened and out of her element in that grimy little industrial town of Gemansk. She'd had no sleep, had spent the last day and a half desperately trying to keep a man alive—a man who'd taken his own life the moment she'd left him.

Randall had been in control and had been unmoved by the impossible situation they found themselves in. He had been a tower of strength, and she'd succumbed to the temptation of giving in to that strength, of lying back and waiting for someone else to make everything all right.

It reminded her of her mother. Passive and nondemanding, she'd let him do everything, from getting their provisions to meeting with Vasili to arranging their escape. She'd been content to stay in that dismal apartment and wait for his return. On her back, she taunted herself. And Randall had even taken care of that, demanding nothing of her but the shimmering, instant response he was so good at eliciting.

He had been sitting at the table when she awoke one morning after they'd been there a little over a week. The room had been filled with the depressing blue-gray light of a grimy industrial dawn, and Maggie wanted to bury her head beneath the scratchy sheet and hide. Hide from the bleakness of the day, hide from the bleakness in Randall's blue-gray eyes. Their lovemaking the night before had been tinged with desperation that left Maggie exhausted and frightened. They hadn't slept more than a few hours, and she felt an unbearable sense of doom hovering over them. The remote expression on Randall's face offered no reassurance.

Not even the smell of freshly made coffee could warm the atmosphere. Maggie sat up in bed and pulled the covers over her breasts in a wasted protective gesture.

He looked up from the paper he had been reading. It was as if the mutual passion of last night had never happened. He'd turned to her time and time again in the darkness, insatiable, driven, wearing them both out with his demands. Sometime during the night, their relationship had changed from one of student and teacher, master and apprentice, to something approaching a dangerous equality. Randall had given her a small part of his soul last night, and he didn't like it one tiny bit.

Tough, she thought, scooting down in the bed and giving him her best smile. Which was a neat trick, considering that her mouth was bruised and swollen from his kisses. It was going to work out, despite his ironclad reserve and the unmistakable existence of a wife. She was going to make him love her.

"We're getting out," he said, and his eyes returned to the paper.

She took in that news with mixed emotions. She was desperate to get away from the squalid little apartment, out into the sunshine again. But here, Randall belonged only to her; here, she had the advantage. Out in the real world things might change far too swiftly. "When?" she said.

"Vasili came by this morning, before you woke up," he said, not answering. "There's a man in the visa office who can be bribed."

"When?" she repeated patiently.

"He's trustworthy," Randall continued, still refusing to answer. "He'll keep his end of the bargain if we keep ours. Vasili took him our new passports."

"And?" Maggie decided to be patient.

"And he decided he'd help. For a price." His eyes still hadn't met hers.

A part of Maggie was slowly dying. "What price?"

"You."

"Are you just going to stand there looking dazed?" Randall's deep voice broke through her abstraction.

She'd been following him mindlessly down the maze of hallways in the old warehouse. Now she managed a wry grin. "I'm glad you know where you're going," she said, ignoring his question.

They were standing outside Caleb's corner office. The smoked glass door was shut and probably locked. Maggie banished the last of her unhappy memories. "How are we going to get in?" she demanded. "And don't look at me—I flunked B and E."

"We don't resort to breaking and entering until we're sure we have to," Randall said. "First we see if it's locked."

He reached out his tanned, narrow hand and tried the brass

handle. It moved, silently and easily, and the door swung open.

"Hell and damnation," Maggie breathed. "Someone's been here first."

# eight

The office had been systematically, thoroughly trashed. Papers were everywhere, covering the industrial green carpeting, the battered desk, the shelves, the grimy windowsills, the upended chairs. In one corner, cans of film had been opened, the winding tape was strewn around the room like a black widow spider's party streamers. Videotapes had been smashed in another corner and thrown in a random fury around the room. One of the windows was broken, letting in a blast of early evening heat to war with the air conditioning. Randall and Maggie stood for a long moment.

"Well," she said finally, "at least we have a good idea what we're looking for. And we know they didn't find it."

Randall looked down at her, a quizzical expression on his face. "Explain."

"Videotapes. Every single videotape in the room has been examined and trashed. Some of the cans of film are still intact, so they clearly weren't looking for film. And the papers were thrown at random—there's no way someone could have gone through them all in the short time Caleb's been at the party."

"All right, I'll accept that they were looking for videotapes," he said slowly. "What makes you think they didn't find it or them?"

"Because the remaining ones were smashed in a fury. That hole in the window looks like it's the size of a videotape. If they'd found what they wanted, they wouldn't have stomped all over the remaining ones."

Randall looked at her, then nodded slowly. "You've

learned a lot in the last five—six years," he corrected himself. His small smile did little to lighten his face.

She didn't return the smile. "I had a little on-the-job training, trying to get out of Gemansk," she said, turning her back on him. "Do you want to see if we can find anything in this mess?"

She could feel his eyes on her back, and she kept it stiff, upright, and waiting—for an excuse, for an apology, for some word of what had never been discussed. But now wasn't the time.

"I imagine they've been thorough," Randall said, his voice level. "Let's go back to the party and see if anyone's in a particularly frustrated mood. Apart from me."

She turned to look at him then. "What are you frustrated about? We've learned something, at least."

He was standing very still, his stormy eyes watchful, his face remote. "You're the one who's gotten so smart all of a sudden, Maggie. You think about it."

"If that's your twisted version of a come-on, Randall," Maggie said, her face flushed, "then you have a hell of a lot of nerve."

"Did you ever doubt it?" he countered. "Let's get back to the party." And turning his back on her, he strode from the office, heading back down the long narrow hallways.

She watched him walk away from her. Watched him leave her, without a backward glance, as he'd done so long ago in Gemansk. And closing the door lightly behind her, she followed him.

In the crowd, the level of noise and smoke and heat had risen appreciably in the ten or fifteen minutes they had been gone to check out Caleb's office. Maggie peered through the mingling people, all dressed soberly in black and dark blue, searching for her sister.

"Oh, my God!" she breathed suddenly. "Mother!"

She could feel Randall's start of interest. "Sybil Bennett? Where?"

"Look for the biggest crowd of men," Maggie said wryly, "and Sybil's in the middle of it."

At that moment, Sybil Bennett caught sight of her oldest, tallest daughter, and her wonderfully husky voice, still with an enchanting trace of British accent, cut across the hubbub. "Maggie, darling!" she cried, and the hordes of young and not-so-young men parted like the Red Sea, leaving a narrow path between Maggie and her mother.

A wry smile lit her face as she surveyed her mother for the first time in almost six months. Sybil Bennett looked as glorious as ever, decades younger than her fifty-four years. Her perfect heart-shaped face was unlined, her raven hair was cleverly unmarred by nasty gray hairs, and her petite, lush figure was perfectly maintained. The famous aquamarine eyes looked up at her daughter's matching ones, and a beatific smile made the angelic face even more beautiful. "Maggie, darling," she said again, holding out her silk clad arms, "come to me!"

Ever the actress, Maggie thought, dutifully obeying her mother and crossing the crowded room. Everyone's eyes were on her. Sybil knew how to set a scene to her best advantage, and Maggie'd learned long ago not to mind. Kate was a different matter. She stood on the sidelines, watching with a troubled expression on her face, then joined Sybil and Maggie.

"Sweetheart." Sybil enfolded her into her scented arms. With a wave of her hand she dismissed her admirers, and they faded away reluctantly, leaving the three Bennett women alone in the crowd. Sybil drew back and surveyed her eldest daughter with a critical eye. "You're too tired, Maggie. And that dress is an abomination."

"Thanks," Kate muttered.

"Is it yours, darling?" Sybil was instantly all charming contrition. "It probably looks wonderful on you. But Maggie needs something more . . . dramatic, more *je ne sais quoi* to go with her spectacular looks. I would have given anything to be a foot taller," she added sadly, and Kate groaned.

"I think five feet one of Sybil Bennett is about all the world can take," she said, and Sybil flashed her a brilliant smile.

"Do you think so, darling? You're probably right. I can be a bit overwhelming. Speaking of overwhelming, Maggie dear, who is that magnificent man lurking behind you?"

Maggie couldn't squash the laughter that bubbled forth at the thought of Randall lurking. She should have known he wouldn't take his dismissal lightly. "Randall Carter, Sybil Bennett," she said.

Sybil's face lit up. "So you're Randall Carter."

"What the hell do you mean by that, Mother?" Maggie demanded, her tolerant good humor vanishing.

"By what?" Sybil said, taking Randall's hand and gazing up at him soulfully. At least Randall didn't appear to be taken in by her. He was smiling down at her. The cynical expression in his eyes showed that he saw straight through Sybil's well-executed artifice.

"How did you hear about Randall?" she pursued, and Randall turned his attention back from her mother, his smile broadening.

"Oh, one hears things," Sybil said innocently. Maggie wasn't fooled for a moment, but now wasn't the time to try to pin her butterfly of a mother down. "Can we leave this depressing party? I've always found cocktail parties loathsome."

"Then why do you go to so many?" Kate demanded.

"They're a necessary evil, darling. Let's go pick up Chrissie and go back to my hotel. Queenie can't wait to see her—she's waited so long to be a grandmother."

"Sybil, you're the grandmother, not Queenie," Maggie corrected her, before Kate could explode.

Sybil shrugged her pretty shoulders. "Do I look like a grandmother?" she questioned soulfully. "We all know Queenie's been a better mother to you girls than I ever was. I'm sure she'll be a better grandmother, too." She battered her luxuriant eyelashes up at Randall. "I'm hopelessly impractical," she cooed, and Maggie saw Kate's hands clench into fists. "Why don't you come with us, Randall? We're going to have a late supper in my suite. Alicia and that charming young giant have promised to join us, and you'd be an admirable addition."

"Charming young giant?" Kate echoed in dismay.

"The one with the wonderful Scots name. Caleb McAllister, wasn't it?" She smiled her bewitching smile, and Kate met it stonily. "We'll have iced champagne and cold salads, and we'll figure a way out of this mess." She leaned closer to her unappreciative younger daughter and said in a loud stage whisper that carried to Maggie's waiting ears, "You can take a shower at my place, Kate dearest. I imagine you haven't wanted to use your own recently."

"Mother!" Kate moaned, sounding adolescent. "Please! Can't you be discreet?" She cast a nervous look at Randall.

"I was whispering," Sybil said, much aggrieved. "Anyway, discretion was never one of my strong points. You'll join us, Randall?"

"Randall's got a lot of things going on," Maggie said hurriedly.

"None of which would interfere with me joining you for supper," he continued smoothly. "What time would you like us?"

"Us?" Sybil raised an eyebrow.

"Maggie and I have a little business to take care of first."

"I don't think—" His hand clamped around Maggie's elbow, with just enough pressure to warn her. "I don't think it'll take too long," she continued smoothly. "We'll meet you back at the Mandrake."

Sybil's eyebrow rose higher still. "Of course, darling. Kate and I have a lot to catch up on. Come along, Kate." Her imperious wave was greeted with a stony look from her second daughter.

"Don't take long," Kate muttered as Sybil drifted away, and she followed in her mother's footsteps.

"What is this business we have to conduct?" Maggie turned back to her unwanted companion. "Kate and Sybil don't get along well. Or shall we say, Kate doesn't get along with Sybil.

Mother is so blissfully egocentric that she never notices when she infuriates people. Particularly her daughters."

"Does she infuriate you?"

"Not anymore. But," she added after a moment's thought, "that's none of your business."

Randall smiled his cool smile. "Of course not," he agreed. "And our business is quite simple. We have to break into Caleb's apartment, see if we can find the missing videotape or tapes, and get back out of there before he returns from Sybil's party."

"Oh." Maggie said blankly.

"Would you rather I did it alone?" Randall asked.

She glared up at him. "We're wasting time, Randall. Let's go."

His gray-blue eyes held the unexpected warmth of approval. "I'm ready when you are, Maggie." And if that simple statement held endless implications, Maggie chose to ignore them.

They stopped long enough to check the phone book, and she breathed a sigh of relief that there was only one Caleb McAllister in Chicago. Kate's unwelcome suitor proved to be a man of surprises. Kate had painted a picture of a stubborn, unimaginative man, and Maggie half-expected him to live in an anonymous cubicle in some large block of condos.

Instead, Randall drove them to a small brownstone that was clearly as charming as Kate's aging apartment building. Each floor held an apartment, and Caleb's commanded the third and top floors. The two tall, well-dressed sneak thieves entered the building and climbed the stairs without encountering even a curious glance.

"What are you going to tell Caleb if he finds out?" Maggie demanded when they reached the third-floor landing.

"That will depend on what we find in his apartment, won't it?" he replied. "If we find something incriminating, we may not have to answer any questions at all."

"How come we're picking on Caleb? Do you think he was

Francis's partner in crime? Kate said they didn't get along well at all."

"That may have been a cover. We're starting with Caleb because we have to start somewhere. Since Caleb's office was searched, it seems as if we're on the right track. Let's just hope we've gotten here before they have."

Maggie stood very still, staring at the door in front of her. "Nasty thought. What if they're still in there?"

"I'll expect you to rout them," he replied simply, trying the doorknob.

Their luck didn't hold the second time—the door was unquestionably locked. Meaning there was no one waiting, Maggie decided, forcing herself to relax.

Randall set to work on the lock and within seconds had it open. "How'd you do that?" she demanded, a note of envy in her voice.

"Tricks of the trade, Maggie. Behave yourself, and maybe I'll show you later."

"Maybe you won't be around later, if I have any luck at all," she muttered gracelessly, following him into the darkened apartment with only a start of nervousness.

"No one's gotten to me yet. I have no intention of dying before my time. Haven't you heard? Only the good die young."

God, why did it still have the power to send shafts of screaming pain through her? She'd let go of Pulaski when she'd had no choice, loving him, missing him, mourning him, and then going on with her life. It was only at odd, unexpected moments when it came crashing in on her again.

"You take the living room, and I'll start with the bedroom," he said, flicking on the lights. "I don't need to tell you what to look for?"

"No. I already told you," she said.

"Couldn't resist it, could you, Maggie?"

"I'm only human," she said modestly, looking around the comfortable apartment with approval.

"Sometimes I wonder," Randall muttered, and disappeared into the bedroom.

She was searching through the videotapes by the VCR when she heard the crash. She was at the bedroom door by the time the huge, black-clad figure emerged on the attack. She was flung halfway across the room before she had time to do more than blink, the breath knocked out of her. She lay sprawled across an upended chair, dazed, and watched the ensuing battle.

Randall had been on the masked creature's heels and caught him before he reached the door. It was a short, dirty little fight, unbelievably savage. All traces of the perfect gentleman were gone from Randall's pale, furious face. He connected more than once, a blow to the side that should have cracked a few ribs, a kick to the groin that should have finished the intruder. But the black-clad figure was seemingly invincible, twisting out of Randall's iron grasp, impervious to pain. Randall slammed the dark figure up against a wall and pinned him there for a timeless moment as he reached up to rip the mask away.

And then the door opened. Caleb McAllister stood there, his face awash with shock and anger. The first intruder used the moment to wrench away, shoving Caleb out of the way and racing out the apartment. Randall was on his heels and disappeared into the night, leaving Maggie draped over the living-room furniture. Her face throbbed from its collision with the chair, and her breath shuddered through her body. He had left her to face a very angry Caleb McAllister.

He stood erect, closed the door quietly behind him, and walked into the living room. Looking down at Maggie, he reached out a large hand to her. She considered it a moment, took it, and he pulled her upright with far more courtesy than she deserved, considering the situation he found her in. Damn it, and damn Randall, too, for not having come up with a believable story in case they were caught. Caleb should have gone straight to Sybil's for supper, but there were never any guarantees in this life. Apparently he'd found a reason to stop by his home between parties. Damn and damn again.

Caleb just looked at her, a long, steady look. "I expect you could do with a drink," he said finally. "I know I certainly could. That should give you enough time to think up a plausible excuse. I just hope you're a better liar than your sister. She always blushes."

"Does she lie to you very often?" Maggie's voice came out a little rusty as her breathing returned to normal. Her pulse was still racing and would continue to race until Randall returned in one piece. Not that she gave a damn about Randall, she reminded herself. She just wanted to know if he'd caught the intruder.

"Often enough. Scotch okay?"

"Scotch would be perfect. Straight, no ice. By the way, why didn't you go to Sybil's?"

"I had a funny feeling that something was going on here. I always trust my instincts." He gave her the drink, dark amber and very potent, and waited until she sank down into the comfortable sofa. "Were you and Carter responsible for the shape of my office, too?"

"No. We're much neater than that. I expect it was the man Randall chased out of here who trashed your office."

"Do you have any idea what he was after? Or what you were after, for that matter?" He was unfailingly polite, almost unimaginatively so, and Maggie could see how Kate could underestimate him. The intelligence in those bright blue eyes belied his innocuous manner. Kate would be well advised to look further beneath his polite exterior—it might be well worth it.

"We didn't know what we were after. Anything that might have some bearing on Francis's death. Your intruder seemed to have zeroed in on videotapes."

Caleb nodded. "Of course."

"Of course?" Maggie prompted, taking a deep, soul-satisfying drink of the Scotch.

"I confiscated the tapes of Francis's newest masterpiece,

*The Revenge of the Potato People, Part Two*. He was ready to send them out to the packagers in Europe, and I wasn't about to do that until he answered a few questions."

"What kind of questions?"

"Simple ones. Like why they were so far over budget. Why several versions were filmed. Why, when *Revenge of the Potato People Part One* lost so much money, he had gone ahead with *Part Two*. Why his biggest customer didn't have a phone, an address, or any record of payment when I tried to track them down."

"Who was his biggest customer?"

"Red Glove Films. They're supposedly located in a small industrial town in Eastern Europe that no one's ever heard of."

Maggie had a curious, sinking sensation. "What town?"

"It's called Gemansk. Why the hell they'd have a film distribution company is beyond me." He shook his head, taking a deep sip of his own drink. "So you want to tell me why you and Carter thought you had the right to break into my apartment? And why you decided to suspect me? Or were you more interested in framing me?"

"Caleb, that man hiding in your apartment who Randall was wrestling with was the bad guy, not us. And, apparently, not you. We didn't really suspect you, Caleb. We just had to start somewhere."

"Why didn't you start with your own sister?"

"Do you think she had something to do with it?"

Caleb looked at her. "I don't know," he said finally. "She knows more than she's saying."

"So do I."

He smiled briefly. "You probably had something to do with Francis's death, too. Am I right to assume *The Revenge of the Potato People, Part Two* has something to do with it?"

"It certainly seems so. In which case, we're all involved, whether we know it or not." Was that the sound of someone in the hallway? Her hands were shaking around the warm glass of whiskey. Caleb didn't indulge in air conditioning, and the room still held the trapped daytime heat. That must have been the reason her palms were sweating as she strained to listen.

He didn't bother knocking. The door was still unlocked, and Randall stepped into the apartment—alone. His perfect black suit was slightly rumpled, his hair was mussed, and there was the beginning of a bruise on his forehead. He looked more human than Maggie had ever seen him, and she took another gulp of her whiskey.

"Could I have one of those?" Randall inquired politely. "I need it."

Without a word, Caleb rose and poured him a drink.

"Did you lose him?" Maggie demanded, wondering why she felt an odd sense of relief.

"I lost him. What a complete waste of time," he said disgustedly.

"Not completely," Caleb said. "I still have the videotapes."

# nine

Randall wasn't accustomed to wishful thinking. He'd managed to avoid that weakness all of his adult life, but when he'd returned to Caleb McAllister's third-floor apartment, bloody but unbowed, he could have sworn that Maggie Bennett had greeted his arrival with heartfelt relief.

Not even his news that he'd lost the intruder had put a shadow on the first real smile she'd given him in six years. The sight of that genuine, warm smile had been like a fist in his stomach. With that glowing look on her face, he had to admit that she was the most beautiful woman he'd ever seen in his entire life. And his desire, his semipathological need to have her, to own her, grew to almost unmanageable proportions.

He'd taken his drink calmly. None of his reactions had showed on his well-schooled face as he sat down beside her, grimacing at his scuffed shoes and rumpled suit. And she hadn't moved away. Step one, he thought with wary relief.

"You still have the videotapes?" he now repeated. "Where? And why, for that matter? Did you think someone might try to take them?"

"I had no idea they were of any particular importance," Caleb said. Randall wasn't sure whether to believe him or not. "They're in a box in the trunk of my car. I was going to take them to my sister's in Evanston. She's a sci-fi buff, and I thought maybe she could tell me if the movies are as lousy as I think they are. And maybe she could tell me what the difference is between the two versions—they look identical to me. Certainly not different enough to warrant the expense."

"And they're still in the car?"

"They were ten minutes ago, when I got here."

"Do you mind if we take them?" Randall made the request politely enough. It wouldn't hurt to give McAllister the impression that he had a choice in the matter.

Caleb's ironic smile made it clear that he wasn't fooled. "It wouldn't do me much good to say no, would it?"

"No."

"Then be my guest. You might consider telling me who the two of you are," he said, pouring himself another, lighter drink and holding up the bottle in silent inquiry. Maggie nodded, and Randall could see her reserve creeping back in around the edges. She'd moved away from him on the sofa. That small piece of body language was inescapable. She was withdrawing, and at that moment he couldn't spare the energy to pull her back. It would have to wait.

"Maggie is Kate's sister," he said, shaking his head at the proferred drink. "There's no mystery about that."

"And you?"

Randall smiled, and he could feel Maggie pull away even further, which infuriated him. Next time he wouldn't let her go. Not until he was ready to. "I'm Maggie's lover." He felt her tense and saw her open her mouth to deny it, then close it again. There was a mutinous look on her beautiful, open face.

"And?"

"And what?"

"Why have the two of you decided to find out who killed Francis? Your . . . mistress"—the slight, ironic inflection made it clear that Caleb wasn't swallowing the tale—"already explained that you were searching my place for clues. Do you have an Agatha Christie fetish, or is there some reason you're out to best the police?"

Randall shrugged. "Just idle curiosity."

"Don't treat other people like fools, Randall," Maggie snapped. "Caleb knows something is going on. Surely if he were part of it, no one would have trashed his office and ransacked his apartment. He wouldn't offer us the videotapes if he were part of the espionage scheme."

"Espionage scheme?" Caleb echoed, shocked out of his usual polite complacency.

*Damn the woman,* Randall thought. "Maybe I will have another drink."

"Maybe you'll tell me what the hell is going on," Caleb said.

"You know, Maggie, you shouldn't be so gullible," Randall turned to her, ignoring Caleb's pugnacious demand. "If McAllister were part of this whole thing, he probably has a partner. What better way to appear innocent than to have him look like a victim, have his office trashed and his apartment searched? And then he could helpfully offer us useless videotapes and keep us busy while he took care of the real dirty business of getting the information out of the country and covering up Francis's murder."

"God, you're suspicious," Maggie breathed, awe and disgust clear on her face.

"You'll find, my dear Maggie, that it pays not to trust anyone. Anyone at all." He watched her withdraw even more, and silently he cursed himself.

"That's fine. You live your life that way, if you can call it living," she snapped. "I prefer to take my chances and trust my fellow man."

"You'll only get your heart broken, and maybe lose your life in the process."

"I'd rather die trusting the wrong person than live trusting no one," she said firmly. "And I think Caleb is worth trusting. We have to take a chance sooner or later."

"I don't have a say in the matter?" Randall said idly.

"You don't have a say in the matter."

"I guess you are lovers after all," Caleb broke in finally. "Strangers don't fight that way."

"We are not lovers," Maggie said icily, "and we never will be. Do you want to speculate about my personal life, Caleb, or do you want to know what's going on?" Her tone was clipped and businesslike, different from anything Randall had heard from her before, and he knew there wasn't any way of stopping her short of dragging her from the apartment, kicking and screaming all the way. And though he might be able to overpower her, six feet and four inches of Caleb McAllister along with six feet of Maggie Bennett might prove his undoing.

He leaned back against the sofa, shrugging, and watched as she edged farther away from him. Another few inches, and she'd be on the floor. It would serve her right. His face ached from the blow their hardy assailant had managed to connect, his knuckles were swollen from his own seemingly useless attempts, and there was nothing he wanted to do more than crawl into a nice king-size bed with the woman beside him. The woman who hated him with a very satisfying passion. He only hoped she was that passionate when he finally convinced her of her fate.

He shut his eyes as she spilled everything to Caleb. She held almost nothing back, damn her, from Francis's body in her sister's bathtub to her cross-town trek to hide it. The only thing she kept quiet about was his own reluctant semi-involvement with Bud Willis and the organization at Langley— she had that much discretion. He'd still have to be doubly careful from now on. He'd told her nothing but the simple truth: he didn't trust anyone. Not even her. And now he had two people he had to watch. It was going to be exhausting.

Never, never had he gone to so much trouble to acquire something as he was going through for Maggie Bennett. He'd spent three years tracking down a Renoir he'd fallen in love with; he'd spent a total of five years, off and on, pursuing the Cellini Venus he'd craved. He wanted Maggie Bennett with the same compulsive craving, and this time he wasn't going to back off. She was the only woman who'd never bored him, and he wasn't going to let her go until she did. It would happen sooner or later—it always did. But until he got her back, he wouldn't be able to free his mind and soul from the insidious trap she'd sprung on him.

She didn't want him, he knew that. She hadn't meant to infiltrate his every waking moment for the last six years and most of his sleeping ones, too. If it were up to her, there'd be at least one continent between them at all times.

But it wasn't up to her, not any longer. He'd waited through her stupid, doomed marriage to the young lawyer, waited through her affair with Peter Wallace, and had been just about to move in on her when she met Mack Pulaski. He'd spent a bad two years then, some of the worst of his life, facing the fact that she was totally out of reach. But Pulaski had died, and Maggie had mourned, and now she was free and less than a yard away from him. And he wasn't going to wait much longer.

He opened his eyes; a weary, cynical expression was on his face. "Are you finished?" he inquired politely. "Are you sure you wouldn't like to tell him your shoe size? Or how we made love on the table in that apartment in Gemansk?"

He'd gotten through to her that time. Her face flushed, her hands curled into fists, and she opened her mouth to yell at him. God, he wanted to stop that mouth with his.

But then she snapped it shut again and smiled a wintry smile that was uncannily like his own. "Can we get the tapes from you when we leave Sybil's tonight?"

"Sure, I'll be glad to bring them. Anything else?" Caleb asked.

"Could we borrow some extra tapes? Do you have any that look like the *Potato People* ones?"

Randall sat up then. "What do you have in mind?"

"I'd think it was obvious," she said sweetly. "It's time for a little action. If you're going to sit there and take a nap, it's up to me to be innovative. If I know Sybil, she's invited half the people from Stoneham Studios for dinner. I wouldn't be surprised if our mysterious intruder is among them. So it wouldn't hurt to set a tiny trap."

"Personally," Randall said, rising with grace that cost him a great deal to maintain, "I think I've seen more than enough action for today." He considered wincing, to see if he could elicit that wonderful look of warmth she'd first shown him, then dismissed the idea. "But I know better than to try to talk you out of it. Will we have any trouble counting on your discretion, McAllister?"

"Of course not."

Randall nodded wearily, unconvinced. "I don't suppose we have a choice. Come along, Maggie. We're due at your mother's before long, and I have to stop off to change my clothes."

"What's wrong with your clothes?" Maggie demanded. "If you just fix your tie and wipe some of the dust from your trousers, no one will notice."

"*I* will notice," he said grandly. "Move it, Maggie. My temper is getting very short."

She did smile at him then, and if it didn't hold the warmth it had earlier, at least it was full of mischievous good humor. "Tough," she said sweetly. "See you at dinner, Caleb."

"You realize," Randall said as they descended the three flights of stairs, "that you're trespassing on your sister's domain?"

"What are you talking about?" She was keeping up with him, her long legs eating up the distance. Sybil was right—the black dress was abominable. And she looked absolutely breathtaking in it.

"Caleb McAllister," he said gruffly. "Your sister's in love with him."

"What made you the expert on love, Randall?" she scoffed. "I didn't think you even believed in its existence."

"Oh, it exists all right. For certain people, for a certain short period of time. I've been around your sister and McAllister at the Studios, seen them together. They fight all the time. Therefore, they're in love."

"Simple equation," she said. "You and I fight all the time. Are we in love?"

He almost fell the rest of the way down the flight of stairs. He looked at her surreptitiously and found her face completely expressionless. "No," he said, halting on the first-floor landing. "Real love, if it exists, is selfless, generous, warm, and tender. Isn't it?"

She was thinking of Pulaski. He could tell by that damnable little half-smile. "Yes," she said.

"And if I loved you, I would have wanted to do anything to save you pain. I would have ached for you when your husband was murdered. I would have done anything to spare you that. That's what real love is all about."

"Yes," she said.

"You know what I felt when I heard Pulaski was killed?" he continued in a ruthless voice, knowing what it was going to do to her, unable to stop himself. "I thought of you, alone and free, and I wanted to celebrate."

Her face went very still and cold. There'd be no snuggling in a king-size bed tonight, or for many nights to come, and he wondered why he'd told her. She'd hated him enough already —why did he have to give her more ammunition?

Maybe it was because he knew things couldn't get any better until she knew the worst. And although he'd kept one tiny thing back, the one thing he knew that was cruel and horrible, at least she now knew the bulk of it. He waited, for the imprint of her strong hand on his face, for her to push him down the stairs.

She'd caught hold of the banister, her hand strong and tanned; Pulaski's damned wedding ring was still on her finger. Slowly, she pushed away, stood upright, and in her cold, still face her eyes were alive, furious, and slightly startled. That look of surprise mystified him. "Interesting," she said in a cool drawl. "You are a very strange man, Randall. Let's not keep my mother waiting." And she continued down the stairs, dismissing him and his topic of conversation.

He stared after her for a long moment. No, she didn't bore him. She infuriated, astounded, confused, and aroused him. It would take a long time to understand her, a long time to grow tired of her. That time would come—it always had before. But it would be glorious until then. And he moved after her, feeling oddly lighthearted.

"You're coming in." Randall's voice didn't allow for disagreement. Maggie nodded. She had no desire to sit in the confines of his Jaguar and wait like a dutiful Moslem wife for her lord and master to return.

"I hope you're not going to spend hours primping," she said, following him through the lobby of the elegant old hotel. "I hate to sit around waiting while someone gets compulsive. I'm not going to twiddle my thumbs while you try to match your socks and cufflinks. My sister Holly's bad enough."

"Maggie, dear, everything always matches anyway," he said, stepping into the elevator.

"I'm sure it does." She wished she could get rid of her feeling of uneasiness. Why did he even care, one way or the other, about her life these last six years? That's the question she couldn't answer. Randall Carter had never been one to give a damn about women, or any particular woman. She knew that because, whether she'd been interested or not, someone had always been eager to tell her the latest gossip about him. He'd divorced his wife sometime after he'd returned from Gemansk, with all the care someone would use to fire a trash collector. He'd gone through beautiful, intelligent women at a sedate, genteel rate, collecting and discarding them like works of art. Except that he didn't discard his works of art, she reminded herself. It had actually surprised her that he even remembered her—there'd been no doubt in her mind that what to her was a devastating experience had been all in a day's work for Randall.

But apparently she'd made some sort of lasting impression. Maybe as the one who'd got away. Except that she hadn't gotten away—he'd thrown her away. So why was he here again? What did he want from her? It couldn't be sex—Randall wasn't the sort who repeated himself. Maybe it was wounded pride? But it was her own pride that had been wounded, not his. Not to mention her heart, her soul—God, the very memory still tightened her nerves.

Thank God she no longer cared. Thank God for Mack,

who'd taught her what real love was all about, so that she would never again have to mistake obsessive craving for the real thing. Thank God that she could look at Randall's tall, elegant body, his thin sexy mouth, and his dark, tormented eyes, and not feel a thing. Not a tiny little thing at all.

"What are you looking at me like that for?" He'd stopped in front of his door and searched through his pockets with uncharacteristic abstraction before coming up with his room key. "Are you afraid I've lured you to my room to have my wicked way with you?"

"Randall," she said sweetly, "I'm not afraid of anything. Least of all you."

He opened the door and ushered her into his elegant hotel suite. The French doors were open to the bedroom beyond, and fresh flowers scented the air-conditioned air. *Lilies,* Maggie thought. The flower of death.

She turned her back on him, strolling toward the windows. "Hurry up, will you? Mother hates to be kept waiting. She won't make her grand entrance until everyone is there." There was no reply from him, and she turned. "Randall?"

He was standing very still, staring at the flowers. There was a note propped against the crystal vase. He moved very slowly and picked it up in one long-fingered hand. "Go back to Washington," he read aloud in an expressionless voice. He stopped reading, crumpling the paper in his hand. "A secret admirer, I suppose."

"Is that all it said?" There was more to it than that—her instincts were too well-honed not to notice his sudden hesitation.

"That's all."

"No threats? No 'or else'? Pretty tame, if you ask me," she scoffed, moving across to him. "Surely they don't expect us just to slink away at the first sign of trouble."

"Maybe they thought it would be worth a try," he said abstractedly.

If he'd been expecting it, she never would have made it. But he was thinking of other things, and it was child's play to grab his arm, bring it down over her knee, and force him to release the paper. Maggie was across the room and out of reach before he even realized what she'd done. The crumpled paper was spread out before her eyes.

"Go back to Washington," she read, "or it will be Gemansk all over again." She raised her eyes to meet Randall's angry, impassive ones. "All right, Randall," she said. "What happened in Gemansk?"

# ten

"You know as well as anyone what happened in Gemansk," he said. "Mullen screwed up, I flew in to get you out, and we spent a week in a squalid little apartment before we split up to make our way home. Those are the essentials."

"But something's missing," Maggie said, determined not to back down this time. "You sent me out expecting me to whore for you and then you disappeared. Don't you think you owe me an explanation after all these years?"

"Why? You didn't whore for me, as you so sweetly put it. Wadjowska gave you the visas without soiling your innocent body."

"How did you know that?"

Randall turned from her. "I know everything that happened in Gemansk six years ago," he said, his voice curiously lifeless.

"That's more than I can say. Why don't you tell me what happened, Randall? You owe me that much."

"I owe you nothing."

There was real rancor there, and anger that mystified Maggie. As far as she knew, she was the wronged party, and she'd held that anger inside her for years. "Not after running out on me?" she questioned lightly.

"Damn you, I didn't run out on you!" he snapped, stripping off his rumpled jacket and throwing it onto the couch. She could see the beginnings of a bruise on his temple, and his high cheekbones were flushed with anger. He glared at her, but Maggie refused to be intimidated.

"Didn't you? It looked like that to me."

"Things aren't always what they seem. I don't have time for this right now, Maggie. We're due at your mother's—"

"My mother can wait. I want to know why you abandoned me in Gemansk. I want to know what that note is talking about. I want to know what the hell happened."

"I don't give a damn what you want to know," Randall said, turning his back on her and heading toward the bedroom. "It's ancient history, and it doesn't bear repeating."

"It's not ancient history to me," she cried, racing after him.

He'd unbuttoned his shirt and was in the midst of shrugging out of it when she caught up with him. "Then that's your problem," he said with deliberate patience. "Do you want to watch me do a striptease or are you going to let me change in privacy?"

She'd caught hold of his arm, and now she dropped it, blushing. "Damn your nasty tongue, Randall."

"You didn't always hate my tongue, Maggie."

That was her limit. She marched from the room with all her dignity, slammed the doors behind her, and threw herself down onto the sofa. The note was still crumpled in her fist, and she tossed it down onto the glass-topped table beside the flowers, grimacing at it. Score another point for Randall. He'd managed to best her again, and there was nothing she could do about it. For years she'd been convinced that something more went on in Gemansk than she'd known about. There were too many holes in the story.

In the end, she'd given up trying to guess what had happened. Maybe it had been wishful thinking on her part; maybe she'd been looking for an excuse for Randall's callous abandonment. She'd even managed to find an excuse for his sending her to Wadjowska's bed—a trip she'd thankfully never had to complete. Sexual barter was a standard weapon in a female operative's arsenal. How could he have known that she wasn't used to trading her body at the drop of a hat?

But of course he'd known. He'd known just how inexperienced she was; he'd probably known just how passionately in love with him she was. And he'd sent her out anyway.

But Miroslav Wadjowska had contented himself with a few lustful glances, a pinch, and a reluctant farewell. And Maggie had raced back to the apartment with the papers tucked into her pocket, only to find Vasili waiting for her and Randall gone.

Vasili, a seventeen-year-old Resistance fighter with the face of an angel, the soul of a poet, and the fighting instincts of a jackal, had left with her. She'd opened the packet of papers Wadjowska had given her and found that Randall's weren't with them; he must have planned to abandon her all along. Vasili had asked no questions; with all the tact of romantic youth, he'd flirted gently with her, coaxing a smile as they crossed the drab industrial city to the crowded train station. He'd ridden to the border with her, saying good-bye in her compartment with a surprisingly soulful kiss. He'd jumped down from the train with buoyant grace, only to be confronted by a squadron of dark-uniformed men.

If only he hadn't run. But he had—he'd taken off on his swift long legs, drawing his enemies away from the train and away from her. As the train pulled out of the station and across the border, she'd watched him get cut down by a spray of bullets. Throughout the years, she'd never been able to rid herself of the feeling that he'd died for her. If it hadn't been for Randall's dereliction, Vasili would still be alive.

"Are you ready?" Randall's voice broke through her memories, and she looked up stonily. He'd changed into another dark gray suit, and he looked perfect, as always. Even the dark bruise on his temple matched his eyes, she thought grimly.

"What are we going to do about your warning note?" she demanded, not moving.

Randall shrugged. "Not a damned thing. I have more important things to worry about than obscure threats. I want to find out what's on those videotapes of Caleb's. The sooner we get through this dinner of your mother's, the better. I don't suppose there's any chance of our ducking it?"

"No chance at all. Besides, I intend to set a little trap—"

"Forget it, Maggie. We don't know enough about our enemy to risk it."

"But that's the whole point—we could find out who's behind this, if we're lucky."

"And if we're not lucky, we could end up in your mother's bathtub. Does your sister own a VCR?"

"Of course—doesn't everyone? We can watch the movies there, if that's why you're asking," she snapped, still ensconced on the couch.

He nodded, apparently taking it for granted. "There's an all-night electronics store over by Evanston. We'll put in an appearance at your mother's and get the tapes from Caleb, then go and pick up another VCR and television and end up back at your sister's. We're going to need two machines if we want to compare prints."

"We're going to be up all night!"

"You don't have to be involved in this, Maggie," he offered politely. "You can go on to your mother's, and I'll take care of everything."

"Over my dead body."

"Then don't complain." He leaned over, and for a moment Maggie thought he was reaching for her. She jerked away, startled, but he was going for the flowers. He picked up the vase and dropped it in the wastebasket by the door. "Let's go."

She rose, tugging at the too-short skirt. "Did you know that Vasili was shot helping me escape?" She hadn't even known she was going to say it—it just popped out.

Randall switched off the light, plunging them both into semidarkness. Maggie felt her usual, instinctive tightening of panic. Then the streetlight filtered through, and she could see his face, could just barely make out the bleak expression. "I knew," he said, his hand on the doorknob, making no effort to open it.

"I consider you responsible," she said, with cruelty that was foreign to her.

He didn't flinch. "So do I," he said. And opening the door, he moved into the hallway without a backward glance.

In Maggie's memory, there were evenings that had seemed longer, but very few. Sybil had surrounded herself with the cream of Stoneham Studios' management; Alicia's grating laugh echoed through Sybil's suite at the Mandrake. When Caleb wasn't looming over a harassed-looking Kate, he was standing dourly in a corner, disapproving of all and sundry. Sturdy, sensible Kate looked ready to fly apart in a thousand directions. Randall moved by her side like the Gray Eminence, the skeleton at the feast.

It had been easy enough for Maggie to abandon him. All the women flocked around him like chattering magpies, and Maggie had slipped away with a wry grin. He hadn't lost his touch over the years. If only there were some way she could figure out what drew women to him, maybe she'd be immune.

Damn it, what was she thinking of? She *was* immune, and had been for six years. Or at least since she had met Mack. But Mack was gone, no longer able to protect her, and she felt herself slipping back into the insidious current, and the more she struggled, the more useless it all seemed.

"Are you all right?" Kate's voice startled her, and Maggie looked up. They were relatively alone in a corner of the vast living room, a small oasis of quiet amidst the revelers.

"I'm fine. I'm more worried about you."

"You needn't be. I'm surviving," she said in clipped tones, pushing a wing of her chestnut hair back from her pale face. "Brian's asked for a postponement on the custody hearing. We won't go back to court for another two weeks."

"Is that good or bad?"

"Depends. If we could have gotten a ruling in my favor with no complications, I would have felt like a new woman. Two more weeks gives us enough time to have this whole situation blow up in our faces."

"Can't you fight the postponement?"

"My lawyer says I can try. I'm just afraid I'd fall apart in court. I figure I'll have to take my chances that you'll be able to clear everything up." She smiled up at her sister, a trusting smile that quivered around the edges. "I'm counting on you, Maggie."

*Damn,* Maggie thought desperately. She wasn't Sybil's daughter for nothing; she had a tiny amount of acting ability, too, and she called on every ounce of it. "Don't worry, Katy," she said, her voice cool and determined. "Have I ever let you down before?"

"No," Kate said, eager to be reassured.

*There's a first time for everything,* Maggie thought. "Well, I won't this time, either. Trust me."

"Sure." Kate's voice was abstracted, her attention lost, and Maggie followed her troubled gaze. Caleb McAllister was bearing down on them, an intent expression in his blue eyes, and Maggie could have been in Timbuktoo for all the attention either of them now paid her. "I think," Kate continued, standing her ground and speaking more to herself than her sister, "that I will get drunk. Queenie's already put Chrissie down in the guest bedroom, and I may just pass out on Mother's sofa." She moved away without another glance in Maggie's direction, pushing past Caleb's advancing figure. She didn't get very far.

"Where do you think you're going?" Caleb demanded, catching her arm.

"To get drunk," Kate said defiantly.

"What do you think that will solve?"

"Nothing," she snapped back.

Maggie stood off to one side, watching, completely ignored by the two combatants. She knew she should withdraw, but for the moment she was too fascinated by a side of her sister she'd never seen.

"Don't be a child, Kate. You've had too much to drink as it is. I think we should go for a walk and let some of your mother's champagne wear off."

"And I think you should go to hell."

Maggie stood watching and made a small bet with herself.

Kate was a strong, stubborn woman, but she'd been through too much in the last few days. Caleb looked equally stubborn, and he had the advantage of being in the right. The best place for Kate right now was alone with him, and she knew it, even if she was fighting it.

"Don't swear," Caleb said automatically. "Did you bring a coat?"

"For Christ's sake, it's ninety degrees out there!"

"Don't swear," Caleb said again, "or I'll keep your mouth so busy you won't be able to say a word."

Kate just stared up at him, temper warring with amazement. And then her stubborn chin shot out. "Caleb," she said in her sweet, polite little voice, "go fuck yourself."

He was very efficient, Maggie had to admit that. Caleb McAllister hauled her sister into his arms and planted his mouth on hers, pushing her up against the wall with gentle strength that was at odds with the temper in his eyes. Kate struggled for a moment; her arms thrashed, her hands pushed at him, but then she slid her arms up around his neck and kissed him back with enthusiasm that didn't surprise Maggie at all.

And then she did slip away, past the oblivious couple, out into the crowded living room with only the slightest bit of an ache in her heart. She wanted to be kissed like that, she wanted to be yanked into someone's arms and held until she gave up fighting what was right and inevitable. She wanted to be loved again.

"Darling, you look so sad." Sybil swooped down on her, emeralds and diamonds flashing at her throat and ears, her jet-black hair a cloud around her beautiful, ageless face. "Were you thinking about Pulaski again?"

In fifty-four years Sybil hadn't learned tact, and she never would. Maggie shook her head, managing a half-smile. "No, Mother. I was thinking about his eventual successor."

"And who is that?"

She should have known Randall would be there, she thought, unable to still the little nervous start his deep voice caused her. She turned to look him straight in those stormy gray blue eyes. "I haven't met him yet," she said firmly. "Mother, we're leaving now."

"But darling, we haven't even served dinner yet."

"Randall and I will get something later." She let herself be enveloped in her mother's scented arms. "Take good care of Chrissie."

"Of course, dear heart. She's delighted to be visiting Queenie and Moomaw."

"Moomaw?" Maggie echoed.

"That's what she calls me. Charming, isn't it? And it doesn't sound depressingly grandmotherly."

Maggie's smile broadened. "It does have that advantage. My children are going to call you Granny."

"Heaven forbid. Give me plenty of warning, darling. And give me time to grow into the part."

"Don't worry, Mother. I have yet to meet Pulaski's successor, remember?"

Sybil's magnificent aquamarine eyes traveled up, way up, to Randall's face, then to Maggie's, then back to Randall's. And she smiled a very knowing smile. "If you say so, dear," she murmured. "Where's your sister spending the night? She said something about my sofa."

"I think Caleb has other plans."

"That tall young man? How very nice. I'll do my best to be discreet."

Maggie shook her head, acutely aware of Randall beside her. "It'll be a losing battle, Mother. Discretion is not one of your many charms."

"But the others make up for it, don't they?" Sybil murmured. "Don't do anything I wouldn't do, darling."

"Is there anything?" Maggie had to ask.

"Not much." Sybil's facelift hadn't erased her dimple, and it showed to perfection. "Take care of her, Randall."

"I have every intention of doing so," Randall said with a thread of amusement in his voice.

"I don't know how we're going to get the videotapes," Maggie warned him as they descended in the empty elevator.

"I don't want Caleb and Kate disturbed. Last time I saw them, they were coming to a long-overdue understanding."

"I wouldn't think of disturbing them," Randall said. "I already got the tapes from him this evening."

"Efficient as ever," she said. "Where are they? Do you have them on you?"

"Maggie, Maggie, do you think I'd do such a silly thing and ruin the line of my jacket?" Randall mocked.

"Silly question," she muttered. "Of course you wouldn't. So where are they?"

"Caleb cornered me the moment he arrived, and I locked them in the car. Apparently he thought about everything you so artlessly disclosed tonight and decided it was time to make a move. It seems that move was on your hapless sister."

"Not so hapless," Maggie said, remembering the dazed look on Kate's face as she wrapped her arms around Caleb's neck. "So we'll have the apartment to ourselves. Just you and me and the Potato People." Her voice was disgruntled, and she could feel Randall's eyes watching her.

"Just you and me and the Potato People," he agreed. "The possibilities are endless."

She laughed then, unable to help herself. "Damn, Randall, I'll be glad when this is all cleared up."

She must have been imagining the look she thought she saw in his eyes. Randall didn't look that way at anybody—not with warmth and longing and tenderness. Those emotions weren't part of his makeup. "So will I," he said, in the cool and distant tone of voice she was more used to. "So will I."

# eleven

"I don't know if I can stand much more of this," Maggie warned. She rolled onto her back and glared up at Randall. "I don't think I'll ever eat potatoes again."

Randall spared a glance from the twin televisions and *The Revenge of the Potato People, Part Two* to look down his elegant nose at Maggie. It was three in the morning, but his only concession to the lateness of the hour was to prop his elegantly shod feet on Kate's coffee table. His tie was still perfectly knotted, his shirt was buttoned, his hair unrumpled.

Maggie, on the other hand, had dispensed with the too-small black dress the moment they'd arrived back at the apartment. She'd searched through all her clothes for what was most likely to irritate Randall and had triumphantly come up with a disreputable pair of cutoffs. Although they unfortunately showed miles of her long, tanned legs, they were still faded, patched, and worn enough to be anathema to the impeccable Randall. She was wearing one of Mack's old denim shirts on top, its shirttails shredded, wearing it because it was the oldest thing she owned, wearing it as some sort of talisman against the powers of darkness. The powers of Randall.

She wiggled her bare toes and looked up at Randall in the darkened room. He'd said nothing at her complaint, merely let his eyes trail over her. She sat up, crossing her legs in front of her. "Aren't you getting sick of this? I'd think French art films would be more your style, not sci-fi epics."

"This is hardly an epic, Maggie," he pointed out. "This is a wretched excuse for wasting film, and I'm just as tired of it as you are. I might remind you that we're not watching it for fun, despite all the popcorn you've been rolling around in. We're watching it for information."

Maggie grinned. She'd insisted on making a tub of popcorn before Randall started the damned movies, and she'd proceeded to spill it all over Kate's beige carpet as she stretched out on the floor to suffer through three viewings of the Potato People. Caleb had six videotapes. The first four were identical and innocent, as far as they could tell. They were on the last lap, and Maggie was ready to give up hope of ever finding anything out.

"Aren't you uncomfortable sitting up there like an undertaker?" she questioned idly, reaching behind her for the glass of wine she'd only managed to spill once, and that time on purpose. "Don't you ever relax?"

"No," he said repressively. "Pay more attention to the movie and less attention to my wardrobe, Maggie. We're getting to the good part."

"The good part?" she echoed in disbelief. "There is no such thing."

"Well, the less horrible part," he temporized. "When the potatoes eat the Empire State Building."

"Randall, the special effects aren't even that good. You can tell that Empire State Building is three feet tall."

"Maggie, stuff your mouth with more popcorn or go to bed," he said. "I'm trying to pay attention."

Maggie turned to stare at the twin televisions. Big, puffy potatoes were rolling down a miniature Fifth Avenue, heading directly toward the Empire State Building. It had been mildly entertaining the first time around, but by the third it had definitely lost all its merit. Not even Maggie's third glass of wine helped. She turned her back on it, scampering to her feet and crossing the darkened room to the sofa. Randall sat unmoving, looking up at her.

She'd had too much wine and not enough sleep. She knew that. She was playing with fire and was about to get burned—

she knew that, too. But even with Mack's shirt wrapped around her, she couldn't resist.

"Randall," she said, her voice teasing. "You're such a stuffed shirt. Can't you at least loosen your tie? Or would your head fall off?"

"Leave me alone, Maggie," he said, his voice a warning—a warning she chose to ignore.

She squatted down beside him. Her bare knees almost touched him, but still he didn't move. For some reason, the memory of Caleb and Kate wrapped in each other's arms still haunted her. She imagined them right now in the king-size bed in Caleb's apartment; *The Revenge of the Potato People* would be miles from their thoughts if they were even thinking at that point. "Come on, Randall," she said, a mischievous smile playing about her mouth, dancing in her eyes. "Prove that you're human like the rest of us."

"I'm human, Maggie. Don't goad me." The potatoes squashed the Empire State Building and neither of them noticed.

"Then loosen up." She reached out to unfasten his tie, but his hand shot out and caught her wrist, stopping her before she could touch him. He was hurting her. Maggie didn't say a word. She only stared at him, her eyes wide and waiting. They could both feel her pulse pounding through her slender wrist.

Somewhere she found her voice. "No, Randall," she said.

He didn't loosen her wrist. "Too late, Maggie. I warned you." And slowly, inexorably, he pulled her to him.

His mouth meeting hers was a shock. The savage hunger, the demand, the need that swept through her at his touch horrified what small part of her brain was capable of thought. Six years might never have passed; he might never have betrayed and abandoned her. She was in his arms, half-lying across him, and she was desperate for more than just his mouth on hers, more than his arms holding her captive, more than his hands on her breasts.

There'd never been any question of not responding. She'd opened her mouth beneath his, moved when he'd pulled her, and then lay beneath him on the sofa, stretched out. Her long bare legs were beneath his trousered ones, her breasts were pressed up against his suit jacket, her arms were wrapped around him and holding him tightly against her as she kissed him back with a need that terrified her.

It had been six years since Randall; it had been two years since Mack or any man had touched her, and her body cried out for it. Maybe she could shut her eyes and pretend she was back in her bed in Boothbay Harbor, pretend it was Mack's hands holding her face, Mack's mouth traveling across her lips, her cheekbones, her eyelids. But the lips were harder, thinner, hungrier, and the hands were uncallused—the hands of a rich man who had never had to work for a living. It wasn't Mack. Mack was dead. The man pressing her into the soft cushions of the sofa was the man who'd betrayed her.

"No," she screamed, but his mouth was on hers, smothering the sound, and her hands were trapped between their bodies. She struggled, and he must have felt it. He reached down, caught her hands, and dragged them away from him. She was very strong, but he was stronger. It took him only a moment to pin her to the sofa; one hand imprisoned her wrists, the other held her face still. She could see his eyes glittering with rage and desire; then his mouth caught hers again, and he kissed her, long and hard—an insult of a kiss that still vibrated with the desire that had sparked between them. And then he pulled his mouth away.

There was blood on his mouth, blood on hers, and she couldn't tell whose it was. He stared down at her for a long moment. "Don't do that again," he said, his voice rough. "You never were a cocktease before, you don't need to start now. I'm not going to play little games with you, Maggie. Don't start something you aren't prepared to finish."

She stared up at him. He was still on top of her, pressing her into the sofa, and he was still fully aroused. "I didn't mean—"

"You did," he contradicted flatly. "And this is the only time you'll get away with it." With a sudden swift movement he rolled off of her, landing on his feet with his usual grace. As she struggled to sit up, his hand reached out and caught her shirt. "And next time don't wear Pulaski's shirt."

"There won't be a next time," she managed, thoroughly sober, thoroughly chastened. She didn't even bother to wonder how he knew it was Mack's shirt. There were times when Randall seemed to know everything. She shivered.

"Won't there?" With swift, economical motions, he stripped off his tie and unfastened the first two buttons of his silk shirt. He tossed the tie at her, and unthinkingly she caught it. "Will that do?"

Even his hair was rumpled. For the moment, Maggie was safe, the danger had passed. She curled herself up in the corner of the sofa. "Fine," she said. "I think we've got more important things to think about than your appearance."

"I've already told you that," he said patiently, turning his attention back to the movies with a calm disregard that she would have found insulting if she hadn't been distracted by her latest discovery.

"Do you see that?" she demanded, moving forward to the edge of the sofa, her voice rising in excitement.

"What?"

"That's how the information is being passed." She gestured toward the twin television sets that had been running cheerfully along, ignored by the two of them. The two screens no longer matched. On one set, potatoes were rolling all over downtown L.A., squashing tourists. On the other, the scantily clad leader of the Resistance was perusing the operating plans of a potato satellite. The long, loving closeup of those plans had already lasted at least a minute, and they didn't look like any potato satellite Maggie had ever seen.

"You're right," Randall said, suddenly businesslike. He quickly backtracked, staring at one television while the potatoes rolled on amidst shrieks on the other. The scene lasted a full five minutes. Three of those minutes were devoted to the blueprint while ridiculous dialogue was carried on in the background. Every nuance of the technical drawing was on screen for long moments, and even the legend "Potato Satellite" emblazoned on top didn't detract from it.

"What do you suppose it is?" Maggie demanded when Randall finally turned from the machine.

"Not a potato satellite. Not a satellite at all, if I'm any judge. I think it's the newest missile the Pentagon's ordered."

"The cruise?"

"Worse than that. This is one of those cute little ones that wipe out everything living while leaving buildings and anything worth money intact. They've had them before, but this one has a much wider range." His thin mouth curled in disgust. "Damn them all."

"Why would you care?"

Randall looked up, startled at her prosaic question. "What do you mean?"

"Exactly what I said," Maggie said. "Why would you care? Your opinion of your fellow man is astonishingly low. Why would it matter to you if there were several thousand fewer?"

"More like hundreds of thousands," Randall said. "And you're right, I don't care much about my fellow man. But I also detest needless waste. Wiping out half the population of a country has never appealed to my sense of efficiency."

"By all means, let's be efficient," Maggie said with a yawn, but her eyes were sharp. "Can we turn off the damned machines yet?"

"Not yet. The movie's almost over. We may as well hold out to the end."

"May as well," she said with a sigh, crawling off the sofa and stretching out onto the popcorn-strewn carpet once more, her head resting on her arms. "Wake me when it's over."

She was asleep before the potatoes had made it to the Grand Canyon. He could hear her deep, steady breathing, with the faint suggestion of a feminine snore, as her long, slender body relaxed into sleep. He sat watching her, watching the television sets, his hands clenched in fists.

He wanted to crawl down beside her and take her into his arms. He wanted to sleep in the popcorn with her, just holding her, listening to her breathing, feeling her warmth. But he sat where he was, watching.

The first VCR clicked off, leaving a fuzzy white television screen. Five minutes later, the second one followed suit. The darkened room was eerie in the flickering light of the television sets. He crossed the room on silent feet, turned off both sets, then moved back to the sofa to turn on the small lamp. She was afraid of the dark—Willis had told him that with great glee. She never had been before, and he had to wonder what had caused that uncharacteristic phobia. He knew it predated Pulaski, and it mystified him—as did everything about her.

There was no way in hell he was going to carry her into her room. She'd have to sleep on the floor and deal with the aches tomorrow. At least it would give her something to think about while she was cursing him.

And curse him she would. Because when she woke up tomorrow morning, he'd be long gone. Now that he knew how the information was being passed, he needed to find out who was receiving it. Who was the intermediary between Stoneham Studios and Red Glove Films? And once he found that intermediary, it would take a very short time to uncover the rest of the mess.

The easiest, fastest way to do that was to go to the source. Back to Eastern Europe, back to Gemansk. He still had more than enough contacts, and although his guilt over Vasili's death had kept him away for six years, he knew it wouldn't take him long to renew those connections.

He looked down at Maggie's sleeping figure. Her thick blond hair obscured her face, obscured the eyes that would be blazing with fury tomorrow when she found he'd gone. He couldn't figure out why the hell she'd started flirting with him tonight. She probably didn't know, either, but it was going to make for a very uncomfortable few nights until he came back and found out why.

It was almost five A.M. Flights to Eastern Europe were notoriously poor, but if he were lucky, today would be one of those days when an airplane was headed in that direction, and he'd be in Gemansk and have the answers he needed before the weekend was over.

In the meantime, there was one last thing he had to do, just to prove to himself that he could, and then stop. He walked silently over to Maggie's sleeping body and squatted down beside her. Very gently, he reached out and pushed the sheaf of hair away from her face. His long fingers caressed her so lightly, she would never feel it. And then he rose and moved away before he could think twice about it.

The door shut silently behind him as he stepped out into the hall. Maggie lay in the deserted apartment, her eyes wide open in the semidarkness. Her instincts were alert, her brain was wide awake. Slowly she pulled herself into a sitting position, shook her cramped muscles, and folded her legs underneath her. "What the hell are you trying to pull this time, Randall?" she muttered out loud. She already knew the answer.

She'd stake her reputation, her career, and her sister's peace of mind that Randall had decided to fly to Gemansk. Leaving her behind, of course. Damn the man. Damn the sneaking, low-living, cowardly bum.

Well, she was going to take that bet. She was going to call the airport and book the first flight for Gemansk, throw everything she could in an overnight bag, and head straight for O'Hare. If Randall wasn't there, if she'd overestimated his resourcefulness, so much the better. She could find the answers she needed just as easily as he could.

But he'd be there—and he'd be none too pleased to see her. The thought was absolutely delicious.

Slovak Airlines had a small, dingy corner in the northeast terminal at O'Hare. Business was far from brisk when Maggie arrived in the late afternoon—the only other customer was a tall, well-dressed gentleman with his back to her. She moved up on him silently and waited with all the patience of a saint as he bought a round-trip, first-class ticket on the flight leaving in just over an hour. He was completely oblivious to her as he dealt with credit cards and window seats with his customary efficiency. For a moment she considered tugging on his jacket like an importunate child, but she resisted the impulse. It would be much more fun to see the look of shock when he turned and saw her.

Trust Randall to travel first class, she thought with a grimace, hoping she had enough credit left on her Visa card to cover her costs. She just might have to suffer along with the peasants in tourist class while Randall swilled champagne with the nobility. Why the hell did a Marxist country have an airline with classes? she thought self-righteously.

Her patience was wearing thin as she waited for him to turn. It had been an endless day, waiting for the one flight O'Hare boasted. Kate hadn't bothered to show up at home, and Bud Willis was nowhere to be found. The anonymous voice at Langley had told her he'd taken a leave of absence, but she didn't believe that for one minute. When it came right down to it, she was just as glad she hadn't been able to reach him. It wasn't that she was adverse to taking information from him; she just wasn't eager to return the favor.

Randall turned, and she waited with delicious anticipation for his eyes to widen with shock and annoyance and for his mouth to thin with irritation. He looked down at her, raised an eyebrow, and handed her her ticket.

"I got you a window seat," he said.

She grimaced. "I shouldn't underestimate you."

"You don't. Not by much, at least. And I shouldn't underestimate you."

She nodded. "True enough. Know thy enemy."

"I thought we were partners."

"For now, Randall. I'm only taking it one day at a time."

He smiled that faint, wintry smile that seldom reached his stormy eyes. It didn't reach them now. "That'll do," he said.

She looked at him, remembering the surreptitious caress in the darkness before he had left her. And she wondered if she dared trust him even for a day.

# twelve

Gemansk hadn't changed in the last six years; it was still the same depressing, gray industrial town, full of downtrodden, beaten people with lost eyes and pale faces. The moment Maggie stepped off the airplane onto the pitted tarmac, depression settled in around her. Randall strode beside her, and she spared a furtive, curious glance up at him. He was clearly lost in his own thoughts; his face was shuttered and closed. But that was nothing unexpected—he'd never been a man with open emotions. His blue-gray eyes were hooded, and his mouth a thin, grim line. She looked at that mouth, remembering the brief moment of hateful, unwanted passion on her sister's couch the night before, and looked away, to the squat, cinder-block building that housed the airport. With every ounce of effort she had, she tried to bring forth the memory of Mack, with his smiling eyes and warm, laughing mouth. But he was fading, leaving her almost more bereft now than his actual death had, and she knew with a desperate certainty that there would be a time when she would reach out for his memory and try to summon him back, and he'd be gone beyond reach, leaving her to Randall's tender mercies.

"I don't suppose you made any arrangements," she said, her voice cold and cranky.

Randall roused himself from his abstraction long enough to smile at her. That smile wasn't reassuring. "What caused this charming mood? You slept almost the entire trip."

Actually, she hadn't. She'd curled up into the cramped, uncomfortable seat that Slovak Airlines considered first class and had shut her eyes rather than have to make conversation with Randall. She'd drifted off for an hour or two as they soared above the clouds, only to wake up with her hand clutching Randall's immaculate shirt-sleeve. She'd released him immediately, pulling back, and he'd said nothing; he'd merely brushed at the creased linen with an absent hand.

"Jet lag," she said dourly now.

He nodded. "You'll feel worse later."

"Reassuring," she muttered.

"I try to be helpful. May I remind you, Maggie dear, that you weren't invited on this particular expedition?"

"Then why did you buy me a ticket?"

"I saw you lurking behind me trying to be inconspicuous, and I knew if I had you shadowing me, you'd be even more obtrusive."

"Damn you, Randall! I know how to shadow someone!" she said furiously.

"You're out of practice. And time and the current situation are too important to risk while you relearn your trade."

"Did anyone ever tell you that you are an unpleasant, condescending bastard?" Maggie inquired in a polite tone of voice.

"Many times." Again that faint smile flitted across his face. "Among other, less complimentary things. My heart isn't breaking."

"You don't have a heart."

He stopped dead on the tarmac, just outside the door to the airport, and Maggie careened into him. His long, hard fingers caught her arms. There was no gentleness in him. His bleak eyes looked down into her defiant ones, and his thin mouth curled into what might have been contempt. But then again, it might have been something else. He started to say something, then thought better of it, and his painful hands released her.

"What were you going to say?" she taunted. "Were you going to tell me you have a heart like anyone else?"

Once more he'd withdrawn behind his masterful defenses. "Maybe," he said. "Except that you're probably right. Hearts and emotions are sentimental weaknesses we can't afford. I'm probably better off without one."

"Haven't you ever loved anyone?" It came out before she could stop it. "Forget I asked that stupid question," she added hurriedly. "I already know the answer."

"Do you?" His voice was rich and deep, and it sent shivers down her backbone. He reached out, opened the door, and held it for her with ironic courtesy. "Far be it from me to disillusion you, Maggie. But try to be a little more romantic. We're supposed to be lovers."

She paused, half in the door, half out. "Why?"

"Why else would we be traveling together?" he replied with great practicality. "Either we're lovers or we're working together. And I don't think we want the local government to think we're here in any sort of professional capacity, do we? Do we?" he prodded gently when she said nothing.

She looked around her before answering. The airport was sparsely populated; their few fellow travelers had long since moved through customs and departed. Only the brown-uniformed officials remained, and the expressions on their broad, slavic faces were identical: curious and suspicious.

With a sigh, Maggie threaded her arm through Randall's and smiled up at him a wide, loving smile that never reached her distrustful eyes. "You're right as always, darling," she said, pitching her voice so that their observers could hear her. Reaching up, she pressed her lips against his hard jaw. She lingered just a minute, and she could feel the tension throbbing through him, feel the pulse beneath her mouth. And then she pulled back, more unnerved than she let on. "We're going to have a marvelous vacation," she added.

He stared down at her, his eyes stormy, his face enigmatic. "I'm sure we are, Maggie," he said, his voice too low for the officials to hear him.

Gemansk customs went smoothly. Too smoothly, she thought, still keeping a besotted simper on her face as she clung to Randall's arm. Their luggage was inspected with only cursory interest, and no questions were asked. All her instincts were aroused. Why should Gemansk be so lax, given the troubled state of the country's internal affairs?

Whatever the reason, the two of them were safely through customs, through the narrow, dour corridors of the dark little airport, and out in the sunshine in a matter of minutes. Maggie immediately released Randall's arm and stepped away from him with nervous speed. He stared down at his crumpled sleeve, smoothed it with an absent gesture, and raised his gaze to Maggie's defiant one. And then his face grew very still as he stared at something, or someone, over her shoulder.

"Taxi, mister?"

Maggie turned and followed the direction of Randall's enigmatic stare. She was barely able to swallow the small scream that welled up in her throat. Standing in front of them, an engaging smile on his youthful face, was Vasili.

But it couldn't be Vasili! For one thing, Vasili was dead; Maggie had seen him gunned down. For another, even if he *were* alive, he'd be years older than the lanky teen-ager who was grinning at them now. She moved back a step and came up against Randall's body; his hand pressed down on her shoulder in reassurance. For once she didn't jerk away.

"We could do with a taxi into town," Randall said carefully. "Do you know a decent hotel? We haven't had a chance to make reservations."

The boy threw back his head and laughed. "Me, I can show you anything you want, mister. You want to see the war memorial? Very impressive, I promise."

She felt Randall's hand relax when the boy made that prearranged response.

"You're Leopold?" Randall asked.

Again that beautiful, flashing grin that matched Vasili's. "At your service, mister. Welcome back to Gemansk. You too, miss."

Maggie winced. Returning to Gemansk had never been high on her list of priorities. But it was too late to worry about that now. She had to concentrate on why they were there, on how thankfully immune she was to Randall's appeal, in order to get through the next couple of days.

Leopold hoisted their luggage and took off at a trot. From the back, his eerie resemblance faded somewhat. He was dressed in the uniform of all teen-agers: faded jeans, a Mickey Mouse T-shirt, and Nikes over neon-green socks. Six years ago, Vasili had managed jeans but nothing else of western culture, and his hair had been shorter than Leopold's long black mop. Yet the resemblance was still unnerving.

"Who—?" she began, but the swift, almost imperceptible shake of Randall's head silenced her question before it had been formed. She didn't need to turn around to know that their exit from the Gemansk airport hadn't been accomplished as easily as she'd first thought. In the fitful summer sunshine, she could see tall shadows behind them. "Who would have thought we'd decide to spend our first vacation in years in Gemansk?" she continued without missing a beat, once more clutching Randall's sleeve as she leaned into him. "I wouldn't call this the garden spot of the world, darling."

"Sightseeing wasn't particularly what I had in mind for the next few days, Maggie," he said in his deep, slow voice. And even though she knew that the words were solely for the benefit of their military escort, and even though they were words she didn't want to hear, she felt a slow, languorous burning in the pit of her stomach.

"We didn't have to travel thousands of miles to make love, Randall."

"With your family always around, we had to do something drastic." His hand reached out and covered hers; his long, thin fingers stroked hers—a warning. The burning flamed a little higher.

She smiled up at him and tossed her blond hair out of her face long enough to get a glimpse of their escort. There were three of them, tall, blank-faced, uniformed men. She looked up at Randall's distant face and clutched him a little tighter, a perfect parody of a clinging, impassioned female. *Was* it a parody? she derided herself.

They'd arrived at Leopold's taxi, a battered Fiat that had clearly seen better decades. Leopold had already stowed their luggage and was standing by the open door, ready to usher them in with all the aplomb of a Helmsley Palace doorman. His soulful brown eyes went to the men following his passengers, then back to them. His face was impassive.

Maggie's heart was thudding beneath her thin cotton suit, and her palms were sweaty on Randall's jacket. He wouldn't like that, she thought with distant amusement, releasing her grip as she started to climb into the car.

"One minute, please." The words were barked out. Maggie slammed her head on the car ceiling, and it took all her shredded self-possession to pull herself back out with at least the appearance of calm.

"Yes?" Randall said haughtily; Randall could be very haughty indeed.

The soldiers ignored him. Their leader was shorter, older, and meaner, and his expressionless face was marred by small, hostile eyes. "You forgot your purse, Miss Bennett."

A shadow crossed Randall's face, inexplicable and instantly gone. "Silly of you, darling," he drawled, holding out his hand for it. "Didn't you notice?"

Maggie cursed herself furiously as she shrugged and smiled sweetly and stupidly at the nasty little man in front of her. He ignored Randall's proffered hand, moved up to Maggie, and handed it to her. It was a large straw bag, almost empty, and when Maggie took it from him she noticed that it seemed heavier than when she'd placed it on the customs desk.

"You should be more careful, Miss Bennett," he said. "If you were to lose your papers, you would have a great deal of trouble leaving our country. We wouldn't want anything to mar your—vacation." The sneer was clear in his voice, the suspicion strong.

Maggie gave him her most dazzling smile, but it left him stonily unmoved. "You're very kind. I promise to be more careful."

"At your service, miss." He bowed, clicked his heels together like a perfect Prussian officer, and moved away, his dark, suspicious eyes lingering.

Maggie stared after him, her fingers clutching the purse, until Randall half-pushed, half-shoved her into the taxi. Moments later, they were careening out of the airport. Leopold was driving very fast, very badly, and he was whistling.

"Of all the stupid, idiotic moves," Randall upbraided her, his voice low and biting. "How could you be so half-witted? What did you have in that goddamned purse, anyway? I suppose now everyone knows why we're here."

"Everyone already knows," Leopold offered from the front seat. His dark eyes met theirs in the rearview mirror. "You can't keep anything from the secret police. You just have to be faster than they are."

"Damn," Randall muttered. "I should have tied you up and left you in the bathtub."

"Listen, Randall, there was nothing the slightest bit incriminating in my purse," she shot back. "If they know why we're here, they didn't learn it from me. Look." She dumped out the contents of the purse onto the tattered cloth seat between them—dumped it out and then sat very still, as a wave of nausea swept over her.

"What is it, Maggie? What's wrong?" Randall was never one to miss her reactions. It was lucky that she wasn't planning to hide anything from him, she thought dizzily.

With a shaking hand, she reached down to pick up the small clutch bag that had fit so easily into the spacious confines of her purse. It was white; the leather was smudged and stained and cracked with age. She opened it, her fingers trembling, and pulled out the passport with Margaret Mullen's name inside, the visa, the money, even the Chanel Number Five. Everything was there, just as she'd left it six years ago when Randall had rescued her from that tiny cemetery shack, rescued her and left Jim Mullen to die by his own hand.

Randall took the white purse out of her hand with surprising gentleness and opened the passport and the visas. He let out a quick, surprised breath. "I'd forgotten that you have a habit of losing your purse," he said after a bit. He stared down at the picture of a younger Maggie, eyeing it objectively. "You're even prettier now," he said, putting the papers back into the clutch bag.

"For heaven's sake, Randall, do you have to be so damned cool about everything?" she snapped, pushing her hair out of her face with trembling fingers.

"Better than being hysterical about something we can't do anything about," he replied, and his common sense angered her even more. "We'd be much better off spending our energy trying to figure out who knows what and why they put this in your purse. I imagine it's a warning. But why didn't they just arrest us at the airport or, even better, refuse to allow us to enter? They could have put us back on the next plane—it's done often enough."

"I would think, mister, that they want you to lead them to members of the Resistance," Leopold offered from the front seat as he careened around a corner.

Maggie pulled herself out of Randall's lap with as much decorum as she could manage. "Then why warn us? Why let us know we're being watched? Surely it would only make us more careful."

Leopold shrugged. "Who is to say? The secret police get as much pleasure from playing with their victims as they get from accomplishing anything. They are very stupid men, usually from the northern provinces." His sneering voice made it clear that he was from the more intellectually gifted southern provinces. "Very bad men, too. We will have to be careful." He veered around another corner, and once more Maggie landed in Randall's lap in a tangle of arms and legs.

Once more she struggled to extricate herself, but this time his long arms wrapped around her, holding her in his lap, and her struggles were useless. "Will you take your hands off me?" she demanded in a furious hiss.

"No. You'll just end up back here the next time Leopold turns a corner, and I'm getting bruised from the impact," he said in his most impassive tone of voice. "Besides, we have company. Don't we, Leopold?"

"Yes, mister," Leopold agreed as the aging Fiat bucked forward with truly impressive speed. "They've been following us for a while now. But not to worry. I, Leopold, will lose them. I'm the best driver in Gemansk, better even than my brother Vasili was in his heyday. You have nothing to fear."

Maggie had stopped her struggles for a moment. "Vasili was your brother?"

Leopold grinned in the rearview mirror, apparently entirely unmoved at his passengers' complicity in his brother's death. Or perhaps he was simply ignorant of it. "One of five," he said proudly. "But none of them are as strong, as brave, as Vasili. Vasili is very much a man."

Randall's arms had seemingly relaxed, and Maggie tried to jerk away from him. She was yanked back into his arms, held there by brute force, and there was nothing she could do short of punching him in the groin to release herself.

"Stay put, Maggie," Randall muttered into her ear, his temper finally overriding his usual calm, "or I'll strangle you."

The Fiat was moving at incredible speed at this point, and the gloomy landscape was whizzing by. Maggie shut her eyes for a moment. "I dare you," she said wearily, leaning her head against his shoulder.

"Don't tempt me." His fingers were no longer biting into her upper arms; they were holding, almost caressing her.

"Hold on," Leopold shouted from the front seat as they once more veered around the corner, probably on two wheels or even on one. And then they were bouncing over a stubbled field, and there was nothing Maggie could do but clutch at Randall and curse under her breath.

A breathless lifetime later, they finally rattled to a stop beneath a bridge next to a dry stream bed. Leopold killed the engine and turned to grin at them proudly. Maggie finally released Randall's arm and opened her eyes in weary relief. There was no one around, no sound or sign of pursuit.

She crawled off Randall's lap, and this time he let her go. His eyes were trained on the front seat. Maggie followed his gaze directly into the barrel of Leopold's gun. He was still smiling that beatific smile.

"And now, mister, you will tell me what happened to my brother Vasili," he said gently.

# thirteen

Maggie sat staring at the gun barrel, staring at Leopold's charming young face, so very like his older brother's. He had the gun trained quite negligently on Randall, obviously underestimating the female of the species, and she considered for a moment whether she could take him. She could, but not without considerable risk to Randall's impeccable gray suit. He wouldn't care to have powder burns in his breast pocket. Regretfully she leaned back against the seat, still alert for possibilities.

"What do you mean?" Randall said with deceptive ease. She could feel the tension running through him; his muscles were coiled and ready to spring at the first sign of weakness. He wouldn't worry about powder burns marring *her* rumpled suit, she thought wryly. She'd better be prepared to duck, and duck fast.

"Don't play games with me, mister," Leopold said evenly. "My brother was shot down by the secret police when you were last in Gemansk. No one will talk about the details of that time, and before I help you any further, I want to know what happened."

"I might feel more talkative if you put that gun away," Randall drawled.

"But I would feel less inclined to listen." The gun stayed where it was. "I'm getting impatient, mister."

"You're asking the wrong person," Maggie said. "He wasn't there when Vasili was shot. I was."

The gun turned to her. "Then you tell me, miss. Tell me

what you know about what happened to my brother on that day."

"Maggie!"

"Shut up, Randall," she said fiercely. "He has a right to know what happened to his brother. We don't have anything to hide. God knows, I've felt guilty enough over the years, but it wasn't our fault. Not really."

"I will decide whose fault it is," Leopold said. "What was Vasili doing at the border? Was he going to escape to the west?"

Maggie shook her head. "He was making sure I got out safely. Randall—Randall still had unfinished business, and he sent me out ahead of him. Vasili accompanied me of his own accord. He—"

"You don't need to explain my brother to me, miss. He could never resist a pretty face."

"We took the train to the border. When he got off, the police were waiting for him. He didn't wait for any questions —he ran. And they—they shot him in the back." Her voice was deceptively cool, her eyes anguished at the memory.

"We are trained to run. The secret police have ways of making people talk." Leopold laughed; the cheerful sound was jarring in the stillness. "That sounds like an American movie. Humphrey Bogart, yes?"

"Maybe," Maggie said carefully.

"You still haven't told me who betrayed my brother to the police."

"What makes you think anyone betrayed him?" Maggie said hotly. "No one could have known what would happen. He decided at the last moment to accompany me when Randall didn't—when Randall's plans changed."

"I would appreciate it," Randall drawled beside her, "if you wouldn't try to protect me when you don't have the facts. It only makes matters worse."

Leopold's cold, smiling eyes were old in his young, handsome face. "So why don't you tell me the truth, mister? Did you betray my brother?"

"Yes."

There was a dead silence in the ancient Fiat. Maggie could hear the distant sound of birds in the trees overhead, the rustle of leaves in the wind. She could even hear their breathing —Leopold's rapid and angry, and Randall's even and controlled beside her. Her own heart hammered in sudden shock and disbelief.

"Maybe you'd better explain what you mean," she said sharply. "Leopold is likely to misunderstand and think you literally betrayed Vasili to the secret police."

"I did."

Maggie considered moving away from him on the bench seat. At that point, she didn't even want his blood splashed on her rumpled suit. But she stayed where she was, waiting, knowing there had to be more to it.

She waited for Leopold to cock the gun. He kept it on Randall, but his expression didn't change. "Explain, mister."

Randall shrugged his elegant, unconcerned shrug. "It was a choice given to me. I chose what seemed to be the lesser of two evils."

"Not enough explanation, mister."

"No," Maggie said quietly, "not enough explanation. What happened on that day six years ago?"

His eyes met hers for a long, contemplative moment, and she wished she could read his thoughts as easily as he read hers. But as always, his thoughts and emotions were veiled, masked behind defenses that could never be breached. He looked at her, then turned back to Leopold with his usual self-control, ignoring the gun, ignoring the demands, making his own decision.

"Maggie and I had to get out of Eastern Europe. A bureaucrat named Miroslav Wadjowksa had agreed to provide phony passports. When I delivered the necessary photos, he developed a not-inconceivable passion for Maggie's picture. He agreed to provide the papers if Maggie would be the one to retrieve them and provide a few hours' entertainment at the same time." He looked at Maggie's still profile. "I could have put pressure on him to do it without the added inducement of sex, but I wanted Maggie to be kept busy for a while."

"Why?" Leopold demanded.

"Because I'd been followed for the previous two days. Vasili knew about it and warned me, but he didn't know how much the secret police knew. When Maggie went off to pick up the papers, I went off to distract the police. I mistakenly thought I was clever enough to lead them on a wild-goose chase, away from Maggie, and then escape them on my own. I'd overestimated either my skills or their ineptitude."

"They caught you?"

"They caught me. I must agree with your assessment of the secret police. They are not very nice men. Not very bright, either, but quite adept at finding out what they want to know. They gave me a choice. I could tell them the name of my contact, Vasili, or they would kill Maggie."

Maggie's swift intake of breath seared her lungs and burned her heart. She sat very still, staring at his averted profile, still saying nothing.

"So you decided my brother was expendable—is that how you say it, mister?" Leopold's eyes glittered with rage.

"I decided that Vasili had a better chance of escaping than Maggie. Particularly since I was being—detained—in a back room of the government building where Maggie was getting the passports. After a little—physical persuasion—I gave them the name they wanted, and they kept their part of the bargain. They let Maggie go and went after your brother."

Maggie shivered in the warm summer air. "Randall, they tortured you. You aren't to blame for breaking under the pain."

His smile was wintry. "It would take days of pain to break me, Maggie. I'm not saying I wouldn't, sooner or later. But it would take more than a few broken bones to do it. I gave them Vasili because they already had you in custody. Vasili was still out there, he still had a chance. You would have had no chance at all."

Leopold nodded. "You made the right decision, mister.

They would have killed her without hesitation, and then they would have found out what they wanted from you sooner or later. They are stupid men, but they know their job." He lowered the gun. "They killed Vasili's woman the way they would have killed yours. And Vasili watched, knowing that a word from him would have stopped them. He's had to live with that, and there have been times when I think he would rather have died on the border. But this is a war, and Grilda knew the dangers as well as Vasili."

"What?"

The boy shrugged and dropped the gun onto the seat beside him. "He told me to help you, that you were good people. He sent his special love to you, miss. His wife did not like that one bit, I tell you." He turned back to start the car. "I am sorry I had to hold the gun on you, but I wanted to make sure you were worth risking my life for. I don't take anyone's word, not even my brother's."

"Leopold, what the hell are you talking about?" Randall's cool distance had vanished. "Is Vasili alive?"

Leopold laughed, cheerful in the summer sunshine. "You think a few bullets would stop my brother? He's as alive as you and me, training Resistance groups in the southern mountains. He has four sons of his own. He's very much a man, Vasili is."

"Four sons?" Maggie echoed faintly. "We've only been gone six years."

"It took him a couple of years to recover from his time with the secret police," Leopold said with an apologetic shrug. "He's already got another little one on the way."

"Jesus Christ!"

"Amen," said Leopold piously, yanking the steering wheel. Moments later, they were bumping over the rutted wheat field, back toward the highway.

Maggie leaned back against the seat, gripping the door handle. She wasn't ready to be tossed back into Randall's arms. There was too much information she had to digest before she could decide how she was going to react to all this. She could feel his eyes on her, questioning, but she refused to meet his gaze. Shutting her own eyes, she pressed back against the backrest and did her best to shut out the world.

It was an uphill battle. She could feel his presence beside her, feel the tangible heat of his body, and she knew that all she had to do was relax her death grip on the door handle to be flung once more into his arms. It wouldn't be her fault, and with luck he wouldn't release her this time, either, and she could ride into Gemansk held safely in his arms. . . .

She was out of her mind! There was no longer any doubt of it. His quixotic gesture six years ago, which had almost killed a young man, didn't change anything. Even though it proved he wasn't a completely heartless villain, it still didn't change the essential facts of his nature. Randall Carter was a cold man, incapable of love, laughter, and light. And the power he was once more exerting over her still scared the hell out of her.

The hotel room was small, dark, and depressing. True, it was the epitome of luxury compared with the one-room apartment they'd shared six years ago, but it wouldn't take much to better that dour place. Maggie stared around at the drab green walls, the double bed with its garish orange bedspread, and the worn carpet beneath her feet and sighed.

Before he said a word, Randall made a thorough search of the room to make certain it wasn't bugged. Then he went to the window and dropped the curtain back over the gloomy view. "Next time, let's chase down leads in Monte Carlo," he said. "I'm getting weary of Eastern Europe."

Maggie sank down onto the bed, kicked off her high-heeled sandals, and looked at the man. He was becoming more and more of an enigma. "You want to tell me about it, Randall?" she said.

He stood there at the window, and the fitful sunshine outlined his tall, elegant body. He'd been remote and silent during the ride into Gemansk, centered on his own thoughts, and

Maggie had known there was no way she could break through. Just as there was no way now.

"Tell you about what?" he countered, dropping into the uncomfortable chair with a grimace. "I'm meeting Leopold alone. The fewer people the better. Remember I didn't ask you to come along—you simply showed up."

"That's not what I'm talking about, and you know it," she said ruthlessly. "Not that that isn't a separate issue, and if you think I'm going to wait in this damned hotel room while you go out and have all the fun—"

"Hardly fun, Maggie," he said. "And you know as well as I do that it's easier for two people to elude the secret police than three, especially when one of them is in high heels."

"I brought my Nikes."

"You can jog around the hotel room."

"Randall, you are rapidly losing any gains you might have made in my esteem."

"Good," he said. "Don't be a sentimental idiot, Maggie. That decision six years ago was based on common sense and nothing else. If I thought it would have saved the mission, I would have sacrificed you without a second thought."

For a moment, she believed him. For a moment, she could see him discarding her life without hesitation or a backward glance. Then she let her gaze travel over the shuttered face, the stormy, unreadable eyes, the thin line of his mouth that so seldom curved in a smile, and suddenly she knew he had lied. He wouldn't have sacrificed anyone if he could help it—his guilt over Vasili's supposed death had clearly haunted him.

But her death would have been worse. It wasn't ego or wishful thinking that made her realize that. She looked at that enigmatic face and simply knew.

"You could almost convince me," she said softly, "except that I'm not quite as gullible as you think. I'll tell you what really interests me right now—why you're trying to convince me that you're a cold-blooded monster. What do you want from me, Randall?"

A shadow crossed his face as he answered. "Not a thing,

Maggie, except to have you wait here like a good girl while I go meet with Leopold."

"Good girl?" she echoed in an explosion of anger, knowing he'd goaded her on purpose, knowing and still being livid.

"I promise to save some of the 'fun' for you. I want your word, Maggie. Swear that you'll stay here, or I'll lock you in the bathroom."

"Try it," she taunted, holding her ground as he advanced on her.

He stopped just out of reach. "You don't think I'd do it?"

"No."

"Well, you're wrong," he said softly. "I'd do it, and I'd turn off the lights. There's no window in the bathroom, Maggie. It would be pitch black in there. And you'd be trapped, alone, in the darkness."

She heard his words with a sickening feeling in the center of her stomach. It didn't surprise her that he knew—Randall knew everything. He was a very thorough man, and Bud Willis took particular pleasure in his knowledge of her phobia. She wasn't really surprised that Randall would use that knowledge to terrify her, either.

What surprised her was the look of pain that clouded his eyes as he threatened her with the one thing she wasn't sure she could withstand.

"I'll be here when you get back," she said, her voice low.

He looked at her, measured her response, and then he gave her a short nod. Without another word, he left the room, closing the flimsy door behind him and leaving Maggie to stare after him. Confusion, rage, and determination swamped her as she huddled in the middle of the bed.

*What do I want from her?* Randall asked himself as he moved down the three flights of stairs in the depressing Gemansk Grande Hotel. A good question, but one that he didn't have an answer to.

He wanted to see the shadow of fear lifted from those remarkable aquamarine eyes. He wanted her smiling up at him

131

the way she had six years ago with the trust and love that for some masochistic reason he'd destroyed.

He could have told her what had happened. He could have found her in New York and tried to explain. But he'd rebelled against that, had been unwilling to make excuses for himself when she should have taken him on trust, should have known that the decision he'd made had been inevitable. When he'd finally laughed at his own egocentricity and demanded complete faith while offering nothing in return, and when he'd finally accepted the fact that his need for her overshadowed his ego and his overweening pride, it had been too late. She'd been married to her first husband, a useless little wimp. He'd known it wouldn't last, and he'd bided his time. He waited and waited and waited, and finally his time had come. He had her alone, and yet like some goddamned fool he kept driving her away.

Leopold was waiting in the Fiat, and he whistled as the Gemansk variant of a pretty girl walked by. Once more, Randall felt a clean sweep of relief that Vasili hadn't died. Enough people were on his conscience already; it was a blessed joy to offload at least one soul.

Leopold looked up and waved at him, his broad mouth creased in a friendly grin. Randall stepped out into the Gemansk sunlight. What did he want from Maggie? What he didn't deserve and would never own.

Just her body and heart and soul.


Maggie peered out the grimy window into the industrial daylight of Gemansk. The tiny white Fiat roared off into traffic, out of sight.

It was all ridiculously simple. Red Glove Films was listed in the thin, tissuelike phone directory. Maggie stripped off her crumpled suit and high heels and replaced them with an anonymous pair of jeans, an oversize shirt, and her Nikes. She could blend in with anyone, and her clothes wouldn't interfere if she had to run for it.

She'd be back in the room before Randall returned, and if

he didn't like the fact that his unwanted partner had bested him, that was too damned bad. She'd gotten too used to relying on herself the last few years—she wasn't about to start being passive now, particularly with Randall. If she wasn't very careful, he would swallow her up, leaving her empty and hollow and hopelessly dependent.

No, she was going to make a move herself. And then she'd wait for him with the name of the intermediaries between Red Glove Films and Stoneham Studios, and she'd snap her fingers at his disapproval.

That thought made a broad grin light her face as she let herself out of the hotel room. The delightful fantasy kept her cheerful as she walked straight into the arms of the secret police.

# fourteen

There were times, Maggie thought, when her own idiocy and gullibility amazed her. As if life could be so simple, she mocked herself, searching for a comfortable position in the dark sedan that was carrying her through the city. No comfortable position seemed possible with her wrists handcuffed behind her back. She leaned back against the seat and shut her eyes for a brief moment, ignoring the dark figure beside her.

How could she have been so stupid? The taxi that pulled up in front of her when she left the dubious security of the Gemansk Grande was just a little too convenient, the driver a little too military, his assurance that he knew how to get to the offices of Red Glove Films just a little too pat. They'd traveled three blocks when he'd pulled over and two men had joined them in the taxi, one in the front, one beside her. The man in the front wore a uniform and carried formidable weapons, the man beside her was in plainclothes.

There'd been a brief, nasty battle, one that had ended with the handcuffs on her wrists and a large welt on her captor's face. And then she was shoved into a corner as the taxi took off down the street.

She listened to the man beside her regain his temper and his breathing, and she spared a brief glance for his profile. There was a wide red welt against his pale, pasty skin, and his small dark eyes looked like raisins in a suet pudding. He took a deep, calming breath and turned to meet her gaze. His wide, almost casual grin was oddly, horrifically familiar in the dank interior of the taxi.

"So rude, Miss Bennett," he chided. "When all we wanted to do was give you a proper welcome on your return to Gemansk. You left too abruptly six years ago—and we were delighted you saw fit to visit us once more."

Maggie just stared at him, at the face she knew but had forgotten along the way. "I believe you have the advantage of me," she said politely. "In more ways than one. Have we met?"

The man beside her laughed in surprise and admiration. "You Americans. Always so brave. My name is Miroslav Wadjowska. I am second commandant of what you call the secret police. Welcome to Gemansk."

Maggie inclined her head regally. "You've been promoted since last we met, Mr. Wadjowska. Six years ago you were a visa clerk."

He smiled. "Six years ago I was third commandant of the secret police. You and your friend underestimated us—we knew what you were doing back then."

"Then why did you let us escape?"

A shadow crossed Miroslav's face. "A mistake, I'll grant you."

"Just one? Randall and I got out separately," she said.

His face darkened further. "Two mistakes. My men were so intent on catching that little traitor Vasili Baskinski that they let you cross the border and escape our reach."

"And Randall?"

"Another error, and this one, I must confess, was mine. Any normal man would have been unable to move after the interrogation he got. My men are known for their efficiency, and most people, if they survived at all, wouldn't have been conscious for days. Your friend is just a bit inhuman."

Maggie thought back to Randall's enigmatic face and managed a grin. "He can be."

"You aren't wise to remind us of failures, Miss Bennett. It will only make us more determined not to fail again."

She sighed. "My dear Mr. Wadjowska, what ever gave you the impression that I was wise? Anyone with any claim to wisdom wouldn't have walked into this little trap. Especially since you were kind enough to warn us by sending my old purse along."

He grinned, showing blackened teeth. "It was stupid of you," he agreed. "But no matter how clever you'd been, we would have caught you. The reappearance of your purse was a minor touch to frighten you into making just such a foolish move. We were planning to visit your hotel room the moment your friend and Vasili's brother returned."

"Friend? Vasili's brother?" Maggie questioned innocently.

Miroslav Wadjowska reached over with deceptive ease and slapped her across the face. He was left-handed, and his knuckles slammed into her left cheekbone with stinging force. She blinked for a moment as involuntary tears of pain filled her eyes, but she forced her face into impassivity.

"You've been watched since your arrival. We saw Leopold meet you at the airport, though we did lose you somewhere between the airport and the city. We know that Leopold has followed in his brother's traitorous footsteps. We know that the two of them have gone off somewhere."

"You don't know where?" Maggie read the frustration beneath his bragging tone. "I thought you didn't plan to make mistakes this time."

Another slap, this one more forceful, and her lip was cut against her teeth. "It is only a very small mistake," he said softly. "And they will come after you, I have no doubt of that at all. Carter already gave us Vasili to save your life. I doubt he will hesitate a second time."

"Maybe," she said. "It depends on what you want from him."

"The same that I want from you. We want to know what you are doing here and what you want with Red Glove Films."

Maggie shrugged and tasted the blood on her lips. "We're here on vacation. We fell in love in Gemansk six years ago, and we suddenly got sentimental to see it again and recapture the old magic." She eyed Miroslav's hand warily, wanting to prepare herself for the next blow. His fingers twitched, but he made no move.

"And what did Red Glove Films have to do with it? They've only been in existence for less than a year—surely they weren't part of your sentimental journey?"

"I heard they had great pornography. Our love life has gotten a little stale lately, and"—the slap shut her mouth for a moment, but only for a moment, as her eyes met his with undaunted courage—"and I thought Randall might like to see some Eastern European sex."

The last blow had hurt Miroslav, and he leaned back, rubbing his wrist. "I think, Miss Bennett, that I personally will indulge your interest in Eastern European sex. Or certain unpleasant variations of it. Now tell me your real interest in Red Glove Films."

"I've always wanted to be an actress, and I thought I might get my big break in Gemansk." She steeled herself for another blow, but this time it failed to come. Her face felt raw and swollen and stung with pain, but she was damned if she was going to cower before the bully beside her.

Miroslav Wadjowska smiled as he leaned back against the seat. "You will get your big break in Gemansk, Miss Bennett. That I will promise you." He spoke to the driver in his native language, one that was incomprehensible to Maggie. The driver and his companion laughed, and Maggie felt a sinking in the pit of her stomach. "Relax," he said to her, and his lips were thick and pink and wet. "You have at least an hour before I can devote my full attention to you."

She looked at him out of calm, emotionless eyes. Randall had been tortured and Randall had survived, had even managed to escape. If she couldn't manage such a feat, if she turned out not to be the superwoman her family had taunted her with, at least she would take it with dignity.

She did her best to keep all her senses alert as they made their way through the twisting, unkempt streets of Gemansk. The stolid gray building looked vaguely familiar to Maggie as they drove into the underground parking garage, which looked like a dungeon. The hands that pushed her out of the car and through the subterranean passages were rough, but she forced herself to endure the indignities with an expressionless face worthy of Randall at his most distant. She'd keep that thought in mind, she told herself: no matter what they did to her, she'd let her face be blank and uncaring. Like Randall's.

Miroslav left her in a corner room. There were windows set high in the walls, beyond her reach, and nothing but a spindly chair and a table in the room. In a sudden, unexpected gesture, he unfastened her handcuffs and stuffed them into his pocket. His hand gently brushed her face. It was a small, squat hand with short fingers and dirty fingernails, and it caressed her bruised and swollen face.

"Such a shame to have to bruise you," he murmured, licking his thick pink lips. "I want you to think about it, Miss Bennett. I can bruise you in many worse places if you don't cooperate. And I will find out what I want to know sooner or later. There is no need for you to be a heroine. No one expects it of you."

Maggie considered him for a moment. "I expect it of myself," she said finally in a light, determined voice.

He sighed, and his fingers caught the tender flesh of her bruised cheek and twisted it sharply. "You will learn," he said, "and soon." And he left her alone in the little room.

At least it wasn't dark. With a weary sigh, she sank down into the spindly chair and surveyed her hands. Rock steady, she noticed with pride, despite the abraded wrists. She could just imagine the state of her face. Her mouth stung, her head ached, and her palms were sweating. Try as she might to deny it, she was terrified.

She gave herself a good five minutes to sit and feel sorry for herself. Then she tried the door, made certain he'd locked it, and hefted the table and carried it over to the corner beneath the windows. She set the chair on top of it and climbed up with a deft silence that pleased her enough to add to her courage. She could reach the small, rectangular windows, but they were locked.

The glass was smoked, and there was no way she could tell what was on the other side. Possibly armed guards, or one of the main streets of Gemansk, or just an empty field. And even if she could manage to break it, was there any guarantee that her strong, almost-six-foot-tall body would be able to squeeze through the narrow opening?

She had no other choice but to try. Sooner or later, Miroslav was going to come back, and with her luck he wouldn't come alone. Being beaten was something she could face; being tortured was less appealing; but being gang-raped was downright unacceptable. She was going to get out of that room or die trying.

She looked back around the barren room. The spindly chair that just barely held her weight would most likely crumble if she used it to break the window, and then she'd have no way of reaching the aperture. The best she could do was slip off one of her Nikes and use it as protection for her fist.

Damn! Why hadn't she added karate to all the other forms of physical fitness she'd practiced during the past two years? Her body was perfectly fit, lean and strong, but it was not experienced in breaking bricks, two-by-fours, or smoked-glass windows. She slammed her sneaker-covered hand against the glass, then swallowed the moan of pain as it bounced back off. The force of it nearly threw her off the chair.

Didn't it have something to do with concentration? Sending your mind through the barrier ahead of your fist, or something like that? But how could she concentrate when her face was throbbing, her fist was likely broken, and the sound of footsteps and voices passing through the corridor outside her prison brought panic closer and closer?

She closed her eyes, forcing herself to take a deep, steadying breath. She flexed her aching hand within the dubious protection of the shoe, then sighed, accepting the inevitable. She slipped the shoe back onto her foot, formed a fist, and slammed it against the smoked glass.

It shattered around her hand. Maggie stared at it with amazement that almost overrode the pain in her fist. Slowly, carefully she picked the shards of glass out of the way and undid the lock. There were cuts on her hand, long scratches, but they looked worse than they were. They'd stop bleeding shortly, she knew, and they wouldn't leave a trail of blood for the secret police to follow. She opened the broken window and stuck her head out.

It was a parking lot, full of dusty black sedans. And in the far corner, there was one blessedly white Fiat with two figures conferring in the front seat.

She was halfway out the window before Randall and Leopold saw her, and her curses at their obtuseness helped her gloss over the pain in her hand. By the time they reached her, her hips had stuck in the narrow opening. The two of them grabbed her arms and hauled her out with more force than care.

She fell against Randall, her face landing against his chest, and she let out a small moan of pain—a moan he didn't hear beneath the steady curses he was heaping on her head as he half-dragged, half-carried her back to the Fiat.

"You may be a stupid idiot," he was saying as he bundled her into the backseat, cramming her in with their piled suitcases, "but at least you're a capable one. God knows how we would have gotten to you in that damned place. You're just lucky Leopold had someone watching the hotel, or God knows when we would have found you."

"You didn't find me," she snapped, her voice a little hazy with pain. "I got out myself."

The car was dark in the gathering dusk as Leopold zoomed out of the parking lot and into the Gemansk twilight. It was too dark for Randall to see her battered face, too dark for her to do anything about the cuts on her hand. She leaned back in the corner, wanting nothing more than to go to sleep. Jet lag and stress were taking their toll.

"Yes, you did," he agreed doubtfully. "Where the hell did you think you were going?"

"To Red Glove Films."

"Where do you think we were?"

"It would have made life a lot easier if you'd just taken me along," she said wearily. "No, maybe it wouldn't. They might have gotten all three of us."

"You may be gullible enough to have fallen into their trap," Randall said with just enough smugness to pull her out of her lassitude of pain and exhaustion, "but I'm not likely to make the same mistake."

"Wanna bet?" Maggie snapped. "Do you know who picked me up? It was Miroslav Wadjowska. The same man you wanted me to sleep with in return for phony passports. And do you know who he works for? And who he worked for six years ago? The secret police, damn you. This whole thing has been a trap."

"Maggie." His hands reached out for her, but she slapped them away, wincing at the pain in her fist.

"Get your hands off me. I can take care of myself," she said. "I have before, and I will again."

"Shut up." He pulled her into his arms and held her against his strong body as Leopold navigated the streets of Gemansk with speed and skill. She didn't even bother to struggle.

"We've already picked up our things from the hotel. I'm taking you to Saltash," Leopold offered over his shoulder, his teeth a gleam in the darkness. "I don't think Wadjowska knows about it, and if he does, it will still be too hard to find you. You can hide there overnight, and tomorrow I'll take you over the border."

"What the hell good will that do?" Maggie fumed. "We haven't found what we came for."

"Yes, we have," Randall said, his voice a deep rumble in the chest beneath her. "The man at Red Glove Films was very cooperative."

"You're one of the best I've ever seen," Leopold offered Randall with youthful enthusiasm. "Just the right amount of pain, and he was singing like a bird. You should teach me that little trick with the fingers—"

Maggie shuddered, and Randall snapped something in a foreign language at their driver. He turned to Maggie, and his voice was surprisingly soothing. "We found out who he was dealing with. It wasn't Francis most of the time. The deliveries were arranged through someone else. A woman."

"Damn you, Randall, Kate has nothing to do with it," she said passionately, squashing down the sudden doubt and fear.

"I never said she did."

"If you don't mean Kate, who the hell do you mean?"

"Alicia Stoneham."

Dead silence in the rattling old Fiat. "I don't believe you," she said finally. "Why, she's as American as—as apple pie. She wouldn't turn traitor."

"She would to bail out her failing film company. Her husband had built it up from scratch, and she couldn't bear to see it go down the tubes. So she sold classified information to support it, with Francis's complicity."

"Sounds like the plot for a movie," she said in a doubtful voice. "Do you have any proof?"

"Not a speck. Just tons of circumstantial evidence, including motive and opportunity. Alicia's brother is a retired admiral. A forcibly retired admiral who's been very vocal about the shabby way he's been treated. He'd have access to top security documents."

Maggie shook her head, trying to clear away the cobwebs. "It seems awfully farfetched."

"It does, doesn't it?" he replied in a lazy voice. "Most spy scenarios are. But they happen, just the same. The first thing we do when we get back to the United States is have Bud Willis check into Admiral Wentworth."

"He'll love it," Maggie said, wondering if she dared lean her head on Randall's shoulder. Her lip was bleeding again, and Randall wouldn't like blood all over him. No, she'd better stay upright. "That still doesn't explain who killed Francis, or why he was dumped in Kate's bathtub."

"No, it doesn't. It doesn't exonerate your sister from murder at all, only from possible treason."

"You're so comforting, Randall," she said with a sigh.

"I do my best." His hand reached up and cupped the nape of her neck, and the decision about leaning was taken out of her hands. He pushed her face against his shoulder, forcing her to relax. She winced as her abraded skin rubbed against the rough shirt, and then she sighed, releasing all the pent-up tension that had been singing through her nerves. "Go to sleep, Maggie. Leopold's going to go the long way around to get to Saltash, just in case we have anyone following us. We've got a long night ahead of us."

"I'd sleep better if you let go of me," she muttered grumpily, not even bothering to stifle the yawn that swept over her.

He didn't say a word, but his hands kept her a gentle captive in his arms. Through the gathering dusk, she could just see the outline of his profile and the grim line of his lips and nose, and for one sleepy moment she wanted to press her mouth against his and see if she could soften that unsmiling face. But then exhaustion overtook her. Sometime, someday in the distant future, she would begin to understand Randall Carter. But right now she was too exhausted even to begin to make the effort. With a deep sigh, she gave herself up to sleep.

# fifteen

She felt light in his arms. Not like the solid mass of muscle and warm hard flesh that he knew made up Maggie Bennett, but curiously fragile, and it took all his resolve not to tighten his arms around her, hold her closer. Protective instincts were foreign to him, and the determined woman sleeping so soundly and so unwillingly in his arms wasn't the sort to want or need protection.

He'd been ready to storm that dull gray fortress that housed the Gemansk government offices. But Leopold's surprisingly cool head had prevailed, and he'd waited for the dusk to close around them. Then his planned heroics became totally unnecessary as Maggie crawled through that narrow window with her damnable self-possession.

He'd always avoided self-sufficient women. His wife, his lovers, even his one-night stands had been soft, pretty, dependent women who listened to his advice, waited for his decisions, and expected him to lead the way. Maggie had been the one exception. She refused to be led, refused to listen, refused to fit into the mold.

"We have company again, mister," Leopold said cheerfully from the front seat, breaking into Randall's thoughts.

Maggie awoke with a jerk, and he felt her wince in his arms. He had no idea how badly she'd been hurt crawling out of that window, but now wasn't the time to ask. She scrambled off his lap before his hands could tighten.

"Who do you think it is?" she questioned in a slightly husky voice.

Leopold's shrug was eloquent in the darkened car. "It

could be anyone. I would guess that it's Wadjowska. He has a certain reputation, and he won't like it that you got away. You're lucky you got out so fast, miss, before he had time to question you. He likes to hurt women."

Randall could feel her shiver in the darkness. "Does he?" she said coolly. "Then I'm glad I didn't wait around for a white knight."

"You missed your big chance, Maggie," he drawled, his eyes intent, peering through the gloom at her. "It's not often that I bother to rescue damsels in distress. It would have been worth the wait."

She turned to him, and he could see her eyes, wide and curious. "That's not true," she said flatly.

"It wouldn't have been worth the wait?"

"Randall, I had access to classified files when I was with the Company. I don't know what you've been doing for the last six years, but before then, every mission you took was a rescue. Boat people from Cambodia, babies from Viet Nam, political prisoners in Chile and Nicaragua, kidnap victims in Italy. You came to Gemansk to rescue me the first time, remember?"

"I remember."

"So why do you say you don't rescue people?" she shot back.

"Maggie, have you suddenly decided I'm a saint?" he questioned, keeping his voice lightly amused. "It's highly flattering, but I'm still the same man who sent you out to whore with Wadjowska and abandoned you."

"Considering that you were being tortured, I think you have a good enough excuse," she said. "Miroslav was talkative before he locked me in that room."

Irritation and something else swept over Randall. The last thing in the world he wanted was her gratitude. He didn't want her to feel she owed him anything; he wanted her to come to him because of the same deep, irrational, overwhelming need that rode him like a devil. Starry-eyed sentimentality was the last thing he needed.

He shrugged. "What of it? I've been tortured before, and even if I'm damned careful, it's likely to happen again. Does that make me a good man, Maggie? Does that make me someone you can like, respect, and trust?"

She sat very still in the close confines of the rattling Fiat. "No," she said finally, "it doesn't."

So where was his sense of satisfaction at making her see things as they were? Why wasn't he pleased that he'd stripped her of her tentative illusions once more? "Good," he forced himself to say, his voice light. "I want you to see things clearly."

"I think I see things very clearly, Randall," she said, her voice still and calm and very certain. For one rash moment, he wondered whether it would be worth trying. Whether he could trick her into thinking he was worth loving. But as swiftly as the thought came, he dismissed it. His illusions were long gone; such thoughts were only tempting pipe dreams.

"I'm going to take a short cut through the next field," Leopold said from the front seat. "When I get to the bridge, I'll slow down long enough for you both to jump out. There's a row of abandoned houses there. The two of you hide while I try to draw Wadjowska away."

"Will you be all right?" Maggie leaned toward the front seat, concern deep in her voice. Randall felt an unexpected surge of jealousy.

"Sure thing, miss," he replied cheerfully. "They haven't caught me yet, and they won't this time, either. Hold on tight."

He turned the wheel hard, and then they were racketing across the field at a dangerous pace. The bright lights of the pursuing car were no longer visible behind the turn in the road. Moments later, they turned back onto the rutted road, and Leopold slowed down to a crawl.

Randall saw the bridge looming up in the moonlit darkness, and without further hesitation he grabbed Maggie's wrist and opened the door. "Good luck," he said tersely, and jumped out, dragging Maggie with him.

They landed on their feet, but just barely. The Fiat sped up and zoomed down the road, and the two of them began a breathless run toward a cluster of buildings that looked more like shacks than houses.

The moon was bright overhead, illuminating their path, illuminating their silhouettes. The sound of the pursuing sedan roared across the field; its headlights swept over the landscape.

"Keep down," Randall muttered, his hand still clamped like a manacle around Maggie's wrist.

"I am, damn you," she shot back. "I'd run a lot better if you'd let go of my wrist."

"Forget it. I don't want to lose you." He stopped short, grabbed her, and shoved her down into the dirt, covering her body with his. The strong beam from the headlights illuminated the spot where they had been standing moments before.

They lay quietly, barely daring to breathe, waiting for all traces of the sedan to be gone. It seemed to take hours although it was less than a minute.

It was a warm night. A soft summer breeze floated through the trees above them and the moon shone down on their entwined, motionless figures. Some other time, some other night, Randall thought, wanting to draw her against him, wanting to tip her mouth up to his.

But that wouldn't happen. The woman lying motionless beneath him hated him—when she wasn't trying to turn him into some plaster saint. And he'd sworn to himself that he wasn't going to touch her until he had to. One day at a time, like an alcoholic keeping away from the drink that he craved. If he could just get through Gemansk without her. . . .

The secret police were long gone but still they lay there. He wondered if she could feel his erection, wondered if the warm night breeze were responsible for the hardness of her nipples against his chest. And then he pulled away, rising in one fluid movement and holding out his hand for her.

"Let's go," he said, his voice even and unmoved.

She put her hand in his, and he felt her shudder as he pulled her upright. It was a shudder of pain. "Are you all right?"

"Fine," she said flatly. "Let's get out of this damned moonlight. Which house do you fancy?"

"House? Hovel, don't you mean?"

"Now isn't the time to be fastidious. As long as we don't have to share it with rats, I'll take anything."

"You'll be sharing it with me."

She looked at him, her eyes bright in the moonlight, the rest of her face shadowed. "You're not a rat, Randall. No matter how hard you try to convince me."

"No, I'm an absolute prince," he drawled.

"I wouldn't say that, either. I haven't decided what you are," she added, cocking her head to one side. Her hair was silver in the moonlight, rumpled around her shadowed, beautiful face, and he wanted to bury his mouth in that hair.

"Let me know when you figure it out," he said in his coolest voice. "We'll take the middle hovel."

She nodded. "I'll do that. The middle hovel it is."

The hut was dark, too dark to see more than the outlines of furniture. There was a narrow, sagging bed in one corner of the one-room building, and a huge closet-cupboard, a fireplace filled with trash and rubble, and a three-legged table leaning against the wall. The windows were long gone; the openings let in enough moonlight to ease Maggie's momentary panic. She looked around her as Randall shut the door behind them.

"Home sweet home," she said.

"Don't knock it. It's better than Miroslav Wadjowska's interrogation room," he said, moving across the room on silent feet.

A small, errant shudder twisted through her body. "You're right," she said. "Anything's better than that."

She moved away from his too-observant eyes to stare out

the window. She wanted to keep her bruised face out of his sight, but the moonlight illuminated it with cruel clarity.

She heard a sudden, quick intake of breath, and then Randall was beside her, his hand on her chin, gently holding her face up in the bright moonlight. "What happened to your face?" His voice was rough; his own face was in the shadows.

"I look like hell, don't I?" she said with a sigh, touching her cheek gingerly. "I wasn't properly deferential to my captor."

He was very close; she could feel his breath on her face, and she remembered the hardness of his body as it had covered her minutes earlier, remembered her own response. And she felt it happening all over again. His hands touched her face lightly, a benediction at odds with the hard and unyielding Randall she had once thought she knew.

"No," he said, "you don't look like hell." He leaned down, and his lips feathered the scrape across her cheekbone. "You look"—his mouth danced across her bruised chin—"absolutely beautiful"—he gently brushed her eyelids—"and more than I can resist right now. I'm sorry." The words were as soft as his mouth on her swollen lips. Slowly, gently he brushed his mouth back and forth across hers, and she stood mesmerized, motionless, her entire soul concentrated on the feel of his mouth on hers.

This was madness. They were on the run in a country that wasn't known for its record in human rights; the secret police were within screaming distance; and all she could think about was his mouth on hers. Her mouth opened in response to the gentle pressure of his, and his tongue slipped inside, tasting, soothing, inciting, until she crossed the inches of darkness that separated them and moved into his arms, into the shelter of his body that was no shelter at all.

A sound ripped through her absorption—the scrape of a boot on a rough surface, a voice calling across the fields in a guttural, incomprehensible language. Randall's hand replaced his mouth across hers, his long fingers stifling any sound she might have made as his body pressed hers against the wall, holding her still.

It must be the secret police, but how did they know? They couldn't have seen them jump from the car. But Maggie couldn't bother with her questions now, because one voice was very close—and with a shiver of fear, she recognized it as Wadjowska's.

Randall had recognized it, too—she could tell by the sudden stillness, the tension vibrating through his body. Slowly his hand moved away from her mouth, slowly he edged them both toward the closet. His firm hands gave Maggie no chance to resist. The flimsy closet door creaked open into the room. Inside there was velvet-thick darkness.

It was a big closet, an endless, pitch-black closet full of demons, and there was no way in hell that she was going to step inside it, into that dark tomb that would smother the last bit of breath from her. She struggled for a moment, a silent, terrified fight that Randall subdued with no difficulty at all. In moments, she was slammed up against his panting body, a prisoner in his merciless arms.

"You have no choice," he whispered. "If you don't move now, he'll find us and kill us."

She stopped her useless struggle. Even through her terror, she knew he was right, knew that even if death and darkness lay in that closet, it was still not as certain as the death that awaited them out in the moonlit street. She had no choice at all.

He must have felt the fight leave her body. His iron grip relaxed, and carefully he drew her into the closet. There was barely room for the two of them. She had to press up against his body as he shut the door after them, shutting the darkness around them, the silent black darkness of death and madness.

She was shivering and shaking all over; a cold sweat ran down her spine. Her teeth clamped down on her cut lip to drown the scream that fought to break free, and every muscle, every tendon, every nerve in her body was stretched taut.

Then Randall's arms moved around her, gentle and comforting. His warmth surrounded her, his hands kneaded her back with strong, soothing strokes, and his lips pressed against her forehead.

Slowly she began to release the panic, slowly she let go of the tension that held her rigid in Randall's arms. The small, icy core of her began to melt, to melt and flow over him. His mouth moved from her temple down the side of her face to catch her upturned lips.

It was a kiss like no other she had ever received from him. It asked nothing, it gave her everything—hope and comfort and healing when the darkness threatened to suffocate her. She could feel unexpected tears in her eyes and felt their sting as they flowed down her bruised face. She shut her eyes, giving herself up to it, giving herself up to Randall.

When his mouth released her, she sank against him and pressed her cheek against the rough texture of his shirt, ignoring the pain of salty tears and bruised skin, feeling oddly content for the moment.

"Mister!" The word was a hiss of sound filtering into the room. "Hey, mister! Are you here? It's Leopold."

Without releasing his hold on her, Randall pushed the door open. The moonlit room was dazzling in its brightness after the coffinlike depths of the closet. Maggie drank it in like pure spring water, feeling it flow through her veins and bringing her strength and resilience back. With it came presence of mind. She stepped out of the closet and Randall's arms with only a small, desperate pang of regret.

"Where are they?" Randall's voice was clipped, indifferent. The moments in the closet might never have happened.

Leopold laughed. "Me, I have been very clever. The two flunkies have gone chasing after my cousin Tomas. Miroslav is thrashing about in the graveyard, chasing ghosts. He's looking for you, my friend. Do you wish him to find you?"

Randall nodded, a short, satisfied nod. "Can you lead him toward the bridge?"

"I can lead him anywhere," Leopold boasted. "You'll be waiting?"

"I'll be waiting."

He disappeared into the night, and Randall turned to the silently watching Maggie, his face blank once more. "Is it a waste of breath to tell you to wait here?"

"Even that question is a waste of breath," she said.

He reached out and took her hand, holding it in the moonlight. The dried blood and cuts looked no worse than Maggie had expected. "Did he do that to you, too?"

"No," she said. "I did it to myself, breaking the window. It's not as bad as it looks."

"And this?" He turned her hand over, caught the other one, and examined her wrists. They were dark and bruised from the handcuffs, and Maggie had no choice but to nod.

"You already admitted he did this." His hand reached out and feathered across her face.

She didn't pull away. "I'm just glad he's left-handed. He could have wrecked my best side," she added with an attempt at lightness.

Randall's hand moved from the bruised side of her face to the untouched side, the fingers gentle and questing. And then it left her, falling back to his side. "If you won't stay here, at least stay out of sight."

"What are you going to do?"

A savage smile transformed Randall's distant face. "Settle some old debts"—his hand touched her face lightly, one more time—"and a few new ones." And he turned and headed out into the moonlit night.

# sixteen

Her legs were long, her strides rapid, but there was no way she could keep up with Randall Carter when he was determined. The moonlight illuminated his silent, almost ghostly figure as he raced across the stubbled fields toward the narrow bridge, and she crashed along behind him with a fraction of his stealth, falling farther and farther back until he was out of sight in the fitful shadows.

When she finally reached the bridge, breathless, with a stitch in her side, the confrontation had already begun. Leopold stood to one side, watching. His youthful face was intent; for once, no trace of a smile lingered around his generous mouth. His eyes flickered to Maggie, then went back to the two men circling each other like wary dogs.

Miroslav was shorter than Randall by a few inches, but his burly arms and shoulders, his stocky legs, and the ruthless determination on his broad face made him a force to reckon with. Maggie felt panic sweep over her as she tried to figure their chances against him if he managed to best Randall.

And then the combatants' movements brought Randall's face into view, and Maggie's doubts vanished, replaced by something close to shock. At this moment, the eminently civilized, impeccably dressed man looked absolutely savage. She watched with horrified fascination as he closed in on Miroslav, wondering if she were about to see a man die in front of her eyes.

It was a longer fight than she would have expected. Miroslav was incredibly strong, incredibly determined, and despite his shorter height he must have outweighed Randall by ten or twenty pounds; those ten or twenty pounds were all muscle. For the first few minutes, Randall did little more than evade Miroslav's furious attacks, letting his opponent wear himself out. And then, when Miroslav's energy began to flag, when he stood panting, staring at his enemy like a frustrated, maddened bull, Randall moved.

It had been a fight with no rules, but even so, Maggie was still startled to see just how vicious Randall could be. The fight she'd witnessed in Caleb's apartment had been a minuet compared to this. Randall's knee slammed into Miroslav's groin, his hand chopped across his throat, and his fist drove into his stomach. In moments, Miroslav was lying in the dust, groaning and spitting blood.

Randall stared down at him for a long, meditative moment. Maggie shut her eyes, afraid of what would come next. Miroslav's semiconscious body was hauled upright and dragged toward the old stone bridge, and Randall shoved him up against the side of it. His body bounced against the unyielding stone, and Miroslav's moan would have been pathetic if Maggie hadn't remembered exactly who and what he was: chief torturer for the secret police, with more pain on his conscience than Randall could ever deliver.

It might be a close call, though. As Maggie watched and listened in the still, hot night, Leopold moved beside her, equally intent. Randall's voice, speaking to Miroslav, carried on the thick night air. "I owe you a great deal, my friend," he said, his voice rough and eerily polite. "More than I can ever repay." He slammed him against the stone wall again, and Miroslav began to weep.

"But your worst mistake," he said gently, "was being a little too free with your hands today. She said you were left-handed—" His voice was dreamy, almost meditative, as he caught Miroslav's left arm and pulled it upright.

It happened so fast, Maggie almost missed it. Randall slammed Miroslav's left hand against the stone wall with hideous force, shattering the fragile bones. He screamed once, a shrill, high-pitched shriek, and pitched forward in a dead faint. Randall stood above him, looking down without a trace of emotion, and a shudder ran through Maggie's body. Suddenly, the hot summer night was cold and deadly.

Leopold moved to Randall then, taking it all in stride. His matter-of-fact manner was almost as horrifying as Randall's savagery had been. "You didn't kill him?"

Randall lifted his head. His black hair was damp around his forehead, his shirt had ripped during the battle, and there was dust and sweat and exhaustion on his dark face. "Not this time," he said, suddenly weary. "You said you had plans?"

Leopold reached down with hidden strength and hauled Miroslav's unconscious body up and over his shoulder. "I thought he'd make a good birthday present for my brother. He had Vasili for almost a year before he managed to escape."

"Then your brother must owe him even more than I do," Randall said, his eyes glancing over Maggie's still figure and then moving away.

"I think he will enjoy repaying his hospitality, yes," Leopold said jauntily. "You can stay in one of the houses? My cousin Tomas will pick you up before dawn and get you over the border. I don't think you should bother with customs this time around. The secret police will know Miroslav has disappeared, and they know he was after the two of you."

"I agree completely." Randall's cool, polite voice was still shocking, coming from the rumpled, violent man opposite her.

"Meet him here by the bridge, mister. And take care of the lady. She looks like she's seen a ghost." Leopold's voice was amused; the unconscious man across his shoulders was no more burden than a backpack.

"Maybe she has," Randall said. "We'll be in the middle shack if something comes up. Good-bye, my friend. Give my best to Vasili."

Leopold nodded, hefting the body higher. "Good-bye, lady."

She forced herself to move then, to break the paralysis that had kept her weary limbs captive. She crossed the few feet to

Leopold, keeping her eyes averted from the limp body draped over him. "Thank you, Leopold," she said, "for everything." And she leaned over to kiss him lightly on the cheek.

He dropped Miroslav into the dust and grabbed her, planted his mouth on hers, and kissed her with a youthful completeness she hadn't experienced since . . . since his brother. When he finally released her, he had a pleased grin on his face.

"Vasili told me how beautiful you were, lady," he said, hauling the body over his shoulder again, "and he didn't lie. Now I'd better get out fast. Your man is looking like he'd like to do to me what he did to Miroslav. Good-bye, my friends." And he disappeared into the shadows with his burden.

Maggie turned to face Randall. Whatever expression had amused Leopold was gone now, leaving the blank, shuttered look she was so damned used to. There were no words. She looked at him for a long, confused moment.

"Let's go," he said finally, his voice even and polite as if the last half-hour of violence and savagery had never happened. "We'll need all the sleep we can get. It's close to midnight, and dawn is sometime around five."

She held her ground for a moment. "Are you all right?"

"What do you mean?" His answering question was wary.

"Did he hurt you? Did you hurt yourself . . . uh—"

"Did I hurt myself beating the shit out of him?" Randall finished the question smoothly. "No. And he didn't manage to lay a hand on me. I'm fine."

"You're very good, aren't you?" she said, wonder and distrust in her voice. And something else, something she didn't even recognize.

He looked as if he didn't know what answer she wanted. He gave the only answer he knew, the honest one. "Yes." He held out his hand to her, an instinctive gesture, and when he realized what he'd done, he dropped it.

She crossed the few feet to his side, afraid to touch him. "I was afraid you were going to kill him," she said suddenly.

"I wanted to. But I'd promised Leopold." He was watching

her with a combination of patience and curiosity. "Are you coming with me, or are you going to spend the night out here?"

It was a thought. Going back into that run-down hovel with Randall suddenly seemed comparable to climbing into the lion's cage with a ferocious man-eater. She eyed him warily, wondering what she would do if he pounced. And even worse, what she would do if he didn't.

"I'm coming with you."

The shack seemed smaller. The moon was setting, the shadows were deepening, and Randall seemed suddenly much larger than before, filling the spaces around her. He shut the door behind them, quietly, carefully, but she wasn't fooled. All through the silent walk across the field, she could feel the tension thrumming through him, feel the violence still simmering beneath the surface, feel the anger and intensity that she could never understand.

"You take the bed," he said, unbuttoning the remaining buttons on his shirt with deceptive calm.

She stood very still. It was a very small bed, more a sagging cot than anything else, but courtesy and something else dictated that she make the offer. "Where will you sleep? On the floor?"

"I could hardly hover in midair, now could I?" he replied, his thinly veiled temper slipping through.

"Don't be an idiot, Randall," she snapped. "We can share the bed."

He moved then, swiftly, silently, and once more she was reminded of his deadly intent down by the bridge. It wasn't death she had to fear from him, she knew that—unless it was the death of her soul, from loving the wrong man. "It's a small bed, Maggie."

She managed a casual shrug that convinced neither of them. "We can sleep back to back. I'm not worried, Randall. I'm sure you're not about to ravish me. I'm not one to overestimate my charms, and you're very good at resisting what you want to resist."

"Maggie," he said, his voice implacable and frightening in the darkness, "there are times when even you are a fool." Then his hands were on her arms, and she knew the waiting was over, the choice was made, and there was no turning back.

The roughness of his mouth on hers reopened the cut on her lip, and she could taste the blood as she moved into his arms. With a small, deliberate decision, she turned her brain off, turned her mind and memory and doubts away, so that there was only the two of them, entwined in the darkness, his hungry mouth on hers, devouring, demanding, denying the existence of a past or future.

His mouth left hers, and his hands held her still, moving her inches away from his hot, tense body. "Maggie," he said, his voice rough in the darkness.

He was frustratingly out of reach. His voice was the voice of reason, but she fought against it, fought against him, reaching for him. He gave her a small shake. "Maggie," he said again, "do you know what you're doing?"

She started to close in on herself again. "If you don't want me, Randall," she said, "all you have to do is say so."

"How many men have you slept with since Pulaski died?"

She winced at the question, flayed by the memory of Mack. "None of your damned business," she said.

"No one, right? Don't you think I'm a hell of a choice? Do you really want to make it with someone you hate?" His words were biting, intrusive, and she wanted to hide from them. But his hands held her steady, the long fingers biting into her arms.

"Message received, Randall," she snapped. "Get your hands off me, and I'll sleep on the floor."

He made no move to release her. She could feel the heat, the tension flowing from his body. His shirt hung open around his torso, and his lean brown chest was rising and falling rapidly. He wanted her. His eyes told her so, his body told her so. But his words kept pushing her away.

"Did you think that because you slept with me before you met Pulaski somehow this wouldn't count? That you'd still be faithful to your dead husband?"

"Don't!" She thought she'd screamed it, but the word came out a raw murmur of pain.

He shook her, and her head snapped back. Her eyes met his. "Did you ever stop to think that maybe I look at it a little differently? For me, Pulaski doesn't count. I had you first."

She stood very still at the bitter, passionate words. Finally, she found her voice. "What are you waiting for, Randall? An engraved invitation? Don't you want to see if I've gotten any better with practice?"

"You couldn't have," he said flatly, his hands leaving her arms.

"Hopeless case, was I?" She began undoing her buttons, one by one; her eyes never left his.

"You couldn't improve on perfection."

Her hands stopped where they were. The shirt hung open, exposing her skimpy little bra. "I think your memory needs jogging, Randall."

"I think your mouth needs stopping, Maggie." And he suited the action to the words, covering her mouth with his as he pulled her into his arms. His tongue slid past her teeth into the stunned interior of her mouth, and he kissed her long and hard and deep as his hands pushed the shirt off her shoulders and unfastened the bra. He stripped her jeans off and moved her down onto the narrow cot, covering her with his still-clothed body.

And then it was all darkness, warmth, and heat. His mouth was all over her, arousing her, inciting her, devouring her, until she was arching in his arms and weeping against the roughness of his shirt as his hands and mouth brought her to the border of madness and then beyond.

She lay gasping and trembling with reaction, listening to her pulse race and her heart pound. Randall lay, still clothed, half beside her, half on top of her, and he made no move to do more than hold her as she slowly floated back toward sanity.

But sanity wasn't what she wanted. She reached her hand down to touch him, but Randall caught her wrist, and she waited for him to pull her away. But he couldn't do it.

"What did Miroslav do to you, Randall?" she taunted softly. "Geld you?"

He laughed then, a small, surprising sound of amusement. "You did a much better job than he ever did, Maggie," he said, his fingers covering hers and pressing her hand against him. She began to tremble with fierce hunger, and her hands were clumsy as she tried to unfasten his zipper.

Finally he took pity on her, stripping off his pants and looming over her in the darkness. She lay back, waiting, nerves on fire, desire sweeping through her, waiting for him to complete their union. He hovered there for a moment, hesitating, and Maggie's arms reached for him.

He moved then, swiftly, pushing deep into her, shoving her back into the narrow cot with the force of his thrust. Her fingers clutched his shoulders, and her legs wrapped around his narrow hips as she took him, all of him, deep inside her, and her entire body responded with a spasm of pleasure-pain that left her sobbing into the night.

"Open your eyes, Maggie," he said softly.

She had no choice but to obey, opening her dazed eyes to stare up at him. His gray-blue eyes looked silver in the moonlight, and his mouth was a thin line of desire. "I want you to know it's me," he said, punctuating his words with a thrust of his hips. "I don't want you to lie there and pretend it's anyone but me filling you. You feel that, don't you? You know it's me, deep inside you, wanting you, having you. For six years I've been waiting for you, and I'm not going to have you mistaking me for anyone else."

She lifted her hands, running them down the sides of his tense, sweating body. It took all her effort not to clench her fists in his sleek skin. She raised her hips to meet him, tightening around him, and watched with satisfaction as his eyes glazed. "Who am I, Maggie?" he whispered, thrusting into her, his voice raw with passion. "Who do you want? Who do you need? Who do you love?" He pulled away, waiting, demanding her answer, and desperately she clutched at him.

"Answer me, Maggie," he said, his voice a thin thread. "Who do you love?"

Some small, distant, conscious part of her brain told her that now was the time for her revenge. Now she could wound him as he'd wounded her, years ago. All she had to do was say Mack's name.

She looked up at him, shivering with desire and frustration. "You, Randall," she said. "Damn you to hell. You."

He moved then, thrusting into her with a force that shook the flimsy bed, once, twice, three times, and went rigid in her arms, in the same instant that she shattered around him. Together they were swept away, lost in a maelstrom of love, passion, and despair still tinged with fury. Maggie held on to him, her fingers slippery on his sweat-slick shoulders, burying her face against his neck, hiding, as the last of the tremors shook her body.

He held her for a long, timeless moment. He didn't say a word, just held her, and she felt his body relax slowly into the stillness of sleep.

Darkness was all around them. The moon had set, and there was a soft wind whispering through the leaves and dancing across her damp skin. The feel of Randall's strong body pressed up against hers was a mindless comfort that she refused to examine. She was too weary, too replete for second thoughts and recriminations. For now, she would take what he had given and worry about it tomorrow.

She yawned, pressed her body back against him, and rubbed gently like a contented kitten as she sank into the velvet blackness of the summer night. One last thought flitted through her mind before she closed her eyes and gave herself up to much-needed sleep: She could learn to like the darkness.

Randall felt the last bit of tension leave her body. She lay in his arms completely at ease, trusting. He didn't have to look to know what her face would look like. Wet with her tears, her smooth skin would be relaxed in sleep with that look of surprise still lingering around her bruised mouth. He had managed to surprise her with her response to him. He had known that response was there, waiting for him to tap it. Sooner or later she'd accept it, too.

She wouldn't like the confession he'd forced from her. She'd hate him for that, she'd hate him for making her want him. He could live with her hatred—he had for years, because he'd always known it was tied up with wanting that she'd only recognize as love. And making her admit it, even if she denied it like crazy tomorrow, was the only way to tie her to him.

And that was what he'd planned all along; to tie her to him so completely that she could never break free, not until he was ready to let her go. And as the blackness of the Gemansk night closed around him, he wondered for the first time if that day would ever come.

Maggie sighed in her sleep, snuggling closer. Slowly, almost of their own volition, his arms moved around her, cradling her against him. And he realized with a flash of despair that he didn't want to let her go, ever. Resting his chin against her silky mane of hair, he allowed himself a short, troubled sleep.

# seventeen

Maggie sat in the doorway, fully dressed, her bare feet tucked under her, and watched the approach of dawn. It came silently at first, with an infinitesimal lightening of the eastern sky. Probably somewhere over Russia, she thought. Odd that a place she thought of as dark and shadowed would get the sunlight first. The sky began to swell with peach and pearly-gray and crimson stripes that reached into the darkness and banished the night. For once Maggie watched the blackness go with regret. With the darkness went the last of her illusions, the last of her comfort. Daylight would bring stark reality crashing in on her.

The birds came next. Starting with a quiet little chatter of noise overhead, it soon expanded into a full-blown symphony of sound as they called to each other through the trees. Maggie wondered if they were calling to their mates. Did those soft gray-brown Eastern European swallows mate for life?

A soft breeze began to pick up, rustling the trees and rumpling Maggie's hair around her bleak face. It was as gentle as a lover's caress, soft and warm and sweet. Maggie shivered, hugging her arms around her knees.

She knew he was awake, knew he was watching her as he lay perfectly still, his own clothes still a tangle on the floor beside the cot. She could sit there and wait, or she could run from what she couldn't face. He'd stripped her of everything last night, her clothes, her pride, her defenses. She could deal with that—pride and defenses could be rebuilt, clothes were easy to put back on. But he'd done the worst thing possible—he'd stolen Mack away from her.

"It's almost dawn." Her voice was admirably cool and dispassionate in the stillness as she kept her gaze outward. "I'll go find Tomas while you get dressed." She rose in one fluid movement, keeping her back to him.

"Maggie." His voice was deep, smooth, and rich—so unlike Mack's cracked shell of a voice. "Look at me, Maggie."

"Leave me alone, Randall," she said gently, and she closed the door behind her as she ran out into the deserted, dawnlit street.

He watched her go through the gaping shell of the window, watched her race away from him as if a thousand devils were at her heels. And slowly, savagely he began to curse.

It was all much easier than anyone would have expected. Leopold's cousin, Tomas, proved to be the dour member of the family. He was waiting for Maggie with a gloomy expression on his face, with forged papers in his back pocket, in a Mercedes pickup truck of prewar vintage. Maggie didn't even want to consider which war.

The three of them rode for hours, crammed together in the front seat, sharing cheese and fresh bread and very strong coffee for breakfast as they bounced along toward the border. After one look at her shuttered, set expression, Randall had left her alone, keeping up a running conversation with the serious Tomas. Lost as she was in her own dark thoughts, Maggie didn't even notice when they crossed the border into Austria and were finally safe from the long arm of the secret police.

It was still before noon when Tomas dropped them off at the train station with their original passports, complete with forged exit stamps. They made it to Vienna and on to the airport in less than an hour and were on a plane to New York by midafternoon. During all those hours, Maggie didn't speak one unnecessary word to Randall and never once looked him in the eye.

He seemed content to let her be. His curious eyes were on her, but his conversation, too, was restricted to the essentials.

He slept during the long flight back to New York, his long legs stretched out in the first-class seats. He slept while Maggie stared out the window, hollow-eyed, empty, for the seven-hour flight.

The massive sprawling bulk of JFK greeted her weary eyes, and a thousand memories hovered around her like angry bats, waiting to strike. So many times she'd stumbled wearily off a plane; so many times the huge airport had witnessed turning points in her life. There was the time Peter Wallace had met her, sending her off to see Mack Pulaski for the first time. And there was the time she and Mack had flown in from Central America and been reduced to stripping off their clothes in public, courting arrest to keep them safe from one of Mack's many pursuers.

It had bought them some time—two years, in fact—until those pursuers had caught up with him. She moved through customs in a fog, hating the memories that swept over her, hating the throbbing pain. From now on, she wasn't going to fly into JFK anymore. If she couldn't get an international flight to another local airport, she'd fly into Philadelphia and drive up. It might even have been worth the wait for the next flight from Vienna to Chicago.

But that would have meant more time in Randall's company, and she couldn't get away from him fast enough. She was desperate to get back to her apartment, away from him, away from everyone and everything but her memories of Mack. Somehow she had to get him back.

Randall caught up with her as she was heading toward the rows of waiting taxis. His hand was rough on her arm, exerting just enough pain to let her know his calm voice was a ruse. She still refused to meet his eyes, but stood, head down, waiting until he released her.

He made no move to do so. "Where are you going?"

"To my apartment. I need a good night's sleep, Randall."

"So do I."

"I hope you get one," she said in her most polite voice. "You won't be getting one with me."

"I know," he said, and the double entendre sent a red flush into her pale face. She raised her head and focused on a point somewhere beyond his left shoulder. "All right, Maggie," he said finally, his long fingers biting into her arm, "I'll let you go this time. I have a few things to check on in the city anyway. I'll make arrangements for us to fly to Chicago tomorrow afternoon."

"I'd rather take care of it myself."

"I'm sure you would. That, however, is not an option. I'll give you some time to yourself, but tomorrow I'll be at your apartment and you'd better be ready to go." His voice was calm, unmoved, but through her numbness Maggie could feel the tension, the anger vibrating through him. "Understood?"

She considered fighting, she considered turning and taking the next flight to Chicago, but in the end the numbness and exhaustion won out. "Understood," she muttered, dropping her eyes again. "May I leave now?"

"Snotty as ever," he said, but there was an oddly gentle note in his voice. "Yes, you can leave now. I'm presuming you don't wish to share a cab with me?"

"You're presuming right," she snapped. "What time tomorrow?"

"I'll call you."

"I won't be answering the phone."

"It wasn't that bad, Maggie," he said softly.

"Go to hell, Randall." She yanked her arm away from him.

"Are you going to be answering your door?"

"Not if I know it's you."

"Locked doors won't keep me out, Maggie. Nothing will."

She took a deep, steadying breath. "Not even the knowledge that you're not wanted?"

"It might. But that's not an issue right now, is it? Your problem isn't not wanting me. It's wanting me too much."

It was enough to make her head shoot up again. For the first time since they made love, she looked into his eyes, and what she saw there shook her. His eyes were dark, almost pleading, in his weary, unshaven face. Randall Carter, the

166

immaculate, impeccable, invincible, invulnerable Randall Carter looked hot, dirty, sweaty, and tired. And he looked as if he needed, wanted, nothing more than her arms around him.

A trick of the light, a trick of her own exhaustion. But one thing was no trick at all. In his scruffiness, with his shirt hanging loosely around his narrow hips and his grubby face, he looked so damned sexy that her wall of numbness began to crumble. And that was the last thing she could bear.

"I don't want you, Randall," she said, the lie clear and cold in her voice. "I'll travel back to Chicago with you, and I'll see this through to the end for my sister's sake. But I don't want you to ever touch me again. Do you understand?"

The emotion had vanished from his eyes so swiftly, she knew she'd imagined it. "I understand better than you think. Go home, Maggie, and sleep."

As swiftly as the hot anger rushed through her, it vanished. She couldn't even summon up the energy to form a snide retort. All she could do was turn her back on him and head out to the waiting taxis.

He watched her go, his face now showing his anger and threatening despair. She was so damned strong, walking away from him, her shoulders back, her tangled blond hair swaying slightly in the evening breeze. She was strong enough to turn so far inward that he'd never be able to break through. He'd seen it on her face this morning, and he cursed himself for an idiot not to have foreseen her reaction. She was pulling away from him, but there was no way in hell he was going to let her do it.

But right this minute, he had to let her be. He would find a shower and decent clothes, and then he had to track Bud Willis to whatever slimy hole he was lurking in. The first step in cleaning up this mess was stopping Admiral Wentworth and sealing the leak before the media discovered it. The American public wouldn't take kindly to an admiral living off his fat military pensions and selling out his country. But what they didn't know wouldn't hurt them.

* * *

Maggie's apartment had the dry, musty smell of a closed-up place. She wandered through it, stripping her clothes off and leaving them where they lay, turned on the air conditioner full blast, and headed for the shower.

She stood under the pounding streams of hot water for half an hour, letting them beat against her skin as she scrubbed every last trace of Gemansk—and Randall—off it. She thought of Francis Ackroyd lying in her sister's tub and shuddered, then turned up the hot water until it stung her skin in scalding drizzle. And still she scrubbed her body, rubbing it raw, until finally she felt clean and turned the shower off.

The apartment was icy, thanks to her efficient air conditioner, and the blasts of cold air prickled her wet skin. She ignored it. She ignored the telephone, knowing she should call Kate and warn her about Alicia, knowing she should call Sybil and make sure everything was all right, and knowing she would do neither.

She ignored the front door and the second and third locks that she hadn't bothered to fasten. If someone wanted to break in and rape and murder her, she wouldn't stop them. They could be her guest.

She ignored the clothing on the floor, the overworked air conditioner, the lights throughout the apartment. She went blindly into her bedroom, found another one of Mack's old chambray shirts and sank into bed with it. In moments she was asleep.

The sound in her living room awoke her. She glanced up at her digital clock and groaned. It was only five o'clock in the morning, and someone had clearly taken advantage of her unspoken offer to come and murder her. She raised her head off the pillow, then dropped it back again. She only hoped he'd be quick about it.

Her bedroom door opened, letting in a blaze of light. "Rise and shine, Maggie." Randall's hateful voice penetrated her mists of sleep.

She gathered enough energy to raise her head and glare in

his direction. "Go away, Randall," she muttered. "We aren't going to Chicago until tomorrow."

"It is tomorrow, Maggie. Five o'clock in the afternoon, for that matter. Get up, or I'll come over there and get you up."

There was no doubting the threat in his voice. With an immediate surge of energy Maggie rolled off the bed, only then remembering she was wearing absolutely nothing.

At least Randall was unmoved by her nudity. She was still clutching Mack's shirt in her fist, and with remarkable aplomb, she pulled it on, buttoning it with calm fingers. "When's our flight?"

"Later," he said, his voice flat. "I'll make coffee." And he closed the door silently behind him.

She stalled as long as she could while getting dressed. She was chilled from the night in an icy apartment, and only with effort did she remember that it was probably steaming hot outside. When she finally emerged from her room, she was wearing faded jeans and Mack's shirt still around her. She could hear music, faint and jarring, and she followed the sound.

Randall was standing in front of the television, absorbed in a videotape. He was dressed like Randall again, though his linen suit wasn't buttoned and he'd dispensed with his knotted silk tie. Another time, another place, and she might have teased him about it. But with the numbness still on her, she took the cup of coffee he handed her and stared blankly at the television.

"Aren't you going to ask me what tape I'm watching?" he asked her.

"I don't give a damn." She turned away from him. Hordes of brightly dressed gypsies wandering around a field didn't interest her; the random, dissonant chords of music didn't hold any fascination, even as they coalesced into the opening strains of something eerily familiar.

And then there it was: a voice, deep, rich, beautiful, and throbbing with life and warmth, singing a stupid song about being free. Slowly Maggie turned, her face frozen, to stare at the television set.

There was Mack, in his guise as Snake, lead singer of the Guess What, his blond hair hanging to his shoulders, his hazel eyes just the tiniest bit doped up, his mouth wide and sexy as he whirled and strutted, danced and pranced over the stage at Woodstock.

Randall was watching her. "Do you play this every night before you go to bed, Maggie?" he taunted gently. "Do you sit there in Pulaski's shirt and masturbate, pretending he's still alive? He isn't. He died two years ago on a sidewalk in Maine. He's gone, and you're left behind, throwing your life away on a memory—on a dead man."

She stood very still, watching the screen. The small, numb part of her that had atrophied since Mack had died came back to an aching, horrible life. She moved toward the television, mesmerized. Randall's voice was only an irritating buzz in the background as she stared at Pulaski's flying form.

Then Randall's hands caught her shoulders and twisted her around to face him, and there was no hiding from the rage and sorrow in his face. "He's dead, Maggie," he said again, his rich voice bleak, "and you're alive." His strong hands took hold of Mack's chambray shirt and ripped it down the middle.

Something finally snapped. She hurled the coffee at him, screaming at him, rage and despair sweeping over her, washing away the self-control she'd always clung to. A red haze formed in front of her eyes, and she could hear the screaming voice in the back of her brain, knew it was her own but was powerless to stop it. . . .

Her voice was raw, her body ached, her hands felt swollen, and there were tight, crushing bands around her body. She opened her eyes, panting, and found that the tight bands were Randall's arms, holding her. The screaming had stopped at last, and a deep, shuddering sigh left her.

In a matter of a few, mad minutes, she had trashed her apartment. The television was a blank screen of fuzz, the VCR smashed on the carpet. Furniture had been upended, books thrown all over the place, the mirrors and pictures smashed. She looked up at Randall, and there was a welt over his eye where she'd managed to connect. She looked up at him and began to cry.

# eighteen

When she stopped crying, the living room was shadowed in twilight. When she stopped crying, she was lying on the littered floor in Randall's arms, and his suit was rumpled and tearstained beneath her. When she stopped crying, his hard hands gently pushed the torn shirt off her shoulders, and he began to make love to her.

She was too exhausted, too drained to resist or protest. Besides, it made some crazy sort of sense to lie there in the mess and celebrate the life she'd tried to wish away. They made love in complete silence; his hands stripped the rest of her clothes away, and his mouth covered every inch of her body, soothing the aching flesh, claiming ownership with his lips. When his hands cradled her narrow hips and his mouth found her, she tried for a useless moment to squirm away. But his hands were firm, and all the fight was gone from her. She lay floating, removed, and then suddenly, shockingly, she was there—her body convulsed and her raw, torn voice called his name, pleading, demanding.

And he came to her, filling her with his passion, filling the emptiness inside her body, heart, and soul. He moved tenderly with her, giving her time to grow used to him, gently pushing away any lingering restraints until she was clinging to him, burying her face against his muscled shoulder as he drove deep into her.

This time, when reality returned, it wasn't such a shock. The wool carpet was itchy beneath her bare back, his weight was holding her trapped without crushing her, and the buzz of the broken television warred with the hum of the air conditioner. The artificial chill was rapidly drying the sheen of sweat that had covered her body, and she turned her head slightly to look into Randall's dark eyes.

Whatever she hoped to see, it wasn't there. Slowly he withdrew, pulling away from her, his face closed and shuttered. And her face matched his as she watched him.

"What time is the plane?" Her voice was calm, matter-of-fact.

"There are flights leaving almost every hour."

Maggie nodded, picked up her scattered clothes, and rose gracefully to her feet. "It won't take me long to get ready."

He didn't move. "I'll pick things up in here."

"No!" It came out a strangled protest, and it took all her last bit of energy to continue in a smoother voice. "Leave it the way it is. I want to see it like this when I come back from Chicago."

He looked at her oddly then. Something broke through his reserve, and he started to speak. She waited, but he shut his mouth again and turned away. "Suit yourself."

They were heading out of the lobby when a figure materialized beside them, coming out of the shadows with stealth that was second nature to him. "Hi there, sweetcakes," Bud Willis said, his hand connecting with her bottom.

Mack would have broken his arm, Maggie thought. But Mack was dead, gone from her at last, and Randall just watched as Willis made his sleazy moves.

Bud Willis hadn't changed in all the time she'd known him. Whether he was fighting with rebels in a Central American jungle or sitting behind a desk in Washington, he still had that feral expression in his colorless eyes. His once-short hair was now carefully styled, his suit was almost as good as Randall's —and at this point, it was in better shape—and his killer's hands were perfectly manicured. Maggie twisted out of his reach.

"It only needed you to make this day complete," she snarled. "What the hell are you doing here?"

"Ask your friend," Willis offered, and Maggie turned her outraged eyes to Randall.

"He's giving us a ride to the airport," he said calmly.

"I'd rather walk."

"Honeybuns, you wound me," Willis protested. "After all I've done for you?"

"What have you done for me?"

"Why, I sent you Randall, of course. What more could any grieving widow ask? She as good a piece of tail as she used to be, Carter?" he inquired affably. "She's out of practice, but I'm sure a few hours in the saddle will get her back in shape."

It took every ounce of her self-control to keep from fighting back. She stared at Willis in mute fury, biding her time.

"Willis, you're being tiresome," Randall said quietly. "Did you take care of everything?"

"Admiral Wentworth is being watched. The limousine is waiting." He made an extravagant gesture toward the door. "And I've got another name for you: Caleb McAllister."

Maggie heard the name with real dread. "What about him?"

"He's got to be involved in this shit up to his neck," Willis said. "His tracks are all over the place—the asshole doesn't have enough sense to cover up anything. We'll get him anytime we want him. Alicia Stoneham'll be a harder nut to crack."

"I don't believe it."

"Listen, she may be one tough broad but—"

"No, I mean I don't believe it about Caleb."

"Believe it. It's him or your sister, sweetcakes. Take your pick."

"Someone was trying to frame Kate. Maybe someone's trying to frame Caleb, too," Maggie insisted stubbornly.

"Maybe. You making it with him, too? I woulda thought Randall would be enough for you." He reached out and pinched her arm, pinched the bruises Randall's hard hands had left. "You like it rough, don't you? If I'd known, I woulda made more of an effort. I like a woman who appreciates pain."

With a seemingly casual gesture, Randall draped a friendly arm around Willis's narrow shoulders. He smiled a peculiarly sweet smile as Willis's ferret-face whitened in sudden pain. "Don't mess with my woman, Willis."

Willis still managed his skeletal smile as the veins on his forehead stood out. "Your woman, Carter? You're sounding human like the rest of us. Who would have thought we'd hear the great Randall Carter refer to a piece of ass as 'my woman.'" He grunted. "Shit, man, cut that out!"

"I thought you were a man who appreciated pain," Randall said gently.

"Not my own, man," Willis protested. "Tell him to let me go, Maggie."

Maggie only smiled.

A moment later, Willis was released. "Dammit, man, you don't need to get so touchy," he said, rubbing his shoulder. "I was just kidding." The colorless eyes that watched Randall above the smiling mouth were those of a cobra waiting to strike.

"When are you going to move on the admiral?"

"When you give me the word, man," Willis said. "Not a damned second sooner, I promise. You going to wrap this up tomorrow?"

"Yes."

"You going to help him, sugarbuns? Or are you just going to be waiting with your legs spread?"

Randall reached for him again, but Maggie got in the way. "What do you think, Bud?" she said sweetly.

"Jesus, I don't know," he said. "You lie there and pretend he's that dead Polack?"

Maggie moved closer, pressing her soft breasts up against him as she repressed a shudder of distaste. "No, Willis. I pretend he's you." And then she brought her heel down on his instep.

He moved, but not in time. "Ouch, Maggie, there's no need

to be so sensitive! You're acting more like a couple of frustrated spinsters than two people who've been fucking their brains out. We're in this thing together—you don't need to beat up on me."

"Poor Bud," Maggie said sweetly. "I'll tell you what. Why don't you and Randall take the limo to the airport, and I'll get a taxi?"

"Have you got any more information for us, Willis?" Randall inquired with apparent courtesy.

"Nope. Just that we're ready to grab the admiral when you get things sewed up in Chicago. Unless you want to bow out—"

"I'll take care of things. I like to finish what I start."

"Don't let the merry widow keep you from nailing her sister if she's involved. I want Stoneham and McAllister on ice by the day after tomorrow. If you get tired of Mrs. Pulaski here, you can send her back to me for a little discipline. Might as well spread some of the hot Danish around." He reached out to pinch her again.

Maggie had had enough. She lunged for him, but Randall was faster. He caught her around the waist and held her while she struggled, muttering dire threats and insults.

"If I were you, I'd get the hell out of here, Willis," Randall said with a cheerful drawl, his strong hands pressed against her middle as she fought him. "If I let her go, there won't be enough left of you to bury at Arlington."

"Hey, man, I'm going," he said, backing away nervously. "Tell your mother I'm looking forward to seeing her again." And he disappeared back into the night.

"Hell and damnation!" Maggie said. "Put me down!"

Randall obeyed immediately, dropping her onto the marble floor of the deserted foyer. She staggered slightly and stumbled into him, then she quickly righted herself. "Wouldn't you know my damned mother would have gotten involved with a scumbag like him?" she demanded.

"Don't believe everything Willis tells you," Randall said.

She was still staring out into the hot city night. She gave

herself a tiny shake. "No, you're right. I always was too gullible where Bud Willis was concerned. What do you think
about what he said?"

"Which scintillating remark?"

Maggie sighed. "Caleb. Do you think he's really involved?"

"I don't know. I think we can't be sure of anything at this
point."

"It would break Kate's heart."

"You aren't going to say anything to her." Randall's voice
was implacable. It wasn't a request, and it wasn't a suggestion. It was an order.

A dozen possible retorts rose in her mind, starting with
"Says who?" and going downhill from there. She closed her
mouth and promised nothing.

"Do you hear me, Maggie? If he is involved, we can't afford
to have him warned. You're to keep your damned mouth shut,
or I sure as hell will find a way to shut it."

She smiled up at him. He was angry with her; his blue-gray
eyes were stormy, and his sexy mouth was a pinched frown.
She couldn't believe that she'd once thought him passionless
and inhuman. "You know, you're beautiful when you're angry," she said with a mischievous smile, feeling suddenly,
oddly playful. There was something to be said for catharsis,
both emotional and sexual.

"Maggie . . ." His voice held a very definite warning.

"Are we going to Chicago?" she questioned in a dulcet
voice.

He stared at her in mute frustration, then thrust out his
arm for her to take. "We're going to Chicago," he said. And
after only a moment's hesitation, she took it, following him
out into the New York City night.


They were back at Kate's apartment well before midnight.
Randall could see tension begin to build in Maggie as they
deplaned at O'Hare, and he watched it grow during the ride
back into the city in his Jaguar. He knew without false mod-

esty that he was the cause of it. She was wondering where he was planning to sleep tonight.

The apartment was deserted when Maggie opened the door with only slight but telltale fumbling. The matching VCRs were still in place, the curtains were open to the dark Chicago night, and a note was taped to one of the television sets. Before she could reach it, Randall had ripped it off the screen.

"Maggie, where the hell are you?" he read. "Chrissie's still with Sybil—I've gone with Caleb to check out a lead in Wisconsin. Stay put. Kate."

"Damn," said Maggie.

"Indeed," said Randall. "If he's as bad as Bud Willis thinks, your sister might be in deep trouble."

"He's not. I'm sure we can trust him. I have excellent judgment when it comes to people."

"Do you?"

She looked at him then, her face flushed and defiant. "I used to. I think I probably still do."

He kept his face impassive, watching her. He wanted to scoop her up into his arms and carry her off to the bedroom, like a scene in a movie. He didn't move, just watched the tension tick through her body.

"Well, I guess there's nothing we can do now," she said finally, when he said nothing. "What are we going to do about Alicia Stoneham?"

"We're going to find out who's working with her. Whether it's Caleb McAllister or someone else, we need to know before we make our move. And we need more proof than just the word of someone at Red Glove Films."

"How did you get him to tell you?" she asked, and he could see the curiosity burning beneath her nervousness.

He smiled a faint, wintry smile. "You don't want to know, Maggie."

"Maybe I don't," she said with a sigh.

"It's just as well your sister isn't here. I don't trust your ability to be discreet. It would be just like you to blurt out everything about Caleb and Alicia, and the fewer people who know at this point the better."

"You mean you expect me not to say anything about Alicia, either?" she demanded, outraged. "What am I supposed to tell her when she asks where I was?"

"Tell her you were in bed with me," he suggested coolly. "Tell her we had a long passionate weekend in your New York apartment, writhing around on the living room carpet."

The nervousness was leaving her, replaced by healthy anger. "You're such a bastard, Randall," she said.

"I know." He crossed the room, took her resisting hand in his, opened it with no trouble whatsoever, and placed Kate's note inside. His hand reached up and gently traced the bruised side of her face; his thumb brushed her cut lip. "You look like you've been through a war."

She stood very still beneath his hands. And then, to his complete astonishment, a very small, very tentative smile lit her face. "You don't look so hot yourself," she said, raising her hand to touch the welt across his forehead.

It was all he could do not to take her then, not to pull her into his arms and make love to her until they were both exhausted. But they were both exhausted already, and he had things to do.

He couldn't resist, though. He caught the hand that had gently touched his forehead and drew it to his mouth, kissing it with great tenderness. And then he moved away.

"Get some sleep, Maggie," he said, ignoring the startled expression in her aquamarine eyes. "I can't afford to have jet lag impair your efficiency."

"No," she said, "we wouldn't want that."

"I'll be back tomorrow morning. Sleep as late as you can—there's nothing we can do for a while."

"Where are you going?"

"To my hotel. Unless you were going to invite me to stay?" He knew she wouldn't, when he put it that way. And much as he wanted to, he had too many things to do to spend the night curled up against her strong, warm body.

She turned away from him. "Good night, Randall."

Her back was straight and strong; her shoulders weren't the slightest bit bowed under all she'd been through. He paused in the open doorway and looked back at her, and his hand clenched the knob tightly. "Maggie."

She didn't turn. "What?" Her voice was cool, not at all sulky.

"Don't put on another one of Pulaski's shirts. I'll just have to rip it off you again." And he shut the door before she could respond.

The shrill ring of the telephone shattered Maggie's sleep. She moaned in her sleep, hating the nagging, insistent ringing, trying to hold on to the fast-disappearing waves of sleep. She reached out in the wide, empty bed, reached out and found no one beside her. The wave of desolation that washed over her wrenched her out of the last bits of sleep.

Still the damned phone rang. With a curse, she threw back the covers and stumbled out into the living room, past the still-burning lamps that she'd left on to defeat the darkness. When she finally reached the phone, it had stopped ringing; the dial tone that met her ear was a taunt. It took all her willpower not to pick it up and heave it through the nearest window, but willpower was something she was slowly regaining. With only the slightest bit of a slam, she replaced the phone onto its cradle, and an only slightly obscene curse left her mouth when she looked at the clock and found it was a quarter past eight in the morning: too early for her to want to get up after her global trek, too late to have any hope for more sleep.

She moved around the room and turned off the lights, shivering in the early-morning chill. The thin cotton nightgown she'd purloined from Kate's closet provided little protection, and she headed back to her room for a sweater.

She was looking at the empty, rumpled bed with unseeing eyes when she finally realized why she was feeling so unbalanced. It wasn't lack of sleep or jet lag. With sudden, inescapable clarity it came to her, leaving her shaken: She hadn't woken up feeling abandoned by Mack. It was Randall's body she'd reached for through the mists of sleep; it was Randall she wanted.

Mack's chambray shirt met her eyes. Countless times she'd worn it for warmth, for comfort. But Mack was gone, beyond her reach, beyond her sorrow. She picked up the shirt and held it in her hands, but it was only a shirt. It was no longer a talisman of the only real love she'd ever known. She dropped it back onto the bed and turned to find a cotton sweater; the increasing chill now came from inside as well as out.

The phone rang again. Maggie forgot about the sweater and raced back out into the living room, stubbing her foot on the desk. The phone clattered off the desk as she lunged for it, and she ended up on her knees on the carpet, clutching the receiver.

"Maggie." Sybil's perfect British tones were distraught, and irritation swept over Maggie. Sybil spent half her life in crisis, and she was in no mood to deal with her mother's histrionics now.

"Yes, Mother," she said patiently, rising to her feet.

"Thank God, you're back. Maggie, they've taken the baby!"

# n i n e t e e n

Maggie no longer felt the chill of the room—every part of her body had turned to ice. She held the telephone in a frozen hand, and it was all she could do to sink her body into the chair. "Explain," she ordered, and her voice was raw. "No hysterics, no acting, no bullshit. Just tell me what happened."

For once Sybil's ego seemed to have deserted her. "She overslept this morning. She usually wakes Queenie up around seven, so Queenie thought she'd better check. When she went into her room, the crib was empty, and there was a message scribbled on the mirror, saying, 'We have the baby. Don't call the police, we'll be in touch.'"

"What was it written in?"

"For God's sake, I don't know!" Sybil snapped. "What the hell does it matter?"

"It matters. Crayon, Magic Marker—what?"

"Actually, it was the most ghastly shade of fuchsia lipstick, now that I think of it. I can't imagine anyone who would wear that color."

"I know someone who would," Maggie said grimly, thinking of Alicia Stoneham's wide, fuchsia-colored mouth and braying laugh. And her cold, cold eyes. Would she hurt the baby? "How did they get in?"

"Lord, I don't know. Probably through the service entrance in this damned hotel suite. Maggie, what are we going to do? They said not to call the police, but I'm terrified for my little Chrissie."

"Where's Kate?"

"Off with Caleb McAllister, somewhere in the wilds of Wisconsin. Apparently, Francis Ackroyd had a brother living in some ridiculous place up there, and they wanted to see if he knew anything. Maggie—"

"Calm down, Sybil. I know who has Chrissie. And I don't think she'll hurt her—not unless she's forced to. We have to be very careful and not make any stupid moves. Just sit tight, and I'll call you back."

"Let me speak to Randall," she said suddenly. "I want him to tell me not to worry—I think you might lie to me just to calm me down."

"Mother, Randall isn't here," Maggie said with ill-disguised impatience.

"He isn't? Didn't you go off with him for the weekend?"

"Yes. But he's not here. He spent the night at his hotel. As soon as you hang up, I'll call him—"

"You must be a changeling," Sybil said flatly. "I can't believe that a daughter of mine could let a man who looks like Randall Carter get away."

"Maybe I sent him away."

"Oh. That's different. Maybe you're my daughter after all. Did you say a woman has Chrissie?"

Maggie hesitated. Beneath her silly banter, Sybil was clearly distraught, and she owed her that much. "Alicia Stoneham," she said.

"I knew I'd seen that hideous shade of lipstick before! I'm going to cut that woman's heart out. How dare she touch my baby!"

"You're going to sit there and say absolutely nothing, Mother. I don't think Alicia will hurt her, but I don't know for sure. She's desperate, and desperate people do desperate things."

"But—"

"I'll call you back." Maggie slammed down the phone and rose on unsteady feet to go to the hallway. Someone was unlocking the door, and she hoped to God it was Randall.

Kate walked in with a sleepy smile on her face. Her clothing was rumpled, and her short brown hair was a mess. She looked happier than Maggie had ever seen her, and she ached for her.

"Maggie, you're back!" she cried cheerfully when she looked up and saw her sister's silent figure. "Come talk to me while I shower, and we'll go see Chrissie. I'm not going in to work today, and I want to tell you about—what's wrong?" The bright chatter faded as she saw Maggie's eyes.

There was no way to sugar-coat it. "Chrissie's been kidnapped."

Kate stood very still, her face deadly white. "Brian?" she croaked, and for a moment Maggie couldn't even remember who she was talking about.

She shook her head. "Not her father. I wish it were him."

"Then who?"

"Sit down, Kate, and I'll explain everything I know, or think I know—"

"Who kidnapped my baby?" she said, her raw voice skirting the edges of hysteria that Maggie badly wanted to forestall.

"Alicia Stoneham."

That stopped the panic cold. "What?"

"Sit down and I'll tell you."

"I don't want to sit down. I want you to tell me why a woman who's been like a second mother to me would kidnap my baby." Her voice was still dangerously close to the edge.

"You want it in twenty words or less?" Maggie inquired grimly. All bets were off with this new development, and Randall would just have to accept it that discretion had gone out the window. "Francis Ackroyd was helping Alicia sell military secrets to Eastern Europe."

"What?"

"Don't interrupt. She was getting military secrets from her brother, a retired admiral, and she and Francis were incorporating them into their stupid science-fiction movies and sending them to Gemansk. To—"

"Red Glove Films," Kate said numbly. "I've seen the shipping orders. That explains a lot of discrepancies. Go on. Did Alicia kill Francis?"

"I don't know. There's another man involved in all this, and we haven't figured out who he is. He's probably the one who murdered Francis, though why he dumped him here is beyond me."

"Why would Alicia take Chrissie?"

"She knows we're on to her. Her brother is being watched closely, and she must know it's a matter of time before we get her. She must have taken Chrissie as a hostage, to buy her enough time to escape."

"She won't hurt Chrissie," Kate said. That simple assurance took some but not all of the panic from her brown eyes.

"No, I don't think she will. But we have to be careful and not panic her into doing something she'd regret. And of course, it all depends who's working with her."

"I can't imagine . . ." Her voice trailed off as she looked with sudden horror into Maggie's eyes. "You can't believe it's Caleb!"

"We don't know," Maggie said carefully. "An informant has mentioned his name, but informants aren't infallible. He has had plenty of opportunity—"

"No!"

"Kate, anything is possible. For Christ's sake, sit down and let me get us some coffee before I call Randall."

"What does he have to do with all this?" Kate demanded numbly, not moving from her spot by the door. "Where the hell were the two of you this weekend?"

"Randall's a consultant."

"For whom?"

"The CIA," she said reluctantly. "We were in Gemansk, checking out Red Glove Films."

"Were they the ones who said Caleb was part of it?"

"No."

"He's not, Maggie!" Kate said. "He can't be."

"Maybe not," Maggie said. "For what it's worth, my instincts tell me he isn't. But you can't rely on instincts when lives are at stake."

"No, you can't," she said dully.

Maggie stared at her, torn in a thousand directions. She wanted to put her arms around her stricken sister and comfort her; she wanted to race over to Sybil's hotel and see if she could find out anything there; she wanted to go out and confront Alicia Stoneham; she wanted to scour the city until she found Chrissie. And a small, weak part of her wanted to run crying to Randall.

The only logical thing to do was to wait. "Coffee," she said. "I'll make the coffee—you sit down and tell me what you found out in Wisconsin."

"Stop trying to make me sit down," Kate said in a dead voice. "We didn't find out a damned thing. It was a wild-goose chase, and don't tell me that's more proof that Caleb is involved. He was just as taken in as I was." She shivered, turning her despairing brown eyes toward the window. "Is there anything we can do?"

"Not at this point. I'll call Randall and tell him. I'm sure he'll tell us to sit still and wait."

Kate shut her eyes, nodding. "I'm going to lie down."

"Do you want any coffee?"

"Not now. All I want to do is hide for a few moments. . . ." She let it trail, and Maggie watched her out of aching eyes, watched as she stumbled wearily toward her bedroom. The door closed silently behind her, and Maggie let out her painfully pent-up breath.

In the kitchen, there was coffee and a phone to call Randall. She stood watching the coffee perk as she listened to Randall's phone ring and ring and ring.

He wasn't there. At eight thirty in the morning, when she most needed him, he wasn't there. And she wondered suddenly if she'd been the world's biggest fool ever to trust him.

Randall was capable of anything. She'd always known that, and the unexpected violence that had surrounded him in Gemansk shouldn't have surprised her. He would use anything and anybody to get what he wanted. She'd always assumed that they wanted the same things, but now she began to wonder if she'd been much too gullible.

He'd been in town when Francis had been murdered, been at Francis's apartment—the scene of the murder—without anyone knowing, when she'd brought the body back. Someone had let the secret police know they were coming; someone had been one step behind them, closing in on them, breathing down their necks. Someone had been involved in this, and she found it hard to believe that Caleb McAllister had such far-reaching power. Randall was the obvious second choice.

He wouldn't be doing it for the money; Randall didn't need money. He spent what he had on possessions, rare and precious works of art that could be very expensive indeed. But he had no weaknesses, no obsessions, no drug or alcohol addictions; he wasn't a gambler or a spendthrift. If he had turned traitor, if he was in this whole mess up to his armpits, then he was doing it for the same reason he started helping out the CIA: For the thrill. To alleviate the boredom that had stalked him most of his adult life, the boredom that didn't suffer fools lightly.

It was a terrifying thought, and Maggie could understand how Kate would panic at the suggestion of Caleb's involvement. It felt as if the very ground were sinking away beneath her.

Two cups of coffee helped. Sitting by the kitchen window and looking over the city as it came to life helped. Telling herself that even if Randall was a traitor, it wasn't the end of the world, as long as Chrissie was all right, helped.

It wasn't as if Randall meant anything to her, after all. She was immune to him; he had no power over her, no effect on her whatsoever. Sex was merely a biological function that reared its ugly head during moments of stress. She wasn't going to bed with Randall again, ever. She didn't like him or trust him, so it didn't really matter if he was a traitor. Did it?

"You don't answer doors anymore?" His warm, rich voice broke through her abstraction, and she turned from the city landscape to look at him. He'd changed into an artfully rumpled beige linen suit. The welt across his forehead had paled with the passing of hours, and his eyes as they looked into hers were oddly warm and concerned.

"I didn't hear you ring," she said, moving slowly away from the window, watching him out of curious eyes. Could he have betrayed her once again? Not just her, but his entire country? Not just his country, but humanity, by stealing a helpless infant? Was he as monstrous as she sometimes wondered?

"What's wrong, Maggie?" His voice was uncharacteristically gentle.

"Didn't Kate tell you?"

"Is Kate back?" he said, momentarily diverted. "I didn't see her."

"Then who let you in?"

"I've already told you that locked doors don't keep me out. I passed the CIA's course on B and E with flying colors, unlike you. You still haven't told me what's wrong."

"You don't know?"

He frowned, becoming impatient. "I'm not interested in playing twenty questions, Maggie. Why are you looking at me as if I'm Frankenstein's monster?"

"Have you been leading me on?"

His reply was an unexpected burst of laughter. "What the hell are you asking me, Maggie? If my intentions are honorable? If I'm going to make an honest woman of you?"

"I'm not talking about sex, Randall. I'm talking about treason. I'm talking about military secrets and Red Glove Films and Alicia Stoneham."

The light of humor vanished as quickly as it had come. "Maggie," he said meditatively, "the fact that you're a woman isn't enough to stop me from punching you in the mouth for asking something like that."

"Try it."

"What's going on, Maggie?"

"It just occurred to me that I've been awfully trusting.

Someone has known just what we were up to, someone has been on our trail from the very beginning. And I wondered if you hadn't been using me as part of a smokescreen to cover your own involvement."

"You've been doing a lot of thinking. Did you come to any conclusions?" His voice was flat, unemotional.

Maggie watched him out of weary eyes. "Yes."

"You want to tell me what they are?"

All his defenses were up. He was watching her out of those stormy gray-blue eyes and his expression was blank, slightly wary, waiting.

"I decided that I had no choice but to trust you," she said, and his expression didn't change.

"Your vote of confidence is inspiring," he said, and she suspected he still wanted to punch her in the mouth. "Does that mean you're going to tell me what the hell is going on?"

"Chrissie's been kidnapped."

"No, she hasn't."

"Don't be ridiculous, Randall, she most certainly—" The words died in her throat as she stared up at him, incredulity and rage warring within her. "What have you done with her?"

"She's with my sister. I had her fly in from Boston last night. They've got a suite three floors down from your mother at the Mandrake, and Chrissie's having a wonderful time playing with my three-year-old-nephew."

"Why?"

"I had to do something to protect the kid, Maggie. This isn't a parlor game we're playing. People use real bullets, they're desperate, and a baby would be a wonderful pawn. It would have been their next move—I just got there first. Would you rather Caleb or Alicia had gotten her? It looked as if it might come to that."

"So the Almighty Randall decided to make his move, without asking anyone, without telling anyone." She spat out the words. "You couldn't trust me enough to tell me, to save my sister and my mother the anguish of thinking Chrissie might be in danger—"

"It didn't seem to be a risk worth taking."

"You heartless bastard," Maggie said calmly. "Who the hell gave you the right to interfere in our lives? If I had a gun, I would shoot you."

"Then let's be thankful you left yours in New York," he said. "Are you going to stand around in that transparent nightgown, or are we going to see how my plan worked?"

"The very first thing I'm going to do is tell my sister what you've done." She headed for the door, but his tall, lean body was ahead of her, blocking her.

"No, you're not. Chrissie's absolutely fine, and Kate will survive the next few hours. I'm sure you've already told her that Alicia took her, and she thinks Alicia isn't really dangerous. We can't afford to have anyone guess what's going on."

"Are you going to move, Randall?" Maggie asked sweetly.

"Not until I have your word that you won't tell your sister," he said.

Randall was good, and he was fast, but Maggie had the element of surprise on her side. Without a moment's hesitation, she kneed him in the groin.

He moved fast, but not quite fast enough for her to miss entirely. He doubled over with a muffled grunt of pain, and forced herself to move past him into the hallway and raced toward Kate's bedroom. Randall had recovered enough to come after her, but she had a head start. She yanked the door open and burst into the room.

"Kate, Chrissie's safe . . ." The words trailed off as she surveyed the empty bedroom, the still-made bed.

"Flown the coop, has she?" Randall inquired from the doorway.

Slowly Maggie turned to look at him. His face was still slightly pale around the edges, with just a hint of pain lingering around his grim mouth. "She's probably gone after Alicia," Maggie said in despair. "You see what you've done with your damned game-playing? Even if Chrissie's safe, Kate's in danger. If anything happens to her, I'll kill you."

"You're probably right," he said, showing no remorse. "Are you just going to stand there threatening me, or are we going after her?"

Maggie stared at him for a long moment. "It'll take me five minutes."

"Make it three." And he turned from the doorway and headed back into the living room.

She made it in two and a half, still pulling on a battered Nike as she stumbled out of her bedroom. Randall was standing by the window, his body stiff and unyielding. He turned, and his face was impassive. "Are you ready? Or do you want to call your mother first?"

"Why?"

"To tell her Chrissie's all right."

"Learned your lesson, did you? That'll teach you to mess with . . . superwoman." She said the word deliberately, waiting to see his reaction. "Sybil can wait."

"Superwoman, eh?" he echoed. "You'll have to convince me."

"Didn't I just do that?"

He shook his head. "Not by a long shot. Come on, Maggie, let's go catch us some spies."

# twenty

Caleb McAllister was waiting for them as they left the building. The August heat was already baking the air; the smell of exhaust and gas and summer sidewalks rose up and surrounded them in a cocoon of city life. Maggie saw him first, his tall, angular body tense and angry, and she nudged Randall ungently in the ribs.

"Here's your chance to find out if he's involved," she said quietly.

Frustration and something else shadowed Randall's eyes. "One of us needs to go after your sister and make sure she doesn't get herself killed. We don't know for sure that Alicia didn't kill Francis. And even if she didn't, there's another murderer loose if Caleb is innocent. Someone who wouldn't think twice about killing to protect himself."

"You take Caleb," Maggie muttered. "I'm going after Kate."

"Maggie—" But she moved quickly out of reach, directly into Caleb's path. Randall's mouth shut with an angry snap.

"Hi, Caleb. Why aren't you at the studio?" she demanded abruptly.

"The studio's closed on Wednesdays. What the hell does that matter? Listen, Sybil called me—"

"Where does Alicia live?" she broke in.

"42557 Springhill Estates," he said automatically. "I have to talk to you, Maggie."

"Talk to Randall," she said, rushing past him and grabbing the first taxi that was lined up outside the hotel next to Kate's building. She didn't even look back as they zoomed out into the midmorning traffic.

It was a long drive. The taxi driver had an all-news radio station on, and the crackle and buzz rattled Maggie's nerve endings as she prayed she'd be in time.

The built-up newness of the city deteriorated into the shabbiness of the older neighborhoods, then began to brighten up as middle-class suburbs approached. Those thinned out, and random, sprawling estates took their place. Maggie's palms were cold and damp with sweat.

The radio was blaring on about hurricanes in the Gulf, and Maggie shut her eyes for a moment, trying to block out the intrusion. And then her eyes shot open again at the newscaster's laconic tone.

"Admiral Jefferson Wentworth was found dead in his Arlington, Virginia, apartment today, an apparent suicide. Admiral Wentworth served on the Naval Intelligence Committee before his retirement in 1984. The police have not ruled out the possibility of foul play."

Maggie's stomach lurched, and her nails bit into her palms. Why the hell had she left her gun in New York when her sister's very life might depend on it? But she knew why—she'd been too befuddled with Randall Carter. That was another she owed him.

"Gates are closed, lady."

The driver's voice pulled her attention back to the present, and she looked up, startled. Wide iron gates spanned the curving drive that led up to an imposing, utterly tasteless white stone mansion. Kate's slightly battered Datsun was parked at a haphazard angle in front of them, blocking entry. There was no sign of her sister.

"This is good enough," Maggie said, shoving money at the driver and almost falling out of the cab. Her sense of disaster was getting stronger all the time, and it took every ounce of will to calm herself. Panic wouldn't help Kate; calm, rational planning would. First of all, she had to figure how to get past the high stone walls that guarded Alicia Stoneham.

In the end it was easier than she'd imagined. Although the front gates were securely locked, the narrow door in the thick stone wall was unlatched. Maggie simply walked through, breaking into a stealthy run as she reached the other side of the curving drive.

Her Nikes were silent as she raced up the driveway. The cold sweat that covered her body evaporated in the blazing heat, and the last of her panic left her. She was calm and very determined and ready to take on anything.

The voices were loud enough to alert her. Kate's usually soft voice was angry, carrying on the stifling summer air, and Maggie moved around the house to the wide back terrace, following the sound unerringly.

"I want you to tell me where my baby is, Alicia!" The two of them were turned away from Maggie as she lurked by the corner of the big white building. She could see Kate's profile, the tangle of brown hair, the furious eyes, the determination in her mouth.

Alicia waved a cigarette-laden hand at her. Her fuchsia-painted mouth looked garish on her unusually pale face. "How many times must I tell you, honey, that I have no idea where she is? I don't know why you think I'd touch little Chrissie, but if you don't calm down and leave, I'll call the police."

"Do you want to tell them about Francis?" Kate demanded. "About Red Glove Films and your brother and how you're managing to keep Stoneham Studios afloat? I'm sure they'd be very interested in hearing about it."

"I don't know what the hell you're talking about, Kate," Alicia snapped, her horse-face devoid of color. "You must have slipped a cog somewhere. Hell, I can understand it— you've been under a lot of pressure with that stinker of a husband. Why don't you come in and have a drink, and I'll call that sister of yours to come get you? You need a vacation."

"I need my baby!" Kate cried. "Just tell me where she is,

and I won't say a word about the spying. I can keep Maggie quiet, too—she'll do as I tell her."

Alicia leaned forward and stubbed out the turquoise Sobranie on the glass-topped patio table. "I'm afraid we can't count on that," she said suddenly, her voice flat and dead. "You know I hate violence, honey, but you leave us no choice. We're going to have to shut you up." And her hand came up with a small, efficient gun in it, trained directly on Kate's chest.

Maggie froze. If she made any sudden moves, Alicia might shoot her sister, whether she really wanted to or not. Slowly, carefully she edged closer to the corner of the building. The two women were within several feet of her; if she found the right sort of projectile, she could knock the gun out of Alicia's hand. Maybe.

"I don't give a damn what you do to me, Alicia. I just want to know where my baby is."

"I really don't know. We didn't take her. You might ask your sister."

Kate's mouth curved in grim smile. "That'll be a little difficult, won't it, if you're planning to kill me?"

Maggie had already slipped off one of her Nikes, preparing to aim it at Alicia's gun hand. She weighed it in one hand, then lifted her arm overhead to throw it.

"You'll have plenty of chances to talk to her," Alicia said. "Won't she, partner?"

Maggie felt body heat close behind her and saw the shadow on the terrace in front of her. She quickly started to wing the sneaker at Alicia, but an iron hand clamped around her wrist, grinding the bones together. Another hand grabbed her rear. She didn't need to hear the mocking voice to tell her who it was or to assure her that neither Caleb nor Randall had anything to do with this treasonous tangle.

"Not so fast, sweetbuns," Bud Willis murmured in her ear. "Don't you know it's rude to eavesdrop?" And he shoved her out onto the terrace.

"Thank God, Maggie," Kate breathed.

"Don't thank God yet, Kate," Maggie said, her voice thick with self-disgust as she stumbled toward the two women, aided by Willis's rough hands. "I'm not helping matters."

"You surely aren't, and that's the truth," Alicia said, putting the gun back into her pocket. Maggie considered diving for it, but then she felt the unmistakable chill of a larger-barrelled gun in the small of her back, and she forced her muscles to relax. "We're going to have to take care of them both, aren't we?" Alicia asked. "No way around it?"

"No way around it, old lady. We have to cover our tracks as best we can. These two can go with the house; Carter and McAllister at the studio. You've already got your plane tickets."

Alicia nodded, looking very old. "It was worth a try," she said, lighting another cigarette, this time a pink one, and shoving it into the long black holder. "I thought I could save the studio. I should have known it was impossible."

"At least you'll have enough money to keep you and your brother living in style," Bud said, moving around to smile his skeletal smile at Maggie. "And I won't come off too badly, either."

"You're absolutely crazy, aren't you?" Maggie snapped. "Have you been behind this all along?"

"Hell, no. I just cut myself in on the action two weeks ago when I found out what was going on. It seemed like too good a scam to pass up."

"How did you find out about it?"

"That stupid little faggot got cold feet and turned state's evidence. It was pure luck that he got passed over to me. I persuaded him to keep quiet, then came out here last week and cut myself in."

"What happened to Francis?" Maggie prompted.

Willis shrugged. "Well, he seemed so eager to talk, I had to shut him up, didn't I? I thought it was a nice touch, bringing him over to your sister's place. I heard you were due for a visit, and I figured she'd have Superwoman bail her out. I was hoping you'd be the one to find him and not your sister—

maybe it would remind you of the Polack. At least you ended up dragging him around the city. Damned funny."

A light shiver of horror iced her skin at Bud's cheerful malice. "But why did you send Randall here?" she demanded.

"To keep you busy. I knew he'd be so involved trying to get between your legs that the two of you wouldn't notice if hell froze over. And Randall's got the advantage of having no paper work, no records at Langley at all. When he buys it today, no one down there will even notice."

"And you'll get away with a nice sum of money."

"I will indeed. Come along, sweetcakes."

"Where?"

Willis jabbed the barrel of his sawed-off machine gun into her ribs. "Anywhere I tell you. Right, sweetie?" He moved the gun to aim it at Kate.

"Right," said Maggie.

He looked over his shoulder at Alicia, who was calmly smoking her brightly colored cigarettes, her fuchsia mouth vivid against her sickly pallor. "Meet me in the car. We don't have any time to waste—the sooner we're away from here, the better."

"I wanted to call Jefferson—"

"You can call him from the studio," Bud said sharply, and the gun jabbed nervously into Maggie's back again. "Do as I tell you, or you can join these two bitches in the house."

"I'll be in the car," Alicia said, turning her back on them.

"Alicia, you can't let him do this," Kate said suddenly, her voice pleading. "You've been like a mother to me."

Alicia halted for a brief moment, looking at her over her shoulder, and her face was old and drawn. "You should know better than anyone how useless mothers are, honey." And she turned away from them once more, heading down the steps to the front of the house.

"No help from that quarter," Bud said cheerfully. "Get a move on, you two."

They had no choice but to precede him into the deserted,

air-conditioned mansion. "You want to tell us what you have planned for us, Bud?" Maggie asked politely.

"Sure thing, Maggie. Anticipation is half the pleasure," he said affably. "I'm going to lock the two of you in Alicia's bathroom."

"Oooh, sounds dangerous," Maggie snapped.

"There are no windows. No way for you to get out. Everything's nicely soundproofed, so no one can overhear anyone taking a crap. Alicia's sold the house to some developers. Tomorrow morning, bright and early, bulldozers and wrecking equipment are coming by to level this place to make room for nice little condominiums. No one's gonna hear your screams, sweetcakes."

"You don't want them to find our bodies."

Bud shrugged. "I could give a rat's ass. If they find you, fine. If not, it won't matter, either, 'cause we'll be long gone."

"Chrissie—" Kate said, her voice desperate.

"Chrissie's okay." Maggie placed a reassuring hand on her sister's shoulder. "Randall took her to stay with his sister."

Kate stopped still on the wide, curving staircase that Bud had herded them to, ignoring the gun. "Did you know about it?" she demanded.

"He didn't see fit to tell me."

"I'll kill him," Kate breathed, rage and relief filling her eyes.

"You won't need to," Bud said. "I'm planning on doing that myself. But I'll send him your regards. Keep moving."

Alicia's bathroom was the size of a small bedroom, with a sunken tub, three sinks, a toilet that resembled the British throne, and an equally ornate bidet. As Bud had said, there were no windows, and the door had solid, unpickable locks, worthy of someone with an absolute fixation for privacy. Maggie paused in the doorway, looking at Bud out of the corner of her eye, wondering if she had any chance at all. She was more than a match for most men, but Bud Willis was a fighting machine, an inhuman automaton with the jungle instincts of a mamba snake. He was western democracy's version of a terrorist, and she knew she'd stand no chance at all of even coming close to him.

Kate had walked into the room and slumped down on the floor, burying her face in her arms. Still Maggie lingered by the door. Willis was smiling his skeletal smile, his transparent eyes gleeful, and he smelled of sweat and death. "Sorry it has to end this way, Maggie," he said. "I had better things planned for you."

"Such as?"

He shook his head. "I don't want to disappoint you by telling you all about the pleasure you'll be missing. I just want to tell you a little something to make your last few hours a little brighter."

"I don't think I want to hear it."

"I know you don't want to hear it," he said. "You remember that day two years ago? It was a hot day in April, and the tourists were swarming all over Boothbay Harbor. The lilacs were out, and your whole street smelled of them."

She waited, saying nothing.

"It was low tide that morning," he continued, pleasure dancing in his eyes. "And it smelled of seaweed and dead fish, along with the lilacs. Pulaski came out of the house wearing a white shirt. By the time I finished with him, his shirt was red."

"Why?" The word was barely audible; her throat had closed up, allowing no breath through its strictures.

"For fun, Maggie," he said. "For kicks. Because you looked at him like he was Jesus Christ walking on water, and you looked at me I was pigshit. Because I wanted to." Then he grabbed her, caught her numb, lifeless body in his hands, and pulled her against his sweating body, pressing his greedy mouth down onto hers, shoving his tongue into her mouth.

She could feel his erection against her leg, feel his clutching fingers clawing at her arms. She stood motionless, and he pulled away, pushing her into the bathroom and aiming the gun at her. "Sorry I don't have more time," he said. He shut the door on them.

She listened to the sounds of the locks, listened to the muffled tread of his footsteps as he moved away. And then she turned and walked over to her sister's huddled figure, a cold knot of hatred churning her stomach.

"He made a mistake," she said out loud.

Kate raised her head from the cradle of her arms. "What do you mean?"

"He wanted me to be too freaked out to think or do anything. But he misjudged me," she said fiercely. "I'm getting out of here, and when I do, I'm going to kill him. Don't just sit there, Kate. Help me."

"Help you what?" she echoed, dazed but game.

"Help me break down this damned door."


"You mean you let her go after Kate alone?" Caleb demanded, his usually deep voice rising into high-pitched rage.

"Maggie can take care of herself. We weren't sure of you." They were speeding across Chicago as fast as the traffic would allow them, which wasn't fast enough. "Someone had to be in on it with Alicia, and you were one of two possibilities."

"What made you decide to trust me?"

"I don't trust you," said Randall. "I don't trust anyone. I decided you weren't the one involved with Red Glove Films, or you wouldn't have confronted Francis about the money. You also don't have the motive and the connections to screw me up as badly as I've been screwed the last few days. And the other possibility does."

"Who is it?"

"No one you know. A man named Bud Willis." A brief, savage smile lit Randall's dark face. "You can meet him after I finish rearranging him a bit."

"Can't you drive this damned thing faster?" Caleb fumed. "I thought Jaguars were sports cars."

"This is a sedan," Randall said. "And it's the traffic that's slowing us, not the car. I have complete faith in Maggie. They'll be all right until we get there."

"And if they're not?" he said stubbornly, drumming his long, freckled fingers on the leather dashboard.

An odd, twisted look came into Randall's eyes, as if the possibility had never occurred to him, and once it had, it been found completely unacceptable. "If they're not," he said finally, "then I doubt you'll find pieces of Bud Willis big enough to identify." And the Jaguar bucked forward with a roar.

# twenty-one

"Maggie, it's hopeless."

"Nothing's hopeless, damn it," Maggie snarled. "Again!"

Once more they crashed in unison against the flimsy bathroom door; once more they heard the encouraging splinter of wood that still failed to make any headway. "Why the hell didn't I ever take karate?" Maggie fumed, rubbing her aching shoulder. "I could kick the damned door down if I had."

"What makes you think we have any chance at all?" Kate said.

"This house is cheap and gaudy and all show. The interior doors are hollow and flimsy. Come on, Kate. Once more, and put your back into it. Think of Chrissie."

"I'd rather think of Randall Carter and what I'm going to do to him when I catch him," Kate said bitterly.

Maggie managed a wry smile, pushing her hair out of her sweating face. "Then imagine you're slamming into him. Let's try a running start this time. Once more, kiddo! We can do it."

This time when the combined two hundred-plus pounds of female muscle slammed into the door, the crack was louder, and Maggie felt it give. "We've almost got it," she panted. "One more time."

Once more they drew back to the far wall of the sprawling bathroom; once more they raced for the door. Maggie shut her eyes, braced for the blow, expecting to bounce back again. But with a crashing, rending sound, the door split down the middle, and Maggie and Kate tumbled through, landing in a tangle on the hot pink wall-to-wall carpeting that stretched through the hallway.

"You okay?" Maggie questioned, sitting up.

Kate sat with a slightly dazed expression on her face. "We did it!" she murmured. The splintering wood had ripped away her sleeve, and a long, nasty scrape was oozing blood. "We really did it." And she started to laugh.

For a moment, Maggie was prepared to stop the incipient hysteria. And then she realized Kate wasn't hysterical; she was just happy and amazed to be alive. Before Maggie could gather her somewhat scattered wits, Kate had jumped to her feet and was grabbing her sister and yanking her upright.

"Come on, Maggie! We've got to go after them. Randall and Caleb are walking into a trap, and we have to rescue them." Her brown eyes were alight with excitement and determination, and Maggie shook her head.

"Listen, kid, don't get cocky," she muttered. "We broke out of a locked bathroom; that doesn't mean we're ready to save the western world."

"Are you going to sit by and let Randall and Caleb fend for themselves?"

"Serve 'em right if I did. The first thing we're going to do, dear heart, is get the hell out of here. Then we'll worry about saving their lives. Let's move it, kid."

Kate was ahead of her, leaping down the steps. Maggie followed at a calmer, no less speedy pace, shaking her head. A little danger, the ability to rescue oneself, and one got just a tiny bit crazy. Maybe that would help carry Kate through the next few hours, hours that weren't going to be pleasant. She only wished she weren't too jaded to experience some of that euphoria herself. She needed all the edge she could get.

Caleb was yanking at the padlocked gates, cursing with inventiveness that would have impressed Randall at another time. "This is Kate's car!" he shouted over his shoulder. "Don't just stand there, man! Help me!"

"You're not going to be able to break that chain with your

bare hands," he said, his mild tone belying the tension that was vibrating through him. "We've got to find another way in —and fast. Stop wasting your energy."

Caleb promptly wasted more energy cursing Randall, but Randall ignored him, turning his attention to the narrow door set deep into the thick stone walls. It was now locked, but locks were not much of an obstacle to a man of Randall's talents. In moments the door had swung open and Randall was heading up the driveway, his long legs eating up the distance.

Caleb's distant curse floated after him, and then his pounding feet signaled his advent up the driveway. Randall didn't even bother to turn and look; all his attention was concentrated on the front door and the two figures he saw there.

Then Maggie and her sister were running toward him, and he could hear Maggie's strong voice on the sultry breeze: " 'Bout time you showed up," she called when she was within hearing distance.

He stood there, wanting to run to her, but his feet were glued to the ground. He waited as she ran toward him, one shoe missing, her hair streaming out behind her.

She stopped just short of him, mere inches from his arms. Her bruised face was pale and sweaty; her eyes were blazing. And without thinking, he grabbed her, pulled her into his arms, and held her as relief washed over him.

She didn't fight him, much as he had expected her to. She leaned against him, resting for a moment in the shelter of his arms, and he could feel the hot August sun baking down on them.

He moved then, pulled away, and looking down at her. "Are you all right? Bud didn't hurt you?"

"How did you know about Bud?" She moved away, running a nervous hand through her tangled hair.

Randall shrugged. "The more I thought about it, the more sense it made. It had to be someone who knew the international scene and our past well enough to screw things up in Gemansk. Bud was the only logical choice. I don't suppose

Bud and Alicia are tied up somewhere in that monstrosity of a house?"

"No such luck. Bud locked us in the bathroom, thinking we'd be stuck there when the wreckers arrived tomorrow. In the meantime they took off for the studio. I think they're hoping you'll catch up with them there."

"We will," he said grimly. "I would have found you, Maggie. I promise you."

"Maybe," she said. "I'm not sure I trust you."

Kate pulled out of Caleb's protective arms. "That reminds me," she said in a dangerous voice, advancing on him. "What the hell did you do to my baby?"

"I do hope you're not planning to beat me up," he drawled, watching her approach with a jaundiced eye, "because your sister already did the honors."

Kate stopped midstride. "You did?"

Maggie smiled with more than a trace of weariness. "I did. Trust me, little sister."

"If you all don't mind, I think we should get out of here," Caleb interrupted. "If we waste much more time, Alicia and her friend will get away scot-free."

"You're right. We've got to get to the studio," Maggie said, heading for the door set in the stone wall.

Randall's hand caught her arm. "What's this *we*, white man? Don't you think you've been through enough today?"

Maggie remembered Bud's skeletal smile and his cheerful, taunting confession. "Honey," she said, "I've only just begun." And she shook off his hand.

Stoneham Studios was a vast, silent, deserted tomb when the four of them entered.

"Why isn't anyone here?" Maggie whispered to Kate.

"We've always had Tuesdays and Wednesdays off," she replied, looking around uneasily. "We work so many weekends that Alicia decided to change the work week."

"But what about security? A night watchman, or anything like that?"

"No such animal," Caleb offered. "We've been cutting costs right and left, and security was one of the first things to go."

"I wonder how they expected to get you two here," Maggie said, limping forward. She still wore only one Nike, the other having been snatched out of her hand by Bud.

"Probably by telling us you're here," Randall said. "At least they won't be expecting us so soon—we have the element of surprise on our side."

"I'm afraid you don't, honey." Alicia's voice shattered the stillness. "You have to get up real early to pull something over on a tough old buzzard like me." She was standing in the shadows, her cigarette a tiny glow of light. The dimness almost concealed the gun in her hand. She'd taken over Bud's more efficient sawed-off machine gun, and if her face was still pale with strain, her hand was rock steady.

"Beats me how you two got out of my house so fast," she said. "I got locked in that bathroom once, and it took the fire department to get me out."

"You underestimated us."

"I guess we did." She sighed gustily, exhaling blue smoke into the murky darkness. Holding the gun with one hand, she tossed her cigarette onto the floor, then grimaced. "I loved that house. Billy-Bob built it for me, with everything I wanted in it. Guess it didn't mean much once he died. Spent too much time here in this goddamned studio, trying to save his dream. Well, it's too late for that. Too late for everything. Tomorrow everything will be gone. I'll be real glad to get away."

"Alicia," Kate said softly, "you don't really want to kill us."

"Of course I don't, honey," Alicia said. "But I don't see that I have much choice. You all move into the center of the room, real slow and careful. If you put a hand toward your pockets, I'll shoot it off. You hear?"

"We hear," Maggie said grimly, and they all obeyed. Randall's body was tense, ready for the slightest opportunity, and that tension radiated through her own body. Somehow or other, she had to distract Alicia just long enough for Randall to pounce. "What do you think Billy-Bob would think of what you've been doing? Turning traitor, involved in murder?"

"He wouldn't like it," Alicia agreed, and Maggie could see the telltale signs of a slightly relaxed guard. The gun drooped a tiny bit, and her basilisk eyes were somewhat less alert. "But I comfort myself with the knowledge that his ma would be spinning in her grave. Don't move, mister." The gun spun around to train itself on Randall's middle. "I'm faster than you'll ever be."

Randall lifted his hands and shrugged. "I wouldn't doubt it, Alicia," he said, and only Maggie noticed he was still edging closer to the old woman.

"What are you planning to do after you kill us?" Maggie questioned, still trying to divert her attention. "Do you think you'll get out of the country without being caught?"

"Of course we will. That little skunk Willis ought to be good for something. He'll cover things up long enough for my brother and me to get to Peru, and then no one can touch us."

"Has Bud left Chicago for any reason in the last few days?" Maggie questioned softly, fiddling with her tangled hair.

Alicia's eyes were trained on Maggie's nervous hand. "He flew back to Washington to clear up some last-minute details yesterday morning, and he returned on the midnight flight," she said. "What the hell does that matter?"

"I just wondered if he was the one who murdered Admiral Wentworth or if he delegated the responsibility."

Alicia was very still. "What the hell are you talking about, girl?"

Randall was almost in reach. "You've been too busy to listen to the news today. Probably too busy to answer the telephone. Your brother was found dead in his apartment in Arlington. It was supposed to be suicide, but the police think it might be murder. What do you think?"

For one brief, crucial second, the machine gun dropped. It was long enough. Randall made a flying tackle and toppled

Alicia's rangy body, and Maggie caught the gun as it skittered across the cement floor.

With calm efficiency she checked the ammunition clip, shoved it into place, and advanced on the wildly struggling old woman. Alicia grew very still as Maggie placed the snub-nosed barrel against her temple.

"Where's Willis?" she said gently.

"Maggie, for Christ's sake . . ." Randall began, but the anger and disbelief in his face faded as he surveyed Maggie's implacable, deadly expression.

"Shut up, Randall." Maggie's voice was still polite and even. "Where is he, Alicia?" And she cocked the gun.

"Come and get me, sweetbuns." The mocking voice floated down from overhead, and Maggie looked up, way up, into the catwalks that crisscrossed the top of the cavernous sound stage. It was too dark and shadowy to see him, but his soft, evil voice called to her.

"Maggie," Randall's voice was a plea and a warning.

She ignored him, rising and moving out of his reach. "I'm coming, Bud," she said grimly, and headed for the cement stairs.

The higher she climbed, the hotter it became. The air was thick and suffocating, but she refused to pause. She kept moving upward, flight after flight of cement steps, the gun held at her side, ready to jerk upward at the faintest sound, her heart cold as ice. Down below, she could hear the murmur of angry voices, could even pick out Randall's outraged tones, but she didn't look down. Bud Willis was ahead of her, and she was going to do to him what he'd done to Pulaski.

She reached the first catwalk and stepped forward onto the narrow walkway, all traces of acrophobia banished in her determination. The gun was unwieldy, and her palms were sweating, belying her calm. She heard a noise up ahead, a tiny scuffling that was undoubtedly a rat. Whether it was the human variety or a rodent remained to be seen.

She was halfway across the wide room when her instincts warned her. A second later, the walkway shook as Bud Willis dropped onto it from the catwalk overhead, and she whirled around to face him, the gun ready.

He looked like death, a grinning, horrifying personification of the grim reaper. His lips were drawn back in a smile, and the veins stood out in his forehead. Every nerve, every muscle, every cell in his body was geared for confrontation. He also had a gun in his hand, the smaller one Alicia had used before.

"You've got to learn not to let your emotions get in the way," he said patiently. "You'll never be any good until you shut out everything. Anger, revenge, even pleasure. Killing has got to be an instinct, not an emotional experience, unless you're a real expert, as I am."

She aimed the gun at him. "I'll keep that in mind next time."

"Sweetcakes, there isn't going to be a next time," he said sadly.

"You don't think so? You've got a twenty-two pistol, buddy-boy," she mocked. "I've got a sawed-off machine gun. I'm sure you're quite lethal with that, but my firepower far outdoes yours."

"But Maggie," he said softly, "you can't do it. You can't stand there and shoot me in cold blood, no matter what I've done to you and yours. You can't pull the trigger until I fire first—and my first bullet will kill you."

She clicked the gun, one incredibly loud little click that brought it one step closer to a spray of bullets. "Try me."

She could feel the eyes watching them up there on the narrow walkway, feel the tension radiating up toward them with the heat. Bud Willis's grin was etched on his face like a stone carving. "I don't need to. You're a pussy, Maggie, in more ways than one. I'm going to turn my back on you and walk away, and you won't be able to stop me. You won't be able to shoot me in the back. But don't worry, sweetbuns. I'll be back for you." And turning, he presented his back to her, walking away from her down the narrow catwalk.

She watched him go, knowing he was right, hating herself and her own impotence, torn with frustration. Then Willis began to whistle, a cheerful, insistent little song that Maggie knew far too well. It was a song about love and freedom that Mack used to sing when he was Snake the rock star. Something snapped inside.

She leapt at him, dropping the machine gun, but she ignored the sound as it tumbled four flights to the cement floor and smashed. She knocked Willis sideways against the wire handrails, white-hot rage blinding her. Then he slipped away, and she clutched at him, unseeing, with a low wail of helpless fury as she felt him escape. She lay there on the catwalk, panting, listening to the crashes, thuds, and screams that floated up to her. Slowly, she rose up to peer over the edge of the walkway.

Randall was looking up at her, an enigmatic expression on his face. Bud Willis lay at his feet, unmoving; he was either unconscious or dead—Maggie couldn't tell which.

"I do wish," Randall said, his voice floating up to her, patiently aggrieved, "that you'd let me rescue you just once."

Maggie grimaced. "Is he dead?"

Randall nudged him gently with a toe. "I don't think so. More's the pity. Come down, Maggie, and have your explanations ready."

Maggie had pulled herself into a sitting position, and a cold shaking had taken over. Her bones had turned to jelly, her muscles to yogurt, and all she could do was huddle in the heat and feel the cold sweat cover her body. She had never felt so alone in her life, and for one tiny moment she couldn't stand it. She had to ask for help.

"I don't think I can," she said in a strangled voice. "Do you suppose you could come get me?"

A series of expressions flitted over Randall's face. Exasperation, tenderness, and something possibly akin to love. "Watch her," he ordered Caleb tersely, who stood with the battered machine gun trained on Alicia. It was a token gesture; Alicia was a broken woman; her garish fuchsia mouth was slack in her pale, freckled face.

Randall raced up the cement steps, taking them three at a

time with his long legs. Moments later, he drew her trembling body into his arms, wrapped his strength around her, pulled her into his lap, and held her there.

"I know why you did this," he said as his hand brushed the hair out of her tearstained face.

She moved closer, seeking his strength and warmth, cold, so very cold inside. "Why?" she croaked out.

"So I'd get a chance to rescue you after all."

She laughed, a raw, rusty sound, and her fingers clutched his shoulders. "I'm ruining your suit," she said.

"Screw my suit." His hand caught her chin and tipped her face up to his; his blue-gray eyes were tender. His mouth touched hers for a brief moment, and she felt her soul come alive in that kiss. The long fingers on her flesh were soothing, and she wanted to sink into him, lose herself. But it was a weakness she couldn't afford, not right then, and when he moved away, she let him go.

"Has someone called an ambulance?" she asked.

"For Willis or for you?"

*You're all I need,* she thought suddenly, and then wondered if she'd spoken the damning words out loud. False words, she told herself. She didn't need him, didn't want him. And her fingers clutched his shoulders more tightly. "For Willis," she said. "I want him to get a chance to suffer."

"You're going to tell me why," he said, and it was a statement, flat and simple.

She nodded. "I'll tell you why. Later. Are you going to get me down from this place, or are we going to leave Kate and Caleb to explain everything?"

"Sounds good to me. Maybe there's a back way out."

"Randall—"

He rose, pulling her up to stand on shaky legs beside him. The sound of sirens in the distance penetrated the huge old building, getting louder. "I guess we'd better face the music," he said. "Let me do the talking?"

"Don't you always?"

He grinned, a suddenly carefree expression on his usually

reserved face. "If you want to come up with the plausible explanations and still not say a thing, you can be my guest."

Maggie's weary smile mirrored his. "No, thanks," she replied. "I'll leave it up to you."

"Abdicating, Maggie?"

"It's only temporary," she said, yawning. "I'm too tired to think, to fight, or to lie."

"I think I like you this way."

"Enjoy it while you can, Randall," she murmured. "It's not going to last."

"That's all right. It wouldn't be the Maggie I know and love if it did."

That was a hell of a strange word for Randall to use. *Love* —when he didn't even believe it existed. She dared a small, furtive glance, but his face was impassive as always, and she decided it had to be a figure of speech. At that point, she couldn't handle anything more.

"Umph," she said, a noncommittal grunt. "Let's go face the music."

## twenty-two

Sybil Bennett was holding court, surrounded by admiring reporters. She was holding her cherubic granddaughter and regaling everyone with the horror of the last few days and the insidious spy drama that she had somehow managed to become a central figure in.

Her daughters stood by, watching with the forbearance of long habit, listening to their mother's fantasies with an indulgent ear.

"There are times, Maggie," Randall murmured in her ear, "that you still manage to amaze me. Your mother is absolutely perfect. She's got those reporters eating up every word she tells them, and if anything even slightly resembles the truth, no one will notice."

"Mother has her talents," Maggie agreed lightly. "You shouldn't give me credit for siccing her on the media, though. It would have been impossible to hold her back." She peered over at Kate, who usually had less tolerance when it came to her mother's playacting. At the moment she was too involved in Caleb's whispered words to pay the slightest bit of attention.

Maggie sighed. "Happy endings are so nice."

Randall's face was very still. "I suppose they are."

"I mean, look at the two of them. Fighting like cats and dogs a week ago, and now blissfully happy. Slimy old Brian even dropped his custody suit."

"I missed that development. Why did he do that?"

"Not out of the goodness of his heart, you can be sure of that. For one thing, Kate told him to stuff his child support.

For another, his new wife is pregnant, and she decided that she didn't want two infants interfering with her jet-setting life-style."

"Happy ending indeed," Randall said cynically. "How long do you think their marriage will last?"

"You underestimate my sister, Randall, and you underestimate Caleb," she said in an even voice. "This is happy ever after."

"Sure it is, Maggie. I don't underestimate them; I simply don't believe in happy endings and true love."

She looked up at him. "Message received. Over and out." And she turned away from him to watch her mother.

"Don't turn away from me, Maggie," he said, his hand on her arm. "I need to talk to you."

"Go ahead."

"In private." He pulled her, and she resisted for a moment.

"We don't really have anything to say to each other in private, do we?" she countered, a thin note of bitterness in her voice.

"Maybe we do." He pulled again, and this time she went, following him into her mother's deserted bedroom.

He shut the door behind them, and Maggie took the moment to pull away from him. She leaned against the wall and crossed her arms in a defiant attitude. "Talk away, Randall," she offered.

Instead of answering, he crossed the room and pulled her into his arms. She fought for a moment, for an angry, hurt instant, and then she melted into him, opening her mouth beneath his insistent kiss, ignoring the common sense that told her this was useless.

"Maggie, I need you," he whispered against her hair. "You can't even begin to know how much. You're a rare and precious jewel, and I've been obsessed with you for six endless years. I can't let you leave me again." His mouth caught hers again before she could reply, sweeping away her defenses and doubts. She drew her hands up between them, feeling the heat of his chest through the thin linen shirt. Her fingers trembled as she reached for the buttons, wanting the feel of his flesh against her, wanting to lose herself in the mindless pleasure he could give her.

But mindless pleasure wasn't for her, and Randall Carter wasn't for her. She pulled away suddenly, and for a moment he clung to her, his fingers possessive and bruising. Then he let her go.

She moved across the room. As he watched her, his breathing was deep and even; only the stormy depths of his eyes betrayed his emotions—emotions Maggie still didn't quite understand.

She'd give him a chance. "Do you love me, Randall?"

He flinched, and his eyes met hers. "No."

She nodded, hiding the pain his expected answer gave her. "Have you ever loved anyone?"

"No." The single word was a sharp death knell in the room. "If I did, Maggie, it would be you."

She smiled, a wry, accepting smile. "Maybe it would. But that's not good enough. I've been loved the best anyone could ever be loved, Randall. I'm not going to settle for second rate."

"Second rate?" His eyebrow rose.

"Second rate," she said firmly. "You want to collect me, like one of your stupid paintings or pieces of jade. And then when you get tired of me, you'd let me go, seek out another acquisition. Wouldn't you?"

"You might tire of me first," he said, not denying it.

"Randall," she said, and her voice was flat and very sure as she lied to him, "I've tired of you already."

She didn't really expect to fool him, and his expression didn't change. "Are you trying to tell me something, Maggie?"

"Yes. Good-bye, Randall."

He smiled then, a small, cynical smile. And then he moved so swiftly, she didn't have time to dodge. He caught her in his arms, brought his mouth down on hers, and kissed her.

It was a kiss fraught with passion and despair, an ending

and a beginning. The thought of resistance never entered her mind. She twined her arms around his neck and pulled him closer, answering his mouth and weeping inside.

"Not good-bye, Maggie," he said softly, "and we both know it." Then he left her alone in the bedroom looking after him. It was only then that she realized she'd never told him Willis's confession, never explained her murderous chase over the catwalks. But what, in the long run, did it matter?

"Maggie"—Kate charged into the bedroom—"someone's on the phone for you. . . ." Her voice trailed off. "Are you all right?"

"Just fine," Maggie said, smiling very, very brightly. "Who's calling for me?"

"Your boss. Mike Jackson, right? He says you're supposed to come down to Washington. They've moved Willis to Walter Reed Army Hospital, but he's refusing to talk unless you're there."

"That's all I needed."

"Do you think he'll make it?" Kate questioned.

"I don't know. A mortal wouldn't have survived that fall, but Bud Willis isn't quite human. I'll go."

"You'll be back for the wedding? I need a maid of honor."

"I'll be back," Maggie said. "What about Sybil?"

"She's off with some new suitor. All she'll tell me is he's Irish and very mysterious. She keeps muttering something about terrorists and looking tragic."

"Typical Sybil. He's probably a beer-guzzling soccer player."

Kate laughed. "Probably. Will Randall give you a ride to the airport?" It was a delicate probe, and Maggie didn't mind answering.

"Randall's gone."

"He'll be back?"

"So he says," Maggie replied. "So he says." And she didn't know whether that was a threat or a promise.

\* \* \*

Washington was hot and sultry in the late August heat. Even at eight o'clock at night, National Airport was blanketed in blasts of thermal air. Maggie shook back her thick hair and considered chopping it all off.

Mike Jackson, head of Third World Causes and nominally her boss, was waiting for her. His affable face with its barracuda eyes was a welcome sight. "You pick a helluva way to spend your vacations, Maggie." He peered at her closely. "You look exhausted."

"I am." She hugged him.

"You also look better than I've seen you in two years," he said bluntly. "You finally let go of Pulaski?"

"No one ever said you weren't observant," Maggie said wryly. "Is Willis going to make it?"

"Who knows? He's a mess, but it's the good who die young."

"He killed Pulaski, Mike."

"Yes."

"You knew?" She stared at him in astonishment.

"I guessed."

"Why didn't you tell me?"

"What good would it have done? I had no proof, just a gut-level feeling, and you were hurting enough as it was. I figured it would come out in its own good time. Did he tell you?"

"Bragged to me. Told me he did it for the hell of it."

Jackson scratched his balding head. "That doesn't sound like Willis. He usually doesn't do anything unless there's a bottom line."

"I won't even begin to guess what his motives are. I can't imagine why he wants to see me. Maybe to ask my forgiveness?"

"Maybe pigs can fly," Jackson said. "I promised I'd bring you straight to the hospital. He's at Walter Reed, you know. You got any energy left?"

"Enough to see Bud Willis check out," she said grimly.

For a while, it looked as if she'd miss that particular pleasure. He'd lapsed into a coma in the last hour, surfacing every now and then to call Maggie's name, then sinking back. His vital signs were erratic and fading. The doctors looked grim.

"We're not going to be able to save him," the chief surgeon told them as they waited outside intensive care in the huge hospital complex. He shook his head in disgust. "We're losing him."

"It's no great loss," Maggie said coldly.

"Not true," Jackson rumbled. "He knows a hell of a lot that he's not telling."

The surgeon turned to check the myriad tiny screens that were monitoring Willis's fast-disappearing life. "You may as well go in. I don't even know if he'll regain consciousness, but he's not going to get any better."

Maggie headed for the door, but Jackson stayed where he was. She turned to give him a beseeching look. "Aren't you coming in with me?"

He shook his head. "It's something you need to face alone, Maggie. You've come this far. You can go all the way."

She hesitated, her hand on the door. And then she entered the room.

The blue tile room was alive with the hum of machines, pumping fluids into Willis's comatose body, draining them back out again, breathing for him, living for him. She looked at the dying man and felt nothing—no sorrow, no rage, no hatred, no regret. She looked at the shell of the evil man and felt absolutely nothing.

His eyelids flickered open, and his malevolent gaze moved unerringly to her still figure. "You came." His voice was a whisper of sound, but she heard, understood.

"I came." She refused to move any closer, just stood watching him out of impassive eyes.

"Wanted to see me die, didn't you, sugarbuns?"

"Not particularly," she said. "I would have been just as happy to stay on in Chicago for a few days instead of rushing back here."

"I'll make it worth your while," he croaked, his eyes bright with malice. "Come closer, sweetcakes."

"Drop dead, Willis."

He laughed, a painful laugh. "I'll do just that. I just have one little thing to tell you. A small little deathbed confession, to make my passing easier."

"Why didn't you tell Jackson? He could have passed the message along."

"This is between you and me." His breathing was hoarse and labored, and the machines were making erratic noises. "You have a good time screwing Randall?"

"Terrific," she snapped. "Anything else?"

He grinned a semblance of his skeletal smile, and his bruised, bloodshot eyes were shining with glee. "I lied to you, sweetheart. I didn't ice Pulaski for kicks."

The lump of pain formed quickly, filling her stomach and heart and forcing the air from her lungs. "You didn't?" she managed calmly. "You want to tell me why?"

"Randall. Randall Carter paid me twenty thousand dollars to kill Mack Pulaski." He laughed, and the laughter turned into a choking cough. "Have a happy life, sugarbuns." And the machines surrounding him stopped their noisy chirps and beeps and resolved into a lifeless hum.

"I don't believe you." Her voice came out a raw gasp of pain. But Bud Willis was beyond hearing. "I don't believe you," she repeated, reaching out to clutch at his shoulders in desperation. But his body was still and limp, and there was no way she could get the truth from him.

She stood very still as she felt her life drain out with his. As her heart screamed *no,* her brain, her wicked, cold, tormented brain said, *quite possibly.* And that possibility was more than she could bear.

She turned and walked past the crowd of medical technicians that rushed past her to labor over Willis's still body. She walked past Jackson with unseeing eyes, down the hallway, and out into the steamy Washington night.

The thick velvet blackness of evening settled around her, smothering her in its inky stillness, matching the disbelieving emptiness in her heart. And she walked on, into the darkness, into the night.

The thick velvet blackness of evening settled around her, smothering her in its inky stillness, matching the disbelieving emptiness in her heart. And she walked on, into the darkness, into the night.

"I'll make it worth your while," he croaked, his eyes bright with malice. "Come closer, sweetcakes."

"Drop dead, Willis."

He laughed, a painful laugh. "I'll do just that. I just have one little thing to tell you. A small little deathbed confession, to make my passing easier."

"Why didn't you tell Jackson? He could have passed the message along."

"This is between you and me." His breathing was hoarse and labored, and the machines were making erratic noises. "You have a good time screwing Randall?"

"Terrific," she snapped. "Anything else?"

He grinned a semblance of his skeletal smile, and his bruised, bloodshot eyes were shining with glee. "I lied to you, sweetheart. I didn't ice Pulaski for kicks."

The lump of pain formed quickly, filling her stomach and heart and forcing the air from her lungs. "You didn't?" she managed calmly. "You want to tell me why?"

"Randall. Randall Carter paid me twenty thousand dollars to kill Mack Pulaski." He laughed, and the laughter turned into a choking cough. "Have a happy life, sugarbuns." And the machines surrounding him stopped their noisy chirps and beeps and resolved into a lifeless hum.

"I don't believe you." Her voice came out a raw gasp of pain. But Bud Willis was beyond hearing. "I don't believe you," she repeated, reaching out to clutch at his shoulders in desperation. But his body was still and limp, and there was no way she could get the truth from him.

She stood very still as she felt her life drain out with his. As her heart screamed *no,* her brain, her wicked, cold, tormented brain said, *quite possibly.* And that possibility was more than she could bear.

She turned and walked past the crowd of medical technicians that rushed past her to labor over Willis's still body. She walked past Jackson with unseeing eyes, down the hallway, and out into the steamy Washington night.

# HOW DID YOU LIKE THIS BOOK?

Fill out and mail this questionnaire and you will be helping us to bring you the kinds of books YOU like to read.

1. TITLE OF THIS BOOK:

   _____

2. TYPE OF BOOK (check only ONE type):

   | ☐ | ☐ | ☐ |
   |---|---|---|
   | mystery | action/adventure | romance |

3. Please indicate how much you liked or disliked certain things about this book.

   |  | liked a lot | liked a little | disliked a little | disliked a lot |
   |---|---|---|---|---|
   | the female lead | ☐ | ☐ | ☐ | ☐ |
   | the male lead | ☐ | ☐ | ☐ | ☐ |
   | the plot | ☐ | ☐ | ☐ | ☐ |
   | the romance | ☐ | ☐ | ☐ | ☐ |
   | the action & adventure | ☐ | ☐ | ☐ | ☐ |
   | the mystery | ☐ | ☐ | ☐ | ☐ |
   | the location | ☐ | ☐ | ☐ | ☐ |
   | anything else you liked or disliked? | | | | |
   | _____ | ☐ | ☐ | ☐ | ☐ |
   | _____ | ☐ | ☐ | ☐ | ☐ |

4. Do you think the story had
   - ☐ too much romance
   - ☐ just the right amount of romance
   - ☐ too little romance

5. Would you buy another book in this sequence of novels?

   | ☐ | ☐ | ☐ | ☐ |
   |---|---|---|---|
   | definitely yes | probably yes | probably no | definitely no |

6. How did you come to read this book?
   - ☐ I read a book in this sequence before, and I liked it.
   - ☐ I saw it in the store, and it seemed interesting.
   - ☐ Someone told me it was a good book.
   - ☐ Other: _____

7. In the last three months, approximately how many of the following kinds of books have you read?

|  | 0 | 1-2 | 3-6 | 7 or more |
|---|---|---|---|---|
| mystery/detective | ☐ | ☐ | ☐ | ☐ |
| action/adventure | ☐ | ☐ | ☐ | ☐ |
| psychological suspense | ☐ | ☐ | ☐ | ☐ |
| occult/supernatural | ☐ | ☐ | ☐ | ☐ |
| romance series (like Harlequin) | ☐ | ☐ | ☐ | ☐ |
| romance (not series) | ☐ | ☐ | ☐ | ☐ |
| espionage/spy | ☐ | ☐ | ☐ | ☐ |

8. What are your three favorite television shows?

   1. _____

   2. _____

   3. _____

9. In what year were you born?

   _____

10. What is your education?

   ☐ some high school
   ☐ high school graduate
   ☐ some college
   ☐ college graduate
   ☐ more than college

IF YOU HAVE ANY OTHER COMMENTS YOU WOULD LIKE TO MAKE ABOUT THIS BOOK, PLEASE FEEL FREE. WE WELCOME ANY OF YOUR THOUGHTS.

NAME: _____

ADDRESS: _____

_____

PHONE NUMUBER: _____

Please put this questionnaire in a stamped envelope and mail it to:

**Reader Research Program**
**Dell Publishing Co.**
**245 East 47th Street**
**New York, NY 10017**

Thank You.